A Legend's Story

Volume One

Michael Bouey

TABLE OF CONTENTS

PROLOGUE

"You are watching Channel 6 News. I am Adriana Hart and am bringing you the local news in Washington D.C. It seems things are heating up in the current Presidential Election. Senator Walt Michaels has decided to reach out to people to obtain his votes the old fashion way. The senator feels that going door-to-door and talking to voters about his view on politics is the best way to open many of their eyes. He feels that the laws of today are beneficial for keeping order and compliance while maintaining law-abiding citizens. Although in order to do so, the senator wants to create many laws that are more geared towards minimizing unlawful criminal acts. Could this be something that creates a better world or just something that creates a world where people are more prone to conform?

There could be harsh consequences without a hint of clemency. Although it may seem like a good idea, many other senators have become open-minded to creating more of a safe environment for everyone. Senator Donaldson agrees that laws are something that has had an impact on many countries in the world. He asks, "What would the world be like without rules and laws?" To him, it is something that could be looked at more closely so that we can keep the kids of our future alive longer. The senator feels that too many lives are lost. He stated that creating better laws could induce people to not create such heinous acts and would direct us to a brighter future.

Stacy Parks, spokesperson for Senator Lenore Graves, states that the world is not perfect. The world is built on laws to help create order, but also to help create control.

Abraham Lincoln fought for freedom a long time ago, but it still feels like we are fighting for our freedom today. Martin Luther King Jr. had a dream that one day we would coexist together in peace and harmony. Yet even though the world is gray, a mixture of black and white, we all still see color creating chaos. Our choices are always predetermined because of its sometimes outrageous consequences. Although we do have the complete free choice that the government exclaims, none of us want to pay a price we are not able to afford. No one wants to have to spend time behind bars in a controlled environment, like a caged animal in a pet store. But looking at both sides in retrospective, no one wants to live a life in fear. It is good to question and to ask what kind of world we would live in based on governmental or presidential decisions. We do not know what will work best because we are not perfect. This seems to be one of the hard hitting topics debated within this election process. Other topics that seemed to be something the senators felt the need to address are: health care, financial crises, education and terrorism, amongst many others.

We need to realize the world hasn't just been born, we are still growing! We all crawl, before we learn how to walk! Sometimes, when we think we are ready, we try running and we fall down. It is only then that we get back on our feet and try again. It is only then that we learn from our mistakes. No one is perfect, including GOD, which explains the non-perfect human he created. I am Adriana Hart and this has been your Channel 6 news..."

CHAPTER 1

A NIGHT TO REMEMBER

The story begins in Washington D.C. in a suburban neighborhood called Merylgrove Park on the west side part of town. It is night time, a few hours after the sun has set into the horizon. A beautiful white house is illuminated by the street lights. The house is two stories high with black shutters on the windows. A small cloud of smoke emitted from the chimney passing through the air over neighboring rooftops. Not a sound can be heard throughout the streets. You can see people in their houses watching television with their family, playing with their kids, or enjoying board games with loved ones. Although this eloquent house has a unique story which begins here, it is a story that will surely be remembered.

The house belongs to the Lewis family. John Lewis, is the man of the house and is married to his wife, Julie Christine Lewis. Their two beautiful kids have been the centerpiece of their life and they loved them both unconditionally. Their oldest daughter, Jennifer, whom is only six years old, sits on the living room couch watching a cartoon as she giggles and laughs throughout the show. She begins to sing along to the tunes playing from the television as she glances over and notices her mother walking into the living room. Julie places their ten month old son Skylar, whom they call 'Sky' for short, in his crib as she goes to the kitchen to fill the tea kettle with water. While she is in the kitchen she hears a deep voice screaming from the dining room, "Julie, have you seen my wallet?" Julie turns and yells back to her husband, "I think it's over near the stereo where you usually put it!" John rushes into the living room towards the stereo and lifts up papers and CD cases to look for his wallet. As he pushes away some of the scattered things near the stereo, he finds his wallet. "I found it" he yells back. He placed his wallet into his back pocket and gathered his things for a night shift at the Federal Bureau of Investigation where, since being out of the field, he works a desk job doing paperwork for several cases. John throws on his jacket and goes upstairs to grab his briefcase.

A loud cry is heard from the living room as Julie rushes into the room to see what happened. She notices there is nothing wrong and Sky just wanted to be picked up and entertained. As Julie searches around, she finds a toy, as she takes Sky out of the crib to calm him down. Sky takes it from Julie and grasps it in his tiny hands as he rattles it back and forth. He giggles in joy while entertained by the small multi-colored toy.

"Come downstairs, Jesse should be here soon," Julie yells up to her husband. John comes down the stairs dressed in a dark black suit with a blue tie on, which seems to be crooked around his neck. Julie places Sky down and asks John to come over so she can fix histie. John walks over to his wife as she places her hands around the back of his neck to help him. Her loving touch to her husband was easily identified to anyone who had witnessed in person their love for one another as being unconditional and genuine. John glances into her eyes and tells his loving wife that he has something to tell her. Julie's face had a smile smeared up upon it in joy and responds by explaining to him that she as well has something to tell him. She walks into the living room as he follows behind her and bends over to pick up an envelope of pictures off the crystal glass table. "I got the pictures developed from the fishing trip we took with Jesse and Marie,"she says. John takes the pictures and they both begin to look through them. Julie snickers as John gets to a picture of him holding a very small fish next to his best friend, Jesse Dean, whom works at the Bureau with him. Jesse was standing next to him holding an abnormally large fish. He turns to her and asks what was so funny. Julie tries very hard to hold in her laughter and compose herself as she tells him that nothing is funny. She places her hand to her mouth while forcefully trying to wipe the smile away from her face. John watches his wife cover her mouth and try to control herself from laughing at the picture.

"Go ahead and say it! What is so funny?" he states to her. Julie turns to him and responds, "Nothing dear, it was just a really fun day and all those memories are coming back. Now what is it you had to tell me?" John sets down the pictures and reaches into his back pocket as he pulls out a small jewelry box. He turns to Julie and opens up the box, "I went out and bought the children matching necklaces with their names on it. The jewelry store owner said I can come back and add more links to it, so when they get older it will fit around their neck better."

John approaches his son's crib and takes the necklace out of the box that has Sky's name on it and places it around his neck. "It fits like a charm," John remarks. Julie turns towards John, "You spent money on collars for our kids!" she states. Sky looks up towards his mother with an innocent face as he giggles. Julie gives John a sarcastic look. It appears that she is not completely upset, but a little bothered by John's decision. "They're not collars; they are jewelry" states John with a perplexed look upon his face. Julie stands next to the couch with a look of disapproval on her face. She walks over to John and closes the jewelry box that he is holding in his hands and tells him that he should not have spent so much money on jewelry for their kids. "You don't understand that I wanted to get something special for the children." John stated with a sincere tone. His wife looked at him with a distinct grin and replied, "You could have done something special without spending a lot of money is all that I am saying."

A car horn honks as John turns and tells Julie that Jesse is waiting for him and that he has to get going. Julie catches his arm and asks him to hold on a minute as she gathers up the pictures from the fishing trip and hands them to him. "Give these to Jesse and tell him to have Marie give me a call when she can," Julie asked in a soft voice. John nods his head and picks up his briefcase shortly before placing a kiss on his wife's cheek. He walks over to his daughter, whom is steadily entertained by the cartoons on the television, and kisses her goodbye. On the way to the front door, John stops by the crib where young Sky is playing with some toys in his crib, and bends over to kiss his youngest child on the forehead.

"What are you cooking for dinner tonight?" John asked his wife. Julie laughed at the comment considering how she had been working all day doing laundry and dishes. "Cooking? I am not cooking tonight. I decided to order a pizza for Jennifer and I. Maybe we will make it a movie night together once I put Sky to bed," mentioned Julie indecisively.

The car horn honks again and John turns around to give his last goodbye to his family before heading to work. As John walks out the front door, he hears loud rap music coming from the interior of Jesse's car. John walks over and opens the door, leans in and tells Jesse to turn down the music. Jesse had the music so loud he didn't even hear John open the door. He sat in the front drivers' seat rapping along to the hardcore rap that was playing. The music emanated from the car speakers as John forcefully reaches over and turns down the music himself. Jesse turns to him and apologizes to his friend. He impatiently signals him to get into the car so they are not to be late to work again.

John gets into the car and closes the door behind him. "My bad, boss! You know that was my favorite song," stated Jesse with a solemn grin. "Well, let it be YOUR favorite song in YOUR neighborhood," responds John sarcastically. The two of them snicker as they give each other a friendly grin. Jesse puts the car in drive and pulls off down the road. As the two drove down the neighborhood street, Jesse turns to John and tells him he has to stop and get some gas. "Alright, but make it quick. We are always late due to your quick stops," says John.

They pull into a local gas station called 'Wheelers.' The building was brightly lit with neon colors. There weren't many customers in the lot. It seemed to be one of their slow nights for business. Jesse pulls into the gas station and gets out the car. He takes out his credit card and slides it through the machine. Jesse reaches over and takes the gas pump off the handle. John opens his car door and yells over to Jesse that he is going to go inside and grab a coffee. As he gets out of the car and begins walking toward the front door, a black SUV pulls up with tinted windows and three darkly clothed men get out of the car. The man driving the SUV gets out first and turns to look across the car hood at the two other men. "Drake and Jarvis, you have five minutes!" he yells to the two men. Drake turns to the man whom was driving and replies back with a stern response, "Alright Dominic."

John glances over towards Dominic. He notices the brute man yelling at the two other guys he was with. "Hurry the fuck up in there!" the man yelled out. John turns away and continues towards the front entrance of the store, ignoring the altercation. Drake and Jarvis rush into the gas station as John follows in behind them. The two suspicious men walk around inside, while suspiciously glancing over their shoulder towards the store clerk. John then made his way over to grab a cup to pour himself some coffee and take it to the front counter to cash out. Both Drake and Jarvis stood in one of the aisles, staring in the direction towards the front as they force a few items from the counter deep down into their pockets. John hands the clerk a few dollars for his coffee and is handed back the change in return. He picks up his cup and walks out the door right past Dominic, whom is standing next to his black SUV searching for a lighter for the cigarette that is loosely being secured by his lips.

As John walks by, Dominic yells over to him, "Hey buddy, do you have a lighter?" John stops to turn around before responding, "Actually I do have one," he replied. Slowly reaching into his side pants pocket, John pulls out what appeared to be a silver lighter with the American flag on both sides of it. "I recently stopped smoking, so you can keep it," he says as he tosses the lighter over to him. Dominic was mesmerized by the patriotic looking lighter. It was similar to one he remembered from his past.

"I used to have the exact same one," Dominic mentioned. John stepped in closer to engage the conversation more. "Is that so? I know that I got mine from my time in the military when I was younger.

That's CRAZY! What about you?" John remarked. Dominic paused for a minute as it was clear that his past was beginning to play in his head like a movie set on fast forward.

"What the FUCK did you just fucking say motha fucka? Say that fucking word again!" Dominic harshly responded. John started to approach him slowly. "Oh I apologize. I don't know if I offended you. I just meant that it was just strange that we either have seen or owned this exact same lighter," he added. When John got closer he noticed that the man he was talking to seemed upset by something and not just by the lighter that seemed to be causing such an emotional effect that derailed him from their once smooth-going conversation. It was apparent that something else was bothering this man and John didn't want to be confrontational. Dominic's eyes were bloodshot red and watery while he stood there poised in a deep and yet seemingly dark trance.

"Are you okay?" John asked as he responded that everything was fine once snapping back to reality. With a gentle response, Dominic grins and thanks him for the lighter. "No problem!" noted John as he heard Jesse honk the horn in the near distance. This truly was a strange interaction. John nodded his head to Dominic before telling him farewell. The darker truth about it all was the story that was about to be told between these two. They had crossed paths for the first time but unbeknownst to the both of them; it wouldn't be their last and final encounter.

John continued back to the car and opens the door to get in as he places his coffee in the middle cup holder. He turns towards Jesse and tells him that he has something for him. John reaches into his inner suit coat pocket and takes out some pictures. "I almost forgot to give you these pictures that Julie wanted me to make sure you got," John says. Jesse takes the pictures and begins flipping through them. He gets to the fifth picture and stops as he glances at it for a moment. A burst of laughter emerges from Jesse as he tries to catch and compose himself. John leans over trying to glance at the picture that Jesse is laughing so hysterically at.

"What are you laughing at?" John asks with a disdained look upon his face. Jesse shakes his head and replies that he is laughing at nothing as he snickers at the picture once more. "It's just that the fish your holding is so small compared to mine," as he shows John the picture. John looks at the picture and sees Jesse holding a huge fish in comparison to the small fish that he has. In short distaste, John sneers at the picture and turns away. "Maybe you caught the bait I used to catch my fish with!" Jesse continues to snicker. With little patience, John tells Jesse to wrap up his laughter and for them to get moving before they are extremely late for work today. Jesse puts the car in gear and pulls off.

In the distance, Dominic watches them pull off as Drake and Jarvis come out of the gas station. Drake looks over at Dominic,"We are ready to go Dom, what's the first neighborhood?" he asks. Dominic takes a puff off his cigarette and puts it out on the bottom of his shoe. "Merylgrove Park," he responds with concise intent. They all get into the car to pull out of the gas station and around the corner. As they drive down the street, they eventually come to a stop and pull over a few blocks down the road before turning off their headlights as they begin to scope out the surrounding houses. A set of headlights moves casually towards Dominic's car, while they lean back in their seats so not to be seen casing the neighborhood. The light grazes over their face as they turn their heads to the side into the dark shadows to further hide their identity. The three robbers then sit up and take notice to a local pizza delivery car coming towards them. Drake immediately recognized the illuminated signed on top of the vehicle.

"Jay's Pizza? I used to order from there all the time," Drake noted before Dominic quickly told him to shut his mouth. Drake immediately stopped speaking as he had a distilled fear of Dominic. There was very little respect given to Drake by Dominic as he was seen more to be Jarvis's friend and only an acquaintance of his. Plus Dominic didn't come to that upscale neighborhood to have small talk. He wanted to remain focused. A plan to get some money quickly was formulating in his head. Dominic was plotting to find a way to take advantage of this situation and capitalize financially to his own advantage. The smallest mistake made could land them all in jail. The car then pulls into the driveway of John Lewis' home that was only two houses down from where Dominic and his henchmen had parked. The young delivery boy that got out of the car appeared to be in his early twenties, clean cut with a few tattoos that were visible on his arm. He cuts off the engine, leaving the keys in the ignition, with his headlights still on and windows rolled all the way down.

Dominic sits in the car with Drake and Jarvis trying to decipher what is taking so long for him to get out of the car to deliver the pizza. The pizza boy was clearly checking his phone to make sure he had the right address as a dim light could be seen reflected off his face. He then reaches over to the backseat to grab a large pizza box that sat inside of an insulated bag to help keep the food warm. He placed in on the passenger seat and reaches into his pocket to pull out his wallet. He didn't seem to be immediately exiting the car, as he rummages through it to make sure he had some change on his if it was needed. It was not unusual in this kind of neighborhood for many people to pay with larger bills.

Dominic turns to Drake and explains that he has a plan. As he takes out a small hand gun and begins to screw on a silencer attachment, he quietly gets out the car and crosses the street towards the pizza delivery boys' car. The car door opens as the pizza boy then gets out and he reaches in across his own seat to the passenger side to grab the pizza that he was delivering to John's house. As he begins to stand up tall with the pizza in his hand, Dominic runs behind the young man and pistol-whips him to the back of his skull. The pizza boys' head lunged forward as he smashes his face against the top portion of the door and then into his driver side mirror, ripping it off of the vehicle. Dominic cowers over the young gentleman's body and steps his right foot onto the boys' neck to hold him down in place. He lifted the handgun towards the boys' face, who laid there in fear looking up to Dominic as he pleaded for him to have mercy and spare his life. Dominic's eyes still teared up and red from rage and confusion, disregarded the boys' plea and fired two shots into his skull and one into the side of his left cheek, leaving him choking on the blood that filled up in his mouth. The boy didn't blink at all as Dominic stared into his eyes, watching his young life fade away to nothing more than a lifeless shell.

Dominic and Jarvis rushed over and placed the corpse on the young boy into the passenger seat, while his arm hung out of the partially cracked open door onto the ground.

Blood ran down his arm onto the cement as it flowed down to the curbside and into a drain. Jarvis reached over the dead body and flipped off the light coming from the sign above the car.

Inside the house, Julie turns towards the window assuming she heard something from outside, but doesn't bother to go check. She asks Jennifer to go upstairs and grab her purse because she knew that the pizza man will be there soon. The night began with bloodshed and could be foreshadowed to be a night that the Lewis family would not forget. Jennifer gets off the couch and heads upstairs. "Okay Mommy!" Jennifer yells back in compliance as she rushes up the stairs. Julie hears the tea kettle go off and runs into the kitchen to turn it off and clean up the spilled hot water. Jennifer heads up to the bedroom and turns on the light to look for her mothers' purse.

Dominic notices from outside that the upstairs light had been turned on within one of the bedrooms. He signals to Drake and Jarvis to move the pizza boys' body from the front seat and place it into the trunk of the car. "While we are in here, I don't want anyone passing by to notice this motha fuckas' body," Dominic rationally stated. The two darkly clothed men assist Dominic within placing the body into the trunk. They stay behind, closing the door and turning off the headlights of the car, so not to bring any attention to them.

Dominic picks up the hot pizza bag that was dropped by the pizza man and walks with it in hand towards the front of the house. He presses his left ear against the door and rings the doorbell. He hears a women yell from the inside, "Jennifer can you grab the door! I am cleaning up in the kitchen. I will be there in a minute." Jennifer had just sat back down with her mothers' purse now sitting beside her to continue the cartoon she was watching. She grabs the purse and replies, "I got it mommy!" Drake and Jarvis shut the trunk door and walk up to stand next to Dominic as they wait for someone to answer.

The three men stood beside one another at the door patiently waiting for someone to come open it. With Dominic standing with a pizza box in one hand and a pistol with a silencer attached in the other, he knew that whoever opened the door would be in for a big surprise. He tossed the pizza into some nearby bushes to lighten his load as he hears someone vastly approaching the door. Jennifer walks over with her mothers' purse in her hands towards the front door. She unlocks the top latch and places her small hand gently on the handle. There was nothing but the thought of the smell from freshly cooked pizza running through her mind, but there was something different than that awaiting on the other side. Jennifer opens the door up to Dominic who stood there raising his hand holding the silenced handgun that was used to kill the pizza man now towards young Jennifer's head whom stood still in motion while encapsulated in pure fear.

With the barrel about two inches from her nose, he fires off four very quick rounds directly into her as she falls to the ground, spilling over most of the belongings from her mother's purse. He whispers to Drake and Jarvis with specific instructions, telling them to go upstairs and find anything of value. The order came from the man and charge as the two steadily departed and made their way up the stairs. Dominic walks in slowly behind them, now standing over Jennifer's body and with a dark grin perched up upon his face. He looks down at the small girl and points his gun towards her and fires off one more, now deadly, bullet into her young fragile skull. Her blood had been spilled across the floor like a fine red wine, soaking into the cracks of the vinyl flooring, while the gaping hole caused by the exit wound had gushed out an endless stream that drenched her clothing.

It was unbearable to watch as her tiny fingers twitched from the random muscle reflexes she had after the massive shock to her body. The reaction in her fingers slowly began to fade until it was no more, like a dying heart beating down to its last heartbeat. Poor little Jennifer will never get the chance to see the day come where she would graduate from high school or be walked down the aisle at her wedding. These moments had been stripped from her by the deranged Dominic Harvey. He looked down at the small child's body and started to have muddled thoughts in his head that were diluted with disturbing flashbacks of his life starting from when he was exactly around Jennifer's age all the way up to this very night. Dominic's head tilts slightly to the left and his right eye begins to twitch. Shortly after having shot the last round into the innocent young girl, he hears a small clank come from the kitchen. "Jennifer, is that the pizza man?" Julie yells from the other room.

Dominic enters, vigorously pointing his gun around each corner, clearing one room after the other. He stops and notices a vase sitting on one of the tables next to a photo of John and Julie. He remembers John's face as the guy he briefly spoke with at the gas station prior to him coming to this particular house. He thinks to himself about what the odds were that he would come across the same guy whose house he is currently robbing. Dominic picks up the vase and stands around the corner from the entrance to the kitchen. Julie sets down the cloth she was using to clean up the spilled water and begins to proceed towards the front of the house to see if her daughter had answered the door as she had asked.

When she gets closer to the vestibule, she was left in complete shock after seeing her daughters' body on the floor buried in a puddle of her own blood. She begins to clam up and have a nervous break- down with her fingers shaking and heart racing. Julie cringes at the very sight of her little angel laying there with bullet holes in her. Out of nowhere Dominic quickly comes around the corner smashes the vase against Julie's skull sending her plummeting to the ground. Shards of glass from the vase pierced her skin, leaving several open gashes. Sky begins crying in a nearby crib where he can witness what is happening to his beloved mother. Julie begins crawling towards her daughter as Dominic pulls and tugs at her ankle so not to allow her to get any closer to her. He whispers into her ear, "Where's the valuable shit at?" But Julie, still in shock, ignores his question.

Dominic turns Julie's body over and mounts the top of her. He places his gun onto her chest and his hands around her neck to strangle her. As you can see the life slowly exiting Julie's body, she foolishly reaches for the gun, picks it up and points in towards Dominic's face as he strangles her. Julie pulls the trigger, but all she hears is a click from the gun signifying that the gun was empty. When Dominic looks down at her, he slaps her with his right hand, while still choking her with his left. He then reaches to his leg where he had a hunting knife strapped to his ankle as he takes it out and stabs poor Julie in the chest. With a small pause, he laughs with that same demented grin upon his face and then stabs her a few more times. Once he notices that she is dead, he puts away the knife and picks up his gun from her cold grasp and reloads the clip. Sexual impure thoughts began to go through Dominic's head as he ripped away part of her shirt with Julie's breast plopping out. He was stunned by her beauty and saw the opportunity to take advantage of her with the desire to insert himself inside her.

At this point Drake and Jarvis come down the stairs and notice what Dominic has done. They had startled him and he stood up to address his criminal lackeys who came down to show off things they had found. "Hey Dom, look what I got!" Drake states after seeing Julie on the ground partially exposed. Dominic looks over and sees Jarvis holding jewelry, but the only thing Drake has in his possession is an old fashion hat that he is proudly wearing on his head and a few other things of lesser value. He could feel the judgement by both Dominic and Jarvis, however, still speaks up as he was proud at some of the invaluable things he found. "A little style for me while I am out robbing people," says Drake.

Dominic slaps Drake as hard as he could across his face. His head slammed into the wall as he fell down to the ground. The horrific view of blood had been splattered all over the white wallpaper which had come from his lip that had been busted open. "We can't sell a fucking thrift store hat, so get your head together before I blow it right off your goddamn shoulders," yells Dominic. As Jarvis slowly turns his head, Dominic looks over to him to tell him to go out to the car and grab the gasoline. "We have to finish the job. No witnesses!" he adds.

Jarvis walks out the front door and over to their car, which is suspiciously parked two houses down across the street. He reaches into the back seat and pulls out two fairly large gasoline containers. As he walks back to the house, a nosey neighbor named Mrs. Cover, whom lives across the street, notices Jarvis walking back into the house with the containers in hand. She doesn't recognize him or their car, though she didn't want to alert any authorities until she is certain that the man was up to no good.

Jarvis walks through the front door with the containers and asks Dominic what he wants to do with the kid. Sky sits up in his crib looking up towards Dominic, whom is standing over him. Dominic takes out a cigarette and lights it up with the same lighter that was given to him by John at the gas station. The sentimental value it now held. He takes a puff of the cigarette and looks down at young Sky, "I fucking hate kids," he says. Within finishing another puff of his cigarette, he shoots a bullet into the crib that young Sky is in, startling the innocent baby. Young Sky begins to cry hysterically after being stunned by the ghastly discharged weapon had been fired so close to where he laid.

"Put him in the car so you can now at least say that you took something of reasonable value. The life of a child! That is one that holds a value that is priceless," says Dominic as he stares scantly at Drake. Both Drake and Jarvis saw this to be such a contradiction at first, but Jarvis soon began to understand what his enraged boss meant. Drake on the other hand couldn't help himself and spoke up to inquire why he sought Dominic to have such a change of heart after hearing his past statements about his feelings for children. "I thought you hate kids," stated Drake with a confused look upon his face. "I do, but I treasure what I can make this one into. Consider this my second chance and also my retribution. I've never had a son before. I lost HOPE and found LOVE delivered to me from the Sky," replies Dominic poetically.

Without hesitation, Jarvis drenches the bodies of Jennifer and Julie with gasoline. The fumes from tank after tank were becoming unbearable as it soaked into their clothing and the carpet beneath them. He proceeds to do the same with the living room furniture and any other belongings that look flammable as Drake picks up young Sky and began to walk out to the SUV with him. Mrs. Cover notices that a darkly clothed man is carrying young Sky out of the house with a handgun in his back waistband. She frantically picks up the phone to dial the authorities as she stops to notice two more darkly clothed men exiting her neighbor's house. Dominic stops at the front door and turns to Jarvis, "Drake has been messing up a lot lately and I think it's time to show him a little tough love if you know what I mean," he states. Dominic takes the lighter that was given to him by John out of his pocket along with a piece of paper. He stops and glances at the lighter for a moment and then ignites the paper.

Dominic slowly looks to Jarvis with a small pause and says, "Irony gave me this lighter." It was a moment in time so poetic to him as he tosses the paper onto young Jennifer's body, which ignites her and the whole first floor of the house. The flames ravage through the house peeling the decorative wallpaper off the walls and riding its way up the silk drapes, whilst the smoke also sifts out the various slightly open windows. When witnessing this horrific encounter, it sends Mrs. Cover into a panic as she drops the phone and runs over to her front door. She runs out of it making a b-line over to be able to help, when she spots Dominic and Jarvis walking away from John and Julie's home. Dominic takes out his gun after noticing Mrs. Cover out from his peripheral vision running straight at them and fires off four shots at her sending her flying to the ground very quickly, leaving her wounded in the middle of the street. Almost lifeless, Mrs. Cover crawls towards the house slowly still on the road begging for her life and crying out for help. Dominic and Jarvis get into the SUV and place the car in drive and without batting an eye, proceed to drive over Mrs. Cover's body helplessly stranded and bleeding out. As the robbers hear the thud and crack from her skull within the inside of their vehicle, they continue driving as if nothing happened.

The three of them head a few blocks down until they notice a house with their porch lights on. Dominic sees a man pulling groceries from the back of his car and bringing them into his house. "We need to ditch the car!" he insinuates. Dominic then pulls the car over across the street and turns to Jarvis and says with a sarcastic tone, "Are you guys' hungry too?" They both nod their head at the sarcastic comment. The intent was to teach Drake a lesson, but made it seem as if the plan was to ditch the car and find out what kinds of snacks and goodies the man was bringing into his home.

Dominic puts the car in park and cuts off the front headlights. When they begin exiting the car, Dominic stops Drake to tell him to entertain the baby so he doesn't cry and alert the unsuspecting man unloading his groceries. This was a smart play by him to avoid the innocent man hearing them sneak up behind him. When Jarvis and Dominic get out of the car and quietly close the doors behind them, they begin walking in the direction towards the front of the dark colored SUV. Dominic looks at Jarvis, before stating in a low tone, "Drake messed up and action has to be taken." Jarvis glances back at Dominic with a 'not so surprised' look upon his face, knowing that Drake had to be held accountable for not grabbing enough valuable things from the last house. This was an action that could not go without having a disciplined reaction that he would learn from. They had come to that neighborhood because they were all low on money and needed to make some quick cash. Before getting to John's house they all had endured a rough time and had been through the ringer, especially Dominic whom had been through the most. John was known by many people to be your average person, but his story was so much deeper than that. He had been through so much already in his lifetime. It had already been a night so far for John, to what he could reluctantly remember, before it was to soon become one that he would ultimately never forget.

A small pause is given by Jarvis initially before asking how Dominic wanted to go about things. Dominic turns back and glares at Drake, as he does the same back, noticing that something is being said about him. The distinct look between both men etched an uncomfortable feeling with Drake as he tried to comfort the baby some more. Jarvis places a pacifier into young Sky's mouth, who quickly rests his eyes and falls into a deep sleep shortly afterwards. There was a small connection with Jarvis and Sky, though Dominic had taken him as his own. He wanted to have that special child he could raise into society. A son, if you will. He wanted to be a father deep down inside, regardless of his distaste for children. That hatred was derived from other children he experienced within his past and not from someone that was so inculpable, like young Sky.

Dominic whispered to Jarvis explaining that he wanted him to inform Drake that plans had changed and he was expected to redeem himself for his prior mistakes. As Jarvis began walking up to the back side of the SUV, Drake rolls down the window to ask what the problem is. Jarvis explained to him what needed to be done and Drake adamantly begins exiting the car with a chance to prove to his fearless leader, Dominic, that he is capable of completing the job. As Drake walks past Dominic under the assumption that he is going in alone, he is confronted by the leader of the pact and told to take point on this one with them following behind to cover him.

The three robbers began walking towards the vaguely lit house as they follow the unsuspecting man, who is approaching his front door, carrying two fairly large bags of groceries in hand. As the man enters the front entrance of his house, the three robbers lightly sprint up behind him. Drake makes it the closest to him and shoves him down into the vestibule of his beautiful residency. The man drops both bags of groceries and is viciously pushed into a nearby piece of furniture that was containing a few umbrellas. He is over-powered by the three men pummeling him and quickly spots Drake, who takes a small handgun out of the back of his pants. The man couldn't identify any of the thugs, but from the way they were dressed, he knew that they were your average every day thugs out committing crimes within his usually quiet community.

Drake slowly lifts the gun up towards the helpless man's head. The man cowers with fear and begins begging for the robbers to stop, insisting that they could take whatever they wanted. "Just don't kill me!" he pleaded. While Drake remained fixated on the man, about to pull the trigger, Dominic takes out his own gun and shoots Drake slightly above his left kneecap. The bullet passed through his leg, leaving an open exit wound. Drake falls to the ground, with the gun dropping out of his hand as he turns and looks up to Dominic in disbelief. "You shot me!" he exclaimed. Dominic then directs his gun to the unsuspecting man on the floor and fires two shots at him. The bullets pierced through his body like a sharpened blade through a stick of butter. Jarvis takes a look at the man as he lies dead on the floor next to the scattered groceries and bleeding all over the place.

In a small moment of shock, Drake turns up towards Dominic and weeps out, "What the hell Dominic? You shot me. Why?" Dominic moves closer to Drake and squats in front of him. With a small sneer, he glances at Jarvis briefly and then quickly back to Drake. In a distasteful voice Dominic replies, "My dad once told me something that I will tell you. We all make mistakes... this is your chance to learn from yours."

Dominic stands up and walks over to a small table in the main hallway of the man's home and picks up the phone. He dials 9-1-1 and slowly places it to his ear. "There is someone in my house, I can't..." Dominic abruptly stops and drops the phone onto the ground. It dangled back and forth hanging from the cord. He then turns and looks at Drake and fires two shots off into the ceiling. As he immediately holsters his gun, he signals to Jarvis as they both exit the front of the house. Flustered with words, Drake mumbles to Dominic... "Don't do this!"

Dominic turns to Drake and replies, "You did this to yourself, motha fucka!" Jarvis quickly jogs across the street and hops in the black SUV. He starts the car and pulls it up to the curb of the house. Dominic rushes up and hops in as the car then takes off abruptly down the street. Drake watched his former friends abandon him at the crime scene. He tried crawling slowly away, but doesn't make it more than a few feet, before he hears police sirens roaring in the distance. He had been set-up to take the fall, all because he didn't grab enough valuable things. This was an extreme lesson that was forced upon him to be learned by Dominic Harvey.

Meanwhile, back at John's house, embers flow through the air, passing by each house in the neighborhood. The smell of burning furniture and flesh created a wretched stench that would cause a human being to vomit. Several ambulances, fire trucks and police vehicles surrounded the house trying to control the area and the flames that constantly hauled itself throughout each room of the crime scene.

Many news vans piled in to cover this horrific centerpiece. Neighbors stood outside their front doors, as most were on their cordless and cellular phones explaining to other family members and close friends what had taken place inside their quiet neighborhood. All of sudden, headlights from a nearby moving vehicle try to find its way through the madness. John, sitting in the passenger seat of the car, notices where the flames are emerging from. This caused him toreact without thinking as he quickly just assumed that the house had been burned down but the family was okay. He yells out to Jesse to stop the car immediately. John jumped out and pushed his way through the crowd of reporters, medical teams, police and watching spectators. Two police officers notice John trying to get closer to his inflamed household and prevent him from coming any further. As soon as one of the police officers placed his hand on John's chest to stop him from endangering himself, John grabs the officers' hand and twists it behind his own back. He quickly takes out his holstered gun and raises it towards the other officer. Several other officers observe the assault on the fellow co-workers.

John was enraged that he was being prevented from getting close to his own home. Deep down he had to know if his family was safe, and in his mind no one was going to stop him. The other officers that witness John's actions had drawn their weapons, pleading for him to drop his firearm. "Put the gun down!" several of them yelled out. One of the officers, whom recognized John, yells out to him, "John... RELAX! It's me Frank. I know your upset... Your family...they're gone!...ALL OF THEM!" John emotionless stands still as several tears begin to trickle down his face. The officer continues, "Put your weapon down, John! None of us want to fire upon you. Think about your family. You have a choice. We will find these bastards." With an esteemed glance at the officer, John turns to the one he is pointing his gun at and says, "If any of them fire, I am taking you with me...Who has the choice now?"

John releases the other officers' wrist and lowers his gun. All of the other officers follow suit and holstered their weapons. John walks forward towards the house and turns to one of the firefighters as they walk by, "Where are their bodies?" he asks. The fireman, who is covered in dirt and debris and responds to him, "The fire was too hot, we couldn't find the remains." John clutches his weapon and falls to his knees. His head falls to his chest and more tears begin to trickle down his face. He looks at his gun and slowly begins to lift it towards his face to place the barrel of the pistol into his own mouth. Although before the barrel reaches his mouth, a hand grasps his shoulder and startles him. John turns up towards the figure behind him and sees his friend, Jesse, standing there as he tries to help him off his knees. Jesse comforts John by calmly explaining to him what the police had just told him had transpired based on all of the comments by other neighbors that were witnesses to the crime.

"It seemed to be a home invasion and the robbers wanted to cover their tracks. I know our precinct. They won't let this cold heartless son of a bitch get away. They all will be on this case till it gets solved," Jesse proclaimed. With deep regret, Jesse apologizes and directs John to get into the car after offering him to come stay at his house for a while until things got better. Tears of sadness fell down John's face from the warm invitation. Jesse felt bad for all that John had loss on this very night. It became a night that they would always remember and a night they would never forget. The two friends make their way towards the car, as John turns and glances back at the house he grew to love and the family he was leaving behind. They both get into the car and Jesse begins driving to his house, which isn't far from John's address. The whole car ride to Jesse's house, he tries to think about other things he could say to help console his friend. It made it difficult to think of things because every time he looked over he didn't see his friend that he's used to seeing every day. John was broken and emotionless. He was more stunned than a deer in headlights. It was almost as if nothing was processing through John's head; accept the loss of his family. It was difficult for Jesse to try and talk to his friend, so he decided to not say anything on the way to his house.

The car pulled into the driveway of a small one-story house. Jesse doesn't live in the nice kind of house that John did. The house was in good condition, just not as fancy. It was a brick house with many flowers planted outside and several perfectly edged bushes. As Jesse puts the car in park, the front door of his house opened and his wife Marie came rushing out. Her face was red and flustered as she had been crying for the last hour after seeing the news report that her close friend, Julie, and the lovely couples' children had been shot and set on fire within their own home during the arson and home invasion. John and

Jesse got out of the car and Marie runs straight up to John and gives him a hug. "Do you want some clothes? You're all dirty! Come inside and get cleaned up John, I will make something to eat," she offers him as she notices him covers in dirt and other debris.

John shakes his head and tells Marie that he just wants to be alone. She could tell that he didn't want to be bothered, but that didn't stop her humble hospitality. Marie directs him in and shows him to the guest room. She leaves John to himself and reminds him that if he needs anything to just ask. She closes the door behind her and walks down the hallway to her bedroom. With a small pause and glance at Jesse whom is standing in the room already, she begins to break down once more in tears. Jesse rushes over to his wife and tries to comfort her. "What will he do?" Marie asks her husband. He turns to her and responds," He will mourn...He will mourn in his own way. Just give him time." They both get into the master bed and turn on the TV as they prepare to go to bed in hopes to forget tonight's tragic turn of events. The television has the coverage of what happened at John's home being broadcasting on several stations. Marie was still in shock while she watches the newscast just as a means to see her friend's face pop up once more on the screen and remember the good times and laughs they had before trying to get some sleep.

CHAPTER 2
LOCAL NEWSCAST

"This is Adriana Hart with your local news. Thou shall not steal. Thou shall not kill. These are just some of the few commandments broken in this news story. Local resident, John Lewis, comes home to the aftermath of his family and home that is in complete flames. Lewis, currently employed with the Federal Bureau of Investigation doesn't seem to be a target, yet his family was a different story. Neighbors heard faint gun shots at the house and noticed three darkly clothed men enter the home, before the shots and cruel arson attack. Lewis, upon the aftermath, lost a wife, six-year old daughter and ten-month old son. Authorities believe that the men responsible for this endeavor are the same men responsible for killing a nearby neighbor and another shooting a few blocks away. Avery Stanton was found shot in the head lying next to his scattered groceries. Authorities also report a 9-1-1 call just moments before the shots were heard by the operator. Unidentified tracks of blood were left behind that didn't match the victim. Police say that there was a struggle and the suspect was shot and wounded, but yet escaped. Authorities are looking for any possible leads.

If you have any information about this shooting, please contact your local authorities.

In other news, just weeks after his inauguration, President James Jennings speaks at a local rally. The President feels that the crime rate has been going up and of two things should be done about this. He feels that putting more authorities on the street could be the best way for bringing down the crime rate. President Jennings looks at the current state the economy is in and begins searching for options to ensure the safety and comfort of our citizens. The second option suggested by the Vice President and several other sitting senators is to bring in the military under martial law. It goes to show people that laws are meant to protect us and when ignored, consequence is sure to follow. We should all stand back and look at things from the other side of the window. For we may be the ones that build the world up, we are also the ones who foolishly tear it down..."

CHAPTER 3

DEALING WITH LOSS

The sun rises as the light shines through the blinds of John's guestroom windows. The light causes him to start slowly opening his eyes as it beams in onto his face. The day is new to him, yet he is unconsciously still haunted by the one before this morning. His heart is still heavy from the loss of his endearing family, but the pain he is feeling isn't processed just yet. He smells sausage and eggs as the aroma seeps through the room and is suspected to be originating from the kitchen. The heavenly aroma causes his stomach to growl instantly. He jumps up and screams out, "Julie, what are you cooking?"

John notices that there is no one there as he glances around the room and finds all four walls to be different than what he remembered. He realizes it isn't the room he has awoken in for the last seven years. John sits up on the edge of the bed. His total mood changed as he leans over and places both of his hands on his forehead and begins weeping. The bedroom door opens and Marie looks in. "Are you alright!" Marie whispers in a solemn voice. When John responds that he is okay, she offers him some breakfast. "Thanks for offering, I will be down in a minute," he responds. Marie closes the door and walks downstairs to set a place for John at the table.

John gets out of bed and throws on some clothes and walks over to the mirror. He begins to fall into a daze while remembering the flashes of light, flames and siren sounds echoing throughout his neighborhood. John becomes weak and cowers over, when a sudden knock on the door is heard. Jesse walks in to ask his friend if he needed anything. John quickly tries to compose himself and tells Jesse that he is fine.

The two of them exit the bedroom and walk down the stairs to the breakfast room together. As they enter and sit down at the table, Marie notices that she left on the television. Even though the volume was turned down low, John takes notice that it is still covering the theft and arson from his house the night before. Marie notices and quickly turns off the television as John gasps for air and even starts to hyperventilate. "I am sorry about that John. I forgot it was on. I was just keeping up to date with any updates that might be broadcasted," she apologizes whole-heartedly while rubbing her hand on his back to calm him down.

John makes the notion that everything is fine and not to worry about it as he tries to gather himself. Although based upon how John stated that things were fine, there was a sense of sadness and dead silence frolicking in the air after his statement. The awkward silence placed Jesse and his wife in awe. With a quick gesture, Jesse nudges his close friend and tells him that he just got word from headquarters that John could take off as much time as he wanted with pay. John took a small pause and turns to Jesse before replying back, "That's good to hear. Hey, I don't want to seem rude but I think I may have loss my appetite. I think I am going to go for a walk to help clear my mind." Placing down his fork, John stands up, grabs a piece of bacon and stuffs it into his mouth before walking out the house. The door closes smoothly behind him as John begins taking a stroll down the street alone.

So many things are going through his mind as he walks through the neighborhood. He thought to himself why it couldn't have had just been him that was taken or even darker thoughts like why he couldn't have been killed and set on fire with them. This wasn't the right state of mind for him. He loved his wife and kids, but he never suspected to having had lost them all in one night. Everything had been taken away from him in a moment's instance.

After John exited the house, Marie turns to Jesse, "Now why the hell did you say that?" she exclaimed in reference to her husband's comment about being paid after his traumatic experience.. With a confused look on his face, "Say what?" he responded back. Marie glanced at him and explained how certain things are sensitive to John and he doesn't need to be reminded of what happened to Julie and his kids. "Like you leaving on the newscast about what happened?" Jesse remarks sarcastically. Marie gives a look to Jesse that many men have seen from women to make them aware that they have said something out of place. She stands up without saying any further words and begins to leave the room. "What?" Jesse screams out. Marie just ignores him and heads upstairs to avoid further conflict.

The sun shines bright out as it is a beautiful day for John to be outside walking down the street. He notices neighbors walking their dogs, mowing their lawn or even backing out their driveways to head to work. As he passes several houses, he notices a restaurant on the corner. It is a small mom and pops diner called 'Dine In.' He decides to stop in and order a coffee. When he walks in, he is instantly greeted by the hostess with a friendly grin. John is then directed towards a small empty booth where he has a seat by himself and even takes a second to glance at the menu. A waitress comes over to greet him. She is very young as she appears to be in her early twenties. She has long curly blonde hair. There is a pen slicked back in her right ear. With her make-up perfectly applied and a smile upon her face, she pulls the pen out with a pad of paper and looks to John, "Morning, my name is Margaret, I will be your waitress, what can I start you out with?" she gestured. "Just a small coffee for now," he replies. Margaret notices that she won't need the pen and paper for such a small order. She slicks the pen back behind her right ear and puts the notebook away. "That's all you want, honey," she hinted. John nodded with a small grin as a response before the waitress turned and walked away to grab him a small coffee.

John turns and looks over to another table. There is a gentleman with his wife. The man is holding a casual conversation about their weekend together. John then sees that the man is smoking a cigarette. As he places the cigarette up to his lips, John sees the tip of the cigarette light up. He begins to have a small flash back. In his head, he sees puffs of bigger flames. He begins to daydream and as he looks around the diner, the walls begin to become engulfed with flames. The pictures and other cloth-like materials slowly curl up from the fire as smoke and embers flow through the air. Just before the smoke had just reached his table from the man's second hand indulgence, Margaret places a cup of coffee down in front of him which startles him. John comes back to reality and realizes that everything in the diner is still in good shape.

The gentleman across from him takes one last puff and puts out his cigarette into an ashtray that was on the table that they were dining in at. He places money on the countertop and he and his wife get up and exit the diner. "Here is your coffee, you sure you don't want anything else" Margaret asked. "No!" John replied. The waitress could tell something was bugging him. She begins walking away and then does a double take back to his table and places her hand softly onto his shoulder. Margaret recognizes where she knows him from. She glances at him for further confirmation before acknowledging where she recognizes him from. "I know where I know you from now!" she says as if they have known each other for many years. John looks up to her and tries to think of where they had met before as she spills the beans. "I saw you on the news, I am truly sorry to hear about your family," Margaret sympathetically states. John's head slowly looks down as he responds to her that he appreciates the kind words. "Thanks!" he states back as a genuine response.

His expressions hinted to Margaret that he rather not talk about it and she completely understood how he felt and respected his space and privacy. "I didn't mean to make you upset, I just wanted to send my respects," she added. Margaret reaches over and lifts John's chin to eye level with her and glares into his eyes. "Life is temporary; but in death and only because of memories...we can live forever though them," Margaret explained. She tells him to think about it and leaves him to enjoy his cup of coffee. As she walks away, a tear rolls down John's face but he understands what she was trying to convey. He sits alone at the table and continues to enjoy his coffee whiling reminiscing about the good times he had with his wife and kids.

Almost an hour goes by and John glances down at his watch, only to notice how long he has been out. He couldn't find Margaret to thank her for her kind words and cordial customer service, but knew he had to get going or Jesse and his wife might start to be concerned considering he had been there drinking coffee for the last few hours. John places enough money to cover his bill plus a generous tip and walks out of the restaurant on his way back towards Jesse's place. In the distance, he sees the same news team on the street that covered the story at his home invasion. They were doing a newscast in front of a local clothing store. The closer that John got, he overhears the newscaster talking about the politics in the world and the current President.

"...crime isn't the biggest problem we have in the country. Our president feels we are the people responsible for the way the world is becoming. How can we control this? Let's ask what the people think," Adriana Hart banters. John slowly walks behind the female newscaster without acknowledgment hoping to pass by without creating any attention on him. Adriana turns to John, "Sir, can I get a few words from you on the ongoing politics in the world," she screams out to John. Without batting an eye, John ignores her and continues walking down the street. His shrouded indirect response to her was undeniably cold and rude. The newscaster realized that she was heard, but that John wasn't interested. She turns her head slightly and notices another man across the street smoking a cigarette. Adriana quickly signals to her camera man to follow her across the street. They both turn and direct their attention to the man standing against the wall. "Sir, can I get a few words from you," she screams out to him.

The cameraman and Adriana Hart make it safely across the street and ask again if they could trouble him for a moment of his time. The man nods his head and agrees to make a few statements about the way the world is. "What is your name sir?" Adriana questions. She places the microphone up to his mouth as he takes the last puff of his cigarette before flicking it into the distance. "My name is Dominic Harvey!" he replies. Adriana shakes his hand and asks for his views on the world and the way things are becoming in our society with politics. Dominic looks straight into the camera and says, "I can't say that any country is perfect. We all make mistakes. It is the only way that we can learn so that we can better ourselves. Though there is a fine line between wanting to help a nation and wanting money and power. Some have money and power and some do not," As Adriana listens to Dominic express his opinion, she stops him in the middle of his statement to ask what he would do if he were the President of the United States. With a small grin, Dominic responds, "If I was the president, I would outlaw guns. Firearms would only be used by the military officials put in place to protect us. I do like the President's concept of enforcing martial law compared to others that do not. It is smart, but also people need to take time to think about this in comparison to our country. If you want a puppy to be more obedient; you discipline him, right?"

Jarvis approaches Dominic holding Sky in his arms as he notices him being interviewed by the news team. Jarvis pauses and waits for Dominic to finish talking with the young news reporter. Dominic darkly stares into the camera lens before remarking, "A vase that has just been broken can be fixed, but like it or not it's still damaged." The camera slowly pans over to Adriana as she gives her closing statement to the camera. "I consider these valuable words of wisdom from our watchful bystander, Dominic Harvey. For we, the people, are the ones that broke the vase, we are also the ones who can fix it. For the ones whom try to fix it repeatedly, like the government, they are the ones respon-sible for tearing it apart," Adriana states as she turns to Dominic to thank him for his time. The cameraman lowers his camcorder as they begin to pack up their belongings.

Jarvis walks over to Dominic and asks him what that was about. He responds with a casual statement informing Jarvis that it wasn't anything. Dominic stopped mid state-ment and realized that Jarvis brought Sky out into the open and reminds him that someone might recognize him. He smacks Jarvis upside his head and orders Jarvis to take him back to the car and wait for him. Jarvis then begins to walk away with Sky as Dominic takes out one last cigarette and lights it up with the same American flag lighter that he had. That lighter was becoming a sentimental object that he was closely connected to. It reminded him of his father who had the same exact one.

While Adriana and her camera man clean up their be-longings, her cell phone rings. She answers it and begins to have a short conversation. A smile arose on her face by the news she had just received. Dominic finishes his cigarette and begins to walk away. Adriana hangs up her phone and calls out to Dominic trying to get his attention. "Dominic!" she yells. "What do you want?" he responds as he turns around to the dazzling reporter. With a smile on her face, she lets him know that her boss just called and told her that many people have been calling in that quickly about their previous live newscast. With a small sense of confusion on his face, he becomes intrigued with her con-versation. "My boss thinks it would be a good idea to have a rally where you can speak to the people about your views on the politics that are currently taking place and to have our news team there to report those events," she adds cor-dially. Her mood is very mirthful as she is more consumed with the idea that the interview she did with Dominic has helped raise her image as a reporter and even more so to have gained added viewership.

"I don't think that's a good idea. Plus, I am a very busy man," Dominic responds. Adriana isn't the kind of person that takes 'NO' for an answer. She hands him her business card and tells him to call her if he changes his mind. Dominic takes the card as he flicks his cigarette and turns around to head back to his car.

As he approaches his SUV, he pulls out a concealed pistol from his jacket and opens the car door. He gets into the driver seat and quickly places the gun up to the forehead of Jarvis. "If you ever take that fucking baby out in public before the age of four, I will slit your throat and then fire a bullet in this piece of shits' brain just to cover my tracks," he protested cold-heartedly. Jarvis apologizes repeatedly as Dominic lowers the barrel of the gun from his temple. They both turn and look to the back seat of the car. Dominic did want to keep the baby boy he had kidnapped from the burglary, but if someone had happened to recognize him in possession of that baby then he felt that he had to dispose of all the witnesses involved.

"I will take care of this kid until he is older and make him an heir to my empire," Dominic states to Jarvis. The thing that bothered Dominic is that he had nothing that his young apprentice could currently be an heir to. Dominic wanted to be able to give him the world. He pondered to himself as he realized that the world was something the currently powerless Dominic didn't own. He thought for a brief moment about what the world would be like if he made global decisions. What is the world missing? What are some things he could bring to the table? How could he change the world and make it better? Dominic asked him-self these questions as he glanced over and noticed Adriana saying goodbye to her cameraman before there were to part ways. He got into the news van and pulled away as Adri-ana waved goodbye to him. She casually walked down the street and turned the corner into a nearby alley as Dominic looked on with a smile on his face.

Meanwhile, back at Jesse's house, John opened the front door and notices Jesse sitting on the front couch. He calls out to him to ask him what the problem is as he notic-es a disgruntled look upon his face. Jesse explains to him how he got into an argument with Marie. Although when John asked what they got into a fight about, Jesse quickly changes the subject. "It was over something stupid," Jesse briefly added. "Where have you been?" he continues.

John quickly can see that Jesse changed the topic and may not want to talk about it. It was obvious that there was more to the story. He tells Jesse about his trip to a nice little diner around the corner. Jesse laughs and tells his friend that he goes in there quite often and that there are a lot of nice staff members there. John tells him about this one staff member that he met named Margaret. Jesse immediately knows who he is talking about. He tells John how she has been there for about four years and how they have had plenty of interesting conversations. The two sat on the couch and reminisced about the good ole days for several hours. As John and Jesse reminisced some more, they both lost track of time. It was comforting for Jesse to see John laugh and converse after having had gone through such a horrific situation with the loss of his family.

John looks over at the clock and realized it was go-ing on two o'clock in the morning. "It's getting late!" John remarked. Jesse agrees how late of an hour it has gotten and suggests they both get some rest and pick up their conversation that neither of them wanted to end to gain some shut eye. Even though they both enjoyed talking about their fond memories, they realized times are definitely changing. They cannot go back to the way things used to be. But the good thing about it was that they knew the future would hold newer memories for them both.

Several weeks passed by and things between Marie and Jesse weren't getting any better. They continuously got into small fights over stupid things. Most of the things they argued about pertained to John and some related to their actual relationship. Marie felt like they didn't do enough things together anymore. She just felt like John needed to move on and branch out on his own after moping around the house all this time. She was sympathetic towards his loss as she too loss her friend, but it was obvious that John needed to talk to a specialist so that he could properly be able to move on from the loss and not continue to let it hurt him. Jesse and his wife sometimes didn't try to hide their arguments. Sometimes they were so intense, that they just forgot that John was in the house. It became no surprise that his stay was starting not to be so welcomed.

John knew that there was a problem, but he just couldn't figure out if he was a huge contribution or how much to the tension felt in the household. Many fights broke out between Jesse and Marie throughout the next few weeks to follow. Most times they would argue so loud that John would have to step out and have a late night bite to eat just to get out of the house and avoid being imprisoned within the drama that he had partially become involved in. John would go to the nearby diner and usually sit in Margaret's section. She would always work a late night shift.

He grew fond of that diner and became really close friends with Margaret. They shared many conversations and got to know each other very well. John wasn't sure if she was someone he grew to like or if he just enjoyed her company. It was difficult to even try and contemplate having feelings for someone else after losing Julie. The one thing he knew is that it was good to have someone to talk to after feeling like he had lost his best friend to a failing marriage that he had contributed to. John liked being able to escape the madness to clear his mind. Things haven't been the same, though he found a sense of peace within going to that diner and talking with Margaret. She was someone that brought a calming peace to his mind.

It wasn't until one Tuesday night in the month of May, where things became a huge problem. John lied down on the couch to watch television late that night. Jesse came in from being out at the bar and having way more to drink that he had anticipated. The door slammed opened as Jesse stumbled in laughing, though his face was covered in tears. He was incoherently mumbling things under his breath.

"It's genius. Francis and Teddy could help. I can't do this without James either. It's such a great idea," he spouted off with what little words that followed that John was able to understand. Jesse then knocked over a lamp that was close by, as it shattered into pieces. John was startled by the door slamming open and the lamp breaking as is work him up from a deep slumber. "Jesse? Is that you?" John asked. He jumped up to find Jesse in the living room and was highly intoxicated. Jesse cowers over to one knee with his pistol drown. With tears in his eyes he yells out, "Marie!" John rushes over to Jesse as he notices his wife did not respond back so he yells out again, "Marie, where the fuck are you? Get down here!"

As John grabs Jesse by the arms to do his best to re-train him, he pushes his friend off him and into the wall nearby. Marie comes rushing down the stairs, stopping half-way, as she notices what is transpiring. Jesse looks over to his wife and sobs as he tries to converse with her incoherently. "I have tried to make you happy...I tried...I, as a man, would die for you," Jesse whimpered. He wipes tears from his face "I have done everything for you, I love you. This isn't about me or John, this is about us," Jesse mutters, still not making any sense. Marie asks him to put his gun down "Look there is more to everything going on with me. I have something huge to tell you, but I don't want to talk to you while you are drunk," Marie raves.

John gets off the ground and walks over to Jesse to ask him to place his weapon on the floor. Jesse yells back and tells them that he can't do this anymore. As John looks to Marie standing on the staircase, he can't understand what is going on. John asks his friend what he is talking about, but when Jesse tries to respond, he is at a loss for words. "Is this about me? Am I the problem?" John yells back. Marie looks at Jesse and becomes frustrated. With little hesitation she screams out "I can't do this anymore. Put down the gun Jesse! No one is to blame but you! That's it! We're through!" Marie walks down the stairs and grabs her coat and the keys off a table near the couch. She tells Jesse she will be back for her stuff in the morning.

John calls out to Marie and asks her to stay and try to work this out. Marie stops for a moment, almost as if she is going to reconsider and not leave her husband. John knows she has something to say. She wanted to tell him something important, but was holding back. Marie takes a deep breath and with a gulp of confidence she says to John "You feel that you could have saved your wife if you were there for her that night?" John stares into Marie eyes with confusion and guilt. Jesse places his pistol on the ground. "This was Jesse's last chance to save his wife," Marie added as she walked past him and closes the door behind her without looking back.

John walks over to Jesse and sits next to him. He flings his arm around his friend and tries to console him. Jesse looks over to John and asks him what he did wrong. John had little understanding as to what just happened. Jesse and Marie had been fighting for weeks and John's mind had been elsewhere. Was he the factor that helped ruin his best friend's marriage? John didn't have an answer for him, but tells Jesse that the problem can be solved.

John acknowledges that he will gather his things and move into an apartment until he can get a place of his own, so he can help not be part of the problem. "I can't lose the two people that mean the most to me in my life right now," Jesse remarks. It is clear to John that they both have been through a lot, but he looks at his best friend and realizes they both need to set things straight in their own life. "This is something I have to do! While I am gone, do what you can to fix your life and relationship," states John. Jesse wipes away a few more tears with his arm. "Go get some sleep and sober up. Call me in the morning," John adds.

As light peaks through the blinds the following day, it awakens Jesse from a deep slumber. John comes through the Jesse's bedroom door and tells him that he found a motel to stay in for a while until he can afford a place of his own. Jesse rubs his eyes and yawns as he congratulates his friend. He is hung over and remembers various random moments about last night. The biggest one that he remembered was his wife, Marie, walking out on him.

"You don't have to go, man. You are more than wel-comed to stay," replies a less intoxicated Jesse as he gets out of his bed. John thanks him for being a friend, but reminds Jesse that he is doing this for himself as well. "It is time I looked towards moving on in my life and try to get past losing my family," John replies back with a quaint smile. He tells Jesse to get up and get dressed because he wants to go grab breakfast and celebrate them both open-ing a new chapter in their life.

Jesse was very hesitant. He was under the assumption that he hadn't fully loss Marie and continued to have high hopes that he could resolve the issue. Considering how long they had been fighting, it was clearer to John that Marie had built up that anger and frustration. It was also obvious that she wanted to move on and had been fed up with Jesse for a little while now, but how could he tell his friend this. John insisted that Jesse come grab a bite to eat. Jesse threw on some clothes and they both headed out the door towards the local diner. When they got there, they both walked in and immediately asked the hostess if Margaret is working today. She informed them that she had just punched in not too long ago and directs them straight to her section to be seated.

Margaret comes over and says hello to both John and Jesse. "It is unusual to see you both in the restaurant at the same time," states Margaret with a grin aimed right in Jesse's direction. She greets them both and asks them what they want to start off with to drink. They smile at the wholesome waitress and tell her to bring out two cups of coffee. She nods her head and turns around to walk away to go grab the coffee pot.

As they sit next to a window looking out to the street, they see many people passing by. Cars sat at red lights waiting for them to turn green. Many kids could be seen jumping rope and playing hopscotch across the street. A young man stood on the corner talking to another girl as he tries to hit on her. Jesse turns his head to John and says "So much has changed out there." Margaret walks back to the table with a coffee pot in hand and turns over both of their coffee mugs and fills each of them to the brim. "Nothing has changed," she states. John looks at her and tells her that a lot has changed and that nothing is the same as what it used to be. Margaret reaches into the front pouch of her apron and pulls out a dollar bill. "You can look at this dollar bill like you look at the world," Margaret says with a boastful smile. She places it back in her apron as she pulls out four quarters and places them on the table. "It may look different, but it's still a dollar. Nothing has changed, John!" she continues as she picked up the quarters and drops them back into her apron. Jesse tells Margaret that if you use your head, you can turn a dollar into ten dollars and even continue to grow from there. It became a back and forth battle between each other's witty logic. Margaret looked at them both as she shakes her head.

With a whimsical chuckle, she says with a soft voice, "You added more to the dollar, but the dollar never changed. It's like getting a new president, boyfriend or girlfriend. What happened has happened, and no change can be made. No pun intended," Margaret proclaims as she leans over and tops off both of their mugs. She asks if they want anything else besides coffee. They both shake their heads and gestured that they were fine with just the coffee. Margaret told them to shout out to her if they needed anything and walked away to greet another table that had just sat down in her section.

John looked over to Jesse and points out how intelligent Margaret is. "Why don't you ask her out on a date," Jesse blatantly states. "It is apparent both of you could use a good start," he adds. "I have a lot going on in my life and don't need you to playmatchmaker. Plus, how could you be so stupid. She has been smiling your way and throwing signals up in your face since we got here," John retorts.

"What?! You think she likes me?" responds Jesse while trying not to show any indication of him blushing. Margaret had known him the longest and shared many moments and deep conversations with one another. John even knew about a time that she had asked him to walk her home, but when that was brought up, Just used the excuse that he was being a gentleman and that it was late that night that she had got off work and he felt partially responsible for keeping her after hours to chat about things going on in his life. "I just don't need your love advice man. Especially to be paired up with someone that clearly has the hots for you," John acknowledges.

Jesse could look at his friend and tell that he hadn't fully recovered from losing his wife, Julie. It was probably best he thought to himself to just drop that conversation and move on. "Look man, I have something for you. I know how tough it is for you. When I am in that same kind of mood, I turn to God. I know it may sound corny or almost like the right spiritual thing to say, but I am serious. I want to give you my bible. I have ready through it a couple times now and it has really changed my life and outlook on things. Here, I want you to have it!" Jesse suggested as he took a small bible he had out that had been concealed during their conversation. John accepted the bible unsure of how it could impact him or change his outlook the same as it did for Jesse. "Thanks man! I will give it a try and read it when I can," he noted. The two sat there talking for quite a few more hours. John eventually happened to glance down at his watch and hints to Jesse how he had to get going. He places down a twenty-dollar bill and asks Jesse to inform Margaret to keep the change. Jesse nods his head with a friendly gesture and says that he is going to stay a little bit longer and maybe chat some more with Margaret.

John gets up and starts heading towards the entrance. As another customer enters, John steps to the side to let them pass and he accidentally bumps into a gentleman whose back is to him while he is dialing a number on his phone. He turns around and apologizes even though the man never turns around and makes eye contact, but yet just grunts out loud and mumbles underneath his breathe. The gentleman excuses John for bumping him as he continues dialing the phone number. The man looks around the diner as the phone continues to ring on his end. He hears a woman's voice on the other end pickup.

"Adriana Hart, how can I help you?" she states with a professional voice. "This is Dominic Harvey. I was calling you back to discuss that rally idea you told me about," he replies in a scruffy voice. Dominic begins to write down an address and time on a piece of paper. He hangs up the phone and takes a pair of dark black sunglasses out his front suit coat pocket and puts them on. A waitress comes over and directs Dominic to a table. He sits down and orders food as he turns immediately making eye contact with Jesse. It was a surreal moment where the two were unaware to the fact of how they would cross paths in the nearing future. Jesse cordially nods his head to Dominic, as he ignores the gesture and rolls his eyes. A few minutes passed and the waitress brings out his food and Dominic begins eating, while ravaging through his pancakes, bacon and eggs. He looks around the room suspiciously as if he was waiting on someone to join him, while constantly wiping his mouth with his hand, even though there was a napkin beside him.

A gentleman enters the diner and sits down at the same booth halfway through Dominic finishing his meal and hands him an envelope before speaking briefly with him. Jesse was inquisitive about what they were discussing as he never fully took his eyes off this unidentified man, because the man sitting with Dominic was familiar to him. It was Senator Walt Michaels, dressed in what appeared to be a fairly expensive suit. Jesse questioned in his head why the Senator was in their neighborhood apparently conducting business with this suspicious gentleman; however, Jesse ignored the thought and continued to drink his coffee. Eventually, Dominic and Walt stood up and both exited the diner. Dominic left his half eaten food on the table with enough money to barely cover the cost of the meal without a decent tip for his waitress.

A few hours later, John walked through the front door of a motel he was temporarily staying at, which was closer to the city. He walked in and set down two fairly large suitcases that he was carrying. As John sits at the foot of the bed, he looks around to what he will begin to call home for a while. He hears his daughters' voice call out to him as he quickly turns his head only to find that no one is there. Then he hears his wife, Julie, come through the door as she calls out his name. John quickly turns his head and realizes there is still no one there. Their voices still haunt him. With little hesitation, he rushes to the bathroom and splashes water on his face to help bring him back to the world of normalcy. He can't get Sky's laughter out of his head. As he casually walks back into the bedroom, he picks up the remote control and turns on the television. He falls backwards on the bed to relax, while started to read scriptures from the bible that was given to him by Jesse as the Channel 6 newscast plays at a low tone within the background.

CHAPTER 4

POLITICS IN THE NEWS

"Things are heating up with politics. Everyone has views and opinions on the current condition that this country is in. Dominic Harvey, a local citizen, will be speaking at a nearby rally to talk on the current state we are in as a nation. We ran into Dominic not too long ago and he spoke his mind about the way things are going. It goes to show you that the people have an opinion too. Many people have been calling in asking where they can come and hear Dominic speak on the situation and voice their own opinions on the matter. His views and opinions can definitely be closely evaluated. He brings valid logic to the table, but his politics doesn't define his morals. It doesn't define his character! It seems like he could be a goodrunning mate if he ever ran in the next election, but people need to take the time out to get to know him as a person. We always pick our President based on the politics they deliver or they party they belong to, and not if the person is truly good for the nation. We sometimes forget that our individual voice is more powerful than our overall indifferences. Most stay silent when it comes time to vote and are VERY vocal after someone they dislike is elected.

Make the world what you want it to be and not what any politician convinces you that it should be! Many have already begun picketing outside the town hall to voice their opinions, while others may sit at home and watch. People want to be able to discuss issues that we are currently facing. Many believe that the current leadership by our standing President isn't within the best interest of the people.

A stand has to be made and our voices need to be heard. If you're interested in hearing Dominic speak at the rally or even voicing your opinion, come down to the Washington Town Hall tomorrow at noon. It starts with one person standing up for a change to happen. Several people have stated that they could run this nation and make things better, but easier said than done for most. Many can say they have what it takes, but are they willing to take that first step before they run. Many people have allowed this nation to remain in shambles versus lifting a single brick to help build what has been destroyed. Some people choose to follow our current President because they rather dine with the devil they know, than to break bread with the one they know not!

The current President has come from a rich family and also has family within the government. He has been handed everything since birth. Many argue that because of his wealthy historical background that he forgets about the little people. We have become separated into categories of importance to him. To him, there are the people that have and the ones that have not. Just remember that a man isn't defined by his endowment, but by his empowerment."

CHAPTER 5

PRESENT POLITICS

Five years passed and so much had happened within that time. Dominic was in full swing doing rallies and speaking all over the country while his lackey, Jarvis, spent most of his days babysitting Sky. Jarvis was becoming fond of the young kid as he watched this kid grow up. Dominic had many days where there was that same kind of connection, but he also would some days revert back to the time he was that age and scorned with so much hatred.

Sky would get the short end of that stick as Dominic would put him to the test with things that were said and passed down to him. He was almost trying to mold another version of his younger self. Each day that passed within the five years, Sky grew to know Dominic as his father and experienced the world in a different light. The five year old version of Sky now would have been a lot different if his family hadn't been killed or he hadn't been taken from his home and raised by a more sadistic father figure.

Now Sky was watching the world pass him by every day in fast forward. He saw many people come and go through his life. He witnessed Dominic's growth in popularity within the political realm and also how others around him responded to this growth. Dominic was becoming a mass phenomenon as those that listened to him speak were compelled to his every word.

Sky wasn't groomed to deal with such hatred as he spent many months after being born with John and Julie. They treated him with love and respect. It isn't to say that Dominic didn't do the same but he had his own way of doing so. That is the strange thing about it all. People wonder where hate comes from and they don't realize that it is inherited. It is passed down by our hated ancestors, hateful people we encounter and hateful friends that do us wrong. Sometimes we are placed in happy homes and around happy people and those do fine and sometimes it's up in the air and because us training ourselves to block out the negativity. In this case, Sky had no choice. He was conditioned by how Dominic treated him. Every at very young ages up until Sky had turned five years old, he was tested in many aspects. He would be put to the test in how he handled pressure, responded to anger and how he would conquer these things when face to face with them.

So here we are five years later and Dominic's popularity is at an all-time heightened point. He had begun hosting local political rallies at a nearby town hall in Washington D.C and having them recorded and televised. Dominic did this because when he began holding the rallies in other states, they were held once a month, and eventually they became so popular that he decided to hold them once a week. Even this was too much for him, especially with all the traveling he was doing. The news showed up every week from whatever town or city he was visiting and covered things that Dominic and other interested bystanders spoke out about. Eventually enough people came and attended those events that they formed a political Green Party of the

United States of America. This party believed in control over its' people, government and the media.

Dominic spoke at the rally he was at this bright Saturday afternoon that week on how the world is not a truly free world. He stated that we are forced to believe that we live in a free world as we are made to conform through the usage of law and guidance of our government. The things that Dominic spoke about put the current President of the United States on edge as he knew this could be a potential running mate that he should be concerned with. Dominic became a media icon who spoke in defiance against what the current President believed in or put forth. When more people heard Dominic speak over the years, they grew fond of him and made reference to the idea that he should run for President. Though he found this concept to be something that he was not prepared to endure, he never stopped speaking about how much change could be brought to the nation if he was to take on such a prestigious role as the commander in chief.

Sky grew older and was almost about to turn six years old. Dominic still looked at Sky and wanted him to one day be able to have something that he could inherit. Dominic felt that the way to obtaining power and giving his something to become his own was by taking part in these rallies. He felt he could build an army of followers that believed the message he was trying to convey. Every night he pondered to himself and thought that maybe the only way for him to have something of that nature, was to consider running for President of the United States. Dominic filled out the necessary paperwork and obtained enough votes to officially run for office.

As he walked in the doors of the local town hall to tell people of the news, he was greeted by many men, women and children. A lot of people looked up to him because he spoke about a new era where people would be able to actually live free instead of conforming to so many crazy laws and living in fear. This was so ironic because the kind of world he wanted it to really become was similar to the only kind of world he grew up in. He had a chance to see the world from two different sides but he had mainly grown up in primarily one of them. He grew up in a middle class household that eventually became a lower class household. The rough life he had, made him stronger, but also crazier as he had experienced much death at a young age and even got to a point where he was a criminal within his teen years to try and make it out alive on a daily basis. He had no guidance, no role model and no one to look up to. Little did the people know in which had attended this rally that this was the man they looked up to with that kind of backstory and mindset. To them, that didn't matter nor was it prevalent to who that considered following or listening to. They didn't support the crazed killer about to stand before them; they supported his politics and point of views.

As he took to the podium, the crowd began to simmer down to mere whispers. He pulled the microphone a little closer to his mouth and thanked everyone for coming out. The crowd cheered as most were people that helped Dominic to this point and knew what he was about to announce. "At first I didn't think you all would accept me because I didn't come out here wearing a blue or red tie. I didn't think you would accept me because the words that came out my mouth were not ones you always agreed with because they weren't the things you fully believed in and wanted to hear. Though, you have all supported me up to this point and I want to not only talk about this change that we all can have, but get to a position of power where

I can put these thoughts into the everyday law. I am glad to announce that after many days of contemplating, I have decided that we, as a nation, are lost and need direction," he stated with a firm voice. The crowd looked at him with very still eyes. Dominic took a deep breath and said "I am willing to be this nation's map...I have decided to run for President of the United States."

A loud uproar was cast throughout the town hall. People began to shout and chant Dominic's name within glorious praise. He raised his hand to settle everyone down as they conformed quickly to the raising of his arm. "The world will not get better by the rules we follow, but by the leadership provided. We must crawl before we walk and walk before we run!" he exclaimed. As Dominic finishes up his speech, many people were overwhelmed with joy as they try to look forward to a better beginning. He dismisses everyone as the meeting was adjourned and people began to exit the building in an orderly fashion. Jarvis comes toward the front of the podium with Sky and shakes Dominic's hand only to congratulate him on his successful speech and announcement. Sky walks over to Dominic and gives who he believes to be his father a hug. "Good job, dad!" Sky says.

Dominic quickly pushes him away and explains to him that he must never show feeling or emotion like that because it is a sign of weakness. Sky looks at him with confusion. He was too young to understand the message that Dominic was trying to push on him. All he sought was whom he knew as his father and someone he loved pushing him away from the affection and attention he needed at that young age.

Dominic looked at this as a perfect time to teach Sky something about becoming a respected leader. He glances around the room and notices that everyone had exited the building. No one is within clear view. Dominic kneels down and places his right hand on Sky's shoulder. The front door of the building quickly slams open as a women and her small child storm into the room towards Dominic and Sky. Dominic looks up as he gets up off of his one knee to greet the woman, who appeared to be very angry and disgruntle. As the woman approached Dominic she stops about three feet from him and begins screaming at him. She explains that she is against what Dominic is adamantly preaching. The woman continues to rant about how she feels it is because of the laws set forth by President Jennings that keeps her and her child safe and that Dominic is preaching to everyone something that would inevitably cause destruction and possibly even war.

It seems almost as if Dominic is not completely listening to the woman as he rudely turns away from her to continue trying to teach Sky a lesson. The woman, annoyed by Dominic's arrogance and brash demeanor, grabs him by the arm and spin him around. "Are you fucking kidding me?! You hear me! Don't you dare fucking ignore me when I am talking to you, you selfless prick," she screams in hopes that her words and approach will gain his attention. Her actions have the opposite effect, which may result in a decision she would soon shortly regret.

Dominic turns back to Sky and places his hand back onto his shoulder and says "This is a good way to explain what I am trying to do in this world. I want to create a world where we are not afraid of our government. I want to create a world where we are completely free!" Dominic reaches behind him and pulls a handgun out and fires a bullet into the head of the enraged woman. Blood splatters over Sky and

Dominic's face. Her daughter screamed and began to cry as she watched her mother bleed out over the floor.

Dominic reaches into his pocket and pulls out a white handkerchief to wipe the blood from his face. "In the world we live in now, I could go to jail, and even face the death penalty for doing what I have just done. But as I sit here and wait...I listen, and I hear nothing. No one! I am free to do what I want and to me that is true freedom. We are not in that era yet, so therefore we must dispose of all the evidence," Dominic states as he hands the gun to Sky and tells him to kill the woman's daughter who is frozen in fear after watching her mother be executed. Sky stood there looking at what Dominic had just done and was scared for his life. There was still blood from the little girls' mother splattered over Sky's face. He dropped the gun in fear and fell to his knees. Dominic picks up the gun and shoots the woman's daughter for him without the blink of an eye. "In time, you will learn how to be stronger! You aren't there yet. You're being a little bitch and people are drawn to that kind of behavior. The coyotes in the streets would eat you up alive," he denounces.

Jarvis, not bothered by what Dominic had just done, begins to drag the bodies towards the back. Just as he started to grab the carcasses by their lifeless arms, Dominic grabs Jarvis by his. "Have Sky carry the little girl's body out to the car and throw them in the trunk," he commands. Sky stood there confused by the order that was giving to Jarvis. It was almost as if anchors appeared shackled to each of his legs. Sky didn't want to touch the body that he had been told to execute, yet had cowered out of doing so. When Dominic tells Sky once more to help Jarvis and he doesn't move, still stuck dead where he stood, began to irritate the irrational crazed politician. "Did you fucking hear what I just said goddammit? Help Jarvis" he repeats, but yet with a more heightened irritation.

Dominic the places the barrel of his weapon up again Sky's left cheek. The tip of that barrel was still hot from the last bullet he had fired. It started to burn Sky's face as he tried to pull away, but Dominic grabbed him by the back of his head and pulled him in to prevent him from escaping. He felt that this was punishment so he would learn not to ever disobey his orders. Jarvis immediately stepped in. He had been Sky's caretaker for a while and watched over him these past five years. "I am sure he gets the point boss, I will have him help me. So don't you worry! I will bring the car around and we will both throw the bodies in the back and dispose of them later tonight," he added. Dominic tells Sky to wipe off his face and to go get in the car after he helped Jarvis. The events that took place were scarring and everlasting to young Sky. No young child should be witness to such heinous and vial acts, though this was Dominic's crazed and sadistic way of raising Sky and making his point clear.

A few weeks later, Dominic was in the race for Presidency against two senators. One of the senators, Donald Polanski, from California, whom had made a huge impact with the Republican Party based upon the partisan viewpoints he held and another known by many as William Casper, a senator from Virginia whom became more controversial with his liberal ideas when he started various arguments against Dominic for actually deciding to run under the Green Party. He exploited the history of the Green Party; it created an egregious uproar where many United States citizens began turning the other cheek from Dominic and his views. So much of the media began to revolve around Dominic and William that they became the center of attention during the election season. Donald Polanski ended up dropping out of the race half way through, because he was not seen as controversial or popular as the other Presidential candidates. Many debates were held between William and Dominic within those next few weeks as they approached the actual election night.

It wasn't until about a week before that night, the two candidates had a debate and the topic of abortion came up. Senator Casper was completely against it and felt that no one should have the right to kill another living human being. He saw it to be immoral and wrong, considering the unborn child does not have a say or choice within the matter. Whether people agreed or disagreed with him, Dominic brought a sense of logical thinking to the table. Dominic argued that what the senator was saying was hypocritical. Many believe that whether they agreed with Dominic or not, he made sense about the things that he voiced. It could have been a turning point in the election that could have caused many people that were not there to vote for Dominic to actually change their intended vote in his favor.

After Senator Casper spoke about how he disagreed with abortion and how no one should make a choice like that, Dominic took the stand and spoke on the issue. As he took the podium, he heard some people cheer and some sneered as they chanted hateful things out. The crowd began to settle and a voice was heard throughout the auditorium asking Dominic for his views and opinions on the debated issue. Dominic cleared his throat and began to speak. "Senator Casper says that no person should be allowed to take the life of another human being. He feels that it is wrong and that they should have a choice on whether they live or die. I call him a hypocrite! Abortion is no different from a man or woman sitting on death row. And this

I know if a topic he is for. We, as a nation, allow someone else to decide whether another human being lives or dies. You, as a person, cannot disagree with abortion and agree with the death penalty! We all deserve the same freedom. Life isn't based on a choice and neither should death," Dominic voiced with a powerful discretion.

The crowd could be heard erupting throughout the entire auditorium. Many that were there in spite Dominic understood where he was coming from. They all sought him to be someone that whether you agree with him or not, that there was a lot of logical thinking that was backed behind what he preached. We, as a nation, may hate the crimes committed and said hatred that engulfs the world, but the one thing we all agree on is that we all want to have a sense of freedom. Dominic didn't pick a side within agreeing or disagreeing with abortion. He only made it obvious that disagreeing with abortion is wrong in comparison to agreeing with the death penalty. It went to show that one cannot agree with one and disagree with the other or vice-versa and tend to hold that as their legitimate argument.

The night continued on with a debate where Dominic makes more logical points of thinking. The crowd sided more and more with what he said, whether if he agreed or disagreed on certain topics. It was clear how people sought Dominic in the auditorium, but what really mattered was on if the rest of the nation agreed with him.

Another week passed and we have finally reached the moment of truth. It was Election Day and everyone was anxious to find out what history was set in store for the nation. Sky and Jarvis walked into the main room where Dominic was. He was standing around waiting anxiously. They are followed by several other people that are in affiliation with the Green Party. One of the supporters Walt Michaels, a now former Senator, places his left hand on Dominic's shoulder and shakes his hand with the other. He congratulates Dominic on coming so far within the election and comments on the impactful responses given during his debates against Senator Casper. "Well done, my friend!" he respectfully remarks.

The two of them briefly chat, when a man yells out for everyone to quiet down and to turn up the television. Sky walks over to the television and picks up the remote control. He turns up the volume loud enough for everyone to hear it and sets the remote back on the table. Their attention is honed in as they wait to find out who is going to win which states.

The news reporter announces that Dominic won the states of Michigan, California and Texas. The room bursts into an uproar, considering that Texas and California are two huge states to win over within the Electoral College. Senator Casper began to take the nextsix states. Even though they were smaller states, it caused Dominic to be a little concerned. Everyone in the room was silent in suspense as they tuned in for what was to come next. The newscaster reported that Dominic had just won the states of New York, Pennsylvania and Ohio. These were great wins for him, but it didn't stop there as more states were rattled off. She then continued to announce that he had won New Jersey, Florida, Illinois, Georgia, and North Carolina. This gave Dominic two hundred and seventy-one votes, which was enough votes to have won the race and be considered the next President of the United States of America.

When everyone heard the news, the room began yelling out and congratulating Dominic on a job well done. Walt

Michaels came over and popped a bottle of champagne and poured it into several glasses as they were passed out to everyone in attendance. Just before they began to drink till they were all heavily intoxicated, Walt Michaels decided to make a toast. "I am not the most recognizable person to speak here. Many of you may not even know who I am. I agree with the vision of Dominic and have stood by his side through thick and thin, promoting him, handing out fliers, and going door-to- door talking to people. All of these things have proved to me that hard work can pay off. I pray that one day I could be in his shoes as the President. One day I can wear the crown and have all the glory and praise. Until that dream is lived, put your glasses in the air and cheers to the soon to be United States President, Dominic Harvey!" Walt presented with such aspiration. The adults clanked their glasses and toasted the new President as they began to party until the break of dawn.

Several weeks passed as Dominic and Jarvis began to plan for the Inauguration Day. Dominic knew that he reached a point of power that could finally possess something worth passing on to Sky. Whereas he was someone that had a dark past that many did not know about and even if they did they still wouldn't understand, he had proved to be someone that could induce change in the world. The question was if this change would inevitably be viewed as a positive or negative one. They were all soon to find out what nightmare they would fall victim to. If the world knew of his past wrong doings, it would have greatly affected his upcoming plans as President. For every man that seems so innocent, even they have skeletons that are buried and Dominic was one of those people. His crazed sadistic mind was not portrayed within the race to become President, but truly was some- thing that people would soon become exposed to and learn more about a deeper mindset he had hidden behind this political mask he wore with such intense fabrication.

The biggest thing on Dominic's mind was to completely earn the respect of the general public and have the world see him as being genuine and kind. The day finally arrived where Dominic was set to deliver his inaugural speech and oh how it was set to be a memorable one. People crowded in on the front lawn of the Capital building to hear him speak as many others watched around the world from their homes. As the festivities began, Dominic became very impatient. He paced back and forth backstage as he practiced his speech in his head over and over.

Finally, he hears a voice announce his name over the speakers. The people began to cheer as Dominic boldly trotted out to the podium for one last speech before taking on the role as the President of the United States. As he reached the stand, the people yet again settled down and awaited his formal speech. He wasn't as nervous this time as he was before. The jitters had seemingly faded. Dominic stayed focused on the task at hand and had a vision of his own in mind. He sought this to be a piece of cake.

Everyone felt they had selected the right person to be their commander in chief, but little did they know that they were in for a rude awakening. Sometimes, we don't pick people to be our leaders based on the quality of person they are, but yet by the politics they promote and the image they fool us with. Imagine picking captains for a football team. People don't pick the captain based on who is the fastest runner or one who knows the names of all the players on the team. They pick the person based on who displays the necessary qualities that appear to be someone capable of leading the team to victory in their eyes. They look at who the team trusts the most and respects, even if that player may be a child molester and they are just unaware of such sinful history or even if he beats on his girlfriend of wife daily. Those kinds of qualities define the character of who we put in office because they define what kind of person he or she truly is. We cannot go by the things they tell us they will do for us if elected or just because they support certain views we agree with that benefit just us as individuals or our own family. This didn't stop those that supported Dominic, as he was ready to take on this new role and make an effort to change the world. He stepped up to the microphone with this being his motive and drive in mind. There was no fear on his part. He cleared his throat and thanked everyone for coming out and for those watching at home.

As he paused to gain everyone's attention, he began to speak proudly to everyone with a voice of inspiration. "Freedom! I want everyone to think about that word. Freedom is something we all desire. The reality is that we are in a delusion. A delusion where we feel we already possess this so-called freedom. People say we have a freedom of speech, though you can't say bomb in an airport. They say you have the freedom to love whoever you want, but you can't show that emotion in public. It's said that you have the freedom to go wherever you want, but the government has restricted areas; Mexicans can't come here without a visa or green card. I am here to lead you to what true freedom is. Nothing I do will please every single person and I get that. Most may see the changes I will make for this nation as being malignant. No matter how contentious you may feel I am at times, I still have the same mission that I had when you elected me. I want everyone to understand that I want to go down in history with a legacy that will be remembered.

Being the President is just half the battle, gaining a legacy is worth so much more to me. A legend is someone who does miraculous things that are accomplished within his or her life expectancy. Though a legacy...a legacy is composed of the miraculous things a legend has done followed by a limitless life-span. This is the difference between the two. A legacy will never die and I promise you that I will change the way this world is. It will be because of me that we will achieve world peace and a stronger foundation. We may have walked into a dark tunnel, but the further that we travel together through the tunnel you will find that the end...the end is incandescent," he declared.

Everyone rose to their feet and began to applaud Dominic as he raised his hand and waived to the public. It is true that the world needs change, but not the kind of change that Dominic had in store for them. As he took office the following day, he began to have meetings almost every day to address some of the important matters he wanted to change. Though it was a rocky road ahead for him, there were several challenges he faced along the way within his four-year term. Dominic had to persuade a lot of people that what he was doing was the right thing and how it would ultimately lead to people having complete freedom.

Dominic was fast approaching his inauguration. When the day arrived for him to give his speech, many had been in attendance and waited to hear him speak. The speech was unusual as it wasn't the normal Dominic that we were used to seeing. He had to put on this front as business came first and he had just taken on the biggest positon in employment one can obtain in the United States of America. He stood at the podium amazed by the amount of people that showed up to hear what he had to say. The fear was something that he just couldn't let get to him, so he jumped right into speaking to the citizens.

"Is this a dream? That is a question that I have been asking myself for the past couple of days. I have realized that this is a reality for me and soon to be a reality-check for many of you. I saw that because I am part of the Green Party. This party is different because it doesn't share the same views as those to which are considered Democrats or Republicans. The Democrats are against abortion, where the Republicans are not. The Democrats are for gun control and the Republicans are not. Democrats want same-sex marriage and Republicans see the life of a married couple to be shared only through the love of one man and one woman. I can go on and on with the differences these two parties house. Each side has the belief that there party is the way the world should be lead, when it hasn't put more love into the world, but yet more money in others pockets. Both sides, ironically though, believe in the Constitution and the written words it doctrines. You ultimately make the choice, but just because you are given the freedom of speech doesn't mean you have to use hateful words or put each other down. Just because you have the right to bear others, doesn't mean you have the right to kill another. Just because you have the right to be protected by any unreasonable searches or seizures doesn't mean you can do what you want. You all believe in these rights and create what laws are made in addition in them. I say all of this because it is foreseen what direction I will go with this Green Party. Imagine being able to do as you please in a New America. I choose this one before the old America or the one we are fooled into believing is a United America. Imagine equality for all and therefore no worry of having less or more than another human being. I have been elected to make a difference and so I shall. I hear from many people that say that the world won't get better. They blame it on different political parties, races, cultures, generation, laws, government, criminals, rich people and poor people. They say why try because it is what it is and it won't get any better. Others are not to blame. You want others to change an every other person wants others to change. This means, that you are 'others' to other people. You have to make a change. I have to make a change. We have to make a change and we will. I intend to make that said change by taking some views from Republicans and some from Democrats and even some ideas of my own and combining them to give this illustrious freedom I speak of. You won't understand what I mean now. You will have questions, but I don't owe you answers in the small timeframe that I am in office. I owe you results. I will make difficult choices and so will you, yet by the end of it all, we will see the America that we all dreamed for," announced Dominic. People were confused by what he meant within his speech, but they cheered for him anyway. Only time will tell how it will all playout.

Within his four-year term he legalized abortion, marijuana, and immigrants being able to come to the states without the necessity of a Visa or green card. This was only the beginning of how he gave back a true sense of freedom to all Americans. Whereas a lot of people didn't agree with what he was doing, they all soon stood by his side. He held many speeches where people came and attended even though they were in disagreement with what he would speak about, and most times people left with a different perspective on things as his approach left people skewed on theirs. Dominic spoke with such conveyance within his portrayed message that people loved him and respected what things he sought to be a good decision for the nation. Even other countries began to like Dominic and saw the great things he did for giving back a sense of true freedom. He wanted people to understand that they truly had a choice and what they chose was up to them. Other leaders began to ask him for advice and implement the same laws and policies.

Before Dominic was the President, it was true that people had freedom to choose whatever they wanted, but most choices people made were influenced by the possible consequence set forth to create a more conformed nation. As Dominic neared the end of his first term, a vast majority of the nation backed him up within running for re- election. Dominic didn't feel like the things he had done within his first term were complete in obtaining a legacy worth remembering. It was even unclear if he could deliver the results he promised in another four years.

Dominic ran for re-election after completing his first term and was successfully re-elected again. He won the election by a landslide this time and continued to change things within the world to give back that sense of true freedom. His two terms almost completely transpired as Dominic looked back at it all when it was was all nearing an abrupt end. He questioned if he had created the world he truly wanted, legally, or if he conformed as a President to making the changes he was limited to making. Eight years wasn't enough time to give the people what they needed. He had spent so much time, fighting congress on many issues to get things past during his start that this ultimately put a wrench in his start. It wasn't until he gained the respect by his followers and other leaders that it had become smooth sailing within his second term. Though time had been lost, it was time for a new election to be held and another President to take the oath of office.

Sky had now neared the age of fourteen and Dominic did whatever it took to teach him how to be stronger as a man.

Dominic had changed a lot of things within his eight years as President, though he still didn't feel satisfied, like things were truly free for the American citizens. The new Presidential race began and started to become the talk of the town. Many people loved what Dominic had done so far, but it was obvious to the people that he was not as happy with his legacy.

Walt Michaels took a stand and ran in the Presidential race. He wanted to live up to the same kind of image that Dominic had and continue to leave behind a legacy of his own that would be remembered by everyone. Running against him, was a younger man that was a Senator from Texas, by the name of Marcus Sparks and an older Senator of Louisiana named Edward Gills. The politics of Walt Michaels was not of great interest to the public. Even though many knew him as being a part of Dominic's past political party from his first election, it wasn't something that gave him popularity or recognition. Many wouldn't even recognize him as a former Senator from almost ten years ago. That says a lot about the mark he left when he held that chair. Walt Michaels eventually dropped out of the current race because he thought that maybe he wasn't running for Presidency at the right time in his life. He wanted to build more of a fan base and gain more trust from the people.

Senator Sparks and Senator Gills held many debates. They were both in agreement that the way Dominic took over and legalized so many things has created a lesser sense of security. Both of the Senators felt that the laws set forth before his Presidency were not things that were meant to create a sense of conformity, but yet a sense of safety. Dominic watched the television as both Senators put him down and insulted all of the things he worked so hard towards within his two terms as being worthless. He knew that if he stood by and let these Senators completely destroy his name or legacy that everything he had done so far would have been for nothing. This began to enrage Dominic as he sat in the Oval office and he began to ponder what steps he should take from this point on. For everything he had done so far, he didn't want it to have been seen as meaningless.

It was about a week before voting day that Dominic sat at home in the Presidential Suite next to Sky watching the newscast. Senator Gills was being interviewed by a reporter about what his thoughts were if he were to be elected as the President of the United States. The Senator looked into the camera and explained that the current leader, President Harvey, had not lived up to the legacy he promised to create. He reminded the people that within one week, Dominic's time would be up. He also acknowledged that the only thing Harvey had to show for was legalizing things that didn't help the society, lower the crime rate or create world peace. The senator pointed out statistics within how the crime rate has risen in the last three years or so. He also quoted people whom wrote letters that were against the things Dominic did within his two terms.

Senator Gills glanced over to the reporter and told her that he had some advice for the current President. He looked back towards the camera before speaking. "President Harvey, you have talked about how you want to be a legend with a legacy that is truly remembered by us all. You are a joke and you have done nothing to help us grow as a country. You have talked a great deal and in my opinion, as I am sure many others would agree, you haven't lived up to your words and promises. Powerful words don't lead a nation, powerful people do!" he stated with a smarmy grin before handing the microphone back to the newscaster. As the reporter takes the microphone from him, she begins to end the segment with a few closing words of her own.

CHAPTER 6

DIPLOMATIC CHANGE

"Leadership, Change, Legacy! They are all words that were supposed to have meaning for the last eight years. Yet, they are words that everyone is still debating today. One can have leadership and invoke change, but does that make for a legacy. We, as a nation, have all been in agreement that we wanted change, but we have to ask ourselves if we got more than what we asked for or less.

America is like a little kid at Christmas that runs downstairs to see their gifts. Like most children, we are excited that we got what we asked for but ignore the smaller gifts. We play with the toys we really wanted and kick them to the curb and then want something brand new a minute later. Many people leave behind something that impacts or changes other people's lives. Some leave behind, music, art or literature that goes on to inspire others to write or sing or draw. That is a legacy that is worth more than a Presidency.

It is true that you can create a legacy with a Presidency, but it is argued if Dominic Harvey has done so with his allotted time. Sometimes the things that we do that become a legacy that is remembered by so many, doesn't become a legacy until a lot of time has passed. We ask ourselves if Dominic Harvey left behind a legacy and we just have to wait and find out how important it is down the road. Sometimes people come in and say they will do better and don't live up to the things they say which then that causes us to respect what we had prior.

You don't appreciate something until it is gone. Words that are so poorly understood! We all live and learn from the choices we make. Dominic has definitely given us some freedom of choice without consequence. Some feel that they are completely free, while others feel they have no safety and security.

In about a week, we will elect a new President and they will promise us something as well. What they promise us will not be something I feel will change the world for the better! You will always have two sides of the fence. You cannot please everyone, no matter how hard you try. The world is filled with opinions and two sides. Republicans and Democrats! Right and wrong! Left and right! Black and White! His or Hers! Mine or Theirs! Ours or Everyone! We cannot create change in the world, if we are always in debate on how to change it! I am Adriana Hart and this has been your Channel 6 News..."

CHAPTER 7

DOMINANT DOMINIC

About three days before the nation was set to vote on a new President, Dominic contacted the media and called a press conference. When the media heard that the current President was calling this press conference, the word spread instantly worldwide. No one knew exactly what Dominic was planning to discuss at the conference, but things heated up as people began showing up to hear him speak. As Dominic stood in the back room patiently waiting, Sky walked in. "You wanted to see me," he said. Dominic turned towards Sky and told him to have a seat. "Many people are going to say bad things about me after today. They will be upset with me and may even become belligerent because of my actions. I have a legacy to uphold. I want to have something that is worth remembering so that I can pass it on to you. I cannot please these CUNTS, and those that disagree can just fucking go to HELL." Dominic jeered.

Jarvis walked in during the conversation and quickly apologized for rudely interrupting. He explained to Dominic that everyone had arrived and were patiently waiting for his public address. Dominic nodded his head and walked past Sky, exiting the room and closing the door behind him. As he walked down the hallway he turned to Jarvis and stated to him that things were about change. There was just a feeling he had deep down inside of him. Jarvis didn't know exactly what Dominic had planned, though he could tell that this version of his deranged friend was a very cold-hearted person. One he almost didn't recognize. He has seen something similar to this look in Dominic's eyes many times before, specifically the night they took Sky from his home, but this one was way darker and came across as even more demented. That day that Dominic took Sky and killed John Lewis' family was quite a moment in his life that was filled with many spiraling events. Lots of lives were lost that day and hearts broken by it.

Dominic walked through the curtain and took the stage as he was blinded by the flashes emitted from the news and photographers' cameras. News reporters began to scream his name and yell out various questions. "Mr. President, what will todays' sudden news conference cover?" one reporter asked.

"Are you happen with your two terms and how do you think the next President elected will do in office?" asked another. Without missing a beat, he calmed the clamored audience of reporters down. Dominic noticed Senator Gills and Senator Sparks in the back of the room as they looked on with sweat running down their face andnecks. The armpits reeked of a stench that would be recognizable as fear and nervousness. He informed the masses that this conference was going to be brief without any follow-up questioning. He took the microphone from the stand and held it firmly in his hand. The anxious bystanders starred at the President as he began to speak about what was initially on his mind.

"Many people feel that I have not created a legacy worth remembering. I promise everyone that you will remember this day! I have given you change and freedom. Many have sneered at what vision I wanted to set forth, whereas some came around and supported that vision. Now you will all find a sense of true freedom and also have the safety that so many people yearned for and felt had been diminished. There are three days left before you select a new President, and I will give you change today. I will give you freedom! I, Dominic Harvey, am putting this nation in a State of Emergency. I will be using the full force of the military to enforce martial law. I won't govern a world made of glass, but I will mold one made of clay!" Dominic boldly stated as the room burst into an uproar filled with confusion.

Many people began to walk out after hearing what they saw to be an infuriating announcement or began to throw things towards the stage while tumultuously booing the world leader. Some people even spit towards the podium, trying to hit President Harvey with their projectile saliva as a message stating their outrage. "The military will be collecting all firearms. I will ONLY allow military officials, who are meant to protect, the right to bear arms. Anyone caught with a firearm will be subject to death by firing squad. I am announcing a Presidential pardon to all jailed convicts and demanding they be released immediately. Crime is something I cannot get rid of, so why cage all current and future beasts for their crimes? Martial law will be the best part of insuring your safety. People will only be allowed out of their home between the hours of eight o'clock in the morning to eight at night. And lastly, the military will execute any individuals who run against me or tries to take me out of office by political means as the President of the United States. I am Dominic Harvey and this is the start of my legacy. I'M DONE NEGOTIATING!" Dominic stated with a comment that grew increasingly pugnacious as he combatively slammed the microphone down in vexation. The Senators running in the election stood by wit a few other officials clamoring about how what was being done went against their right and wasn't within the control governed to the president. They became rowdy to the point where soldiers lined them up and had them all executed down the row on the live telecast as the footage was cut short soon after the second or third execution.

One bullet after another piecing through each appointed official cranial skulls and chest cavities, succumbing to the horrific televised massacre. The power had been so hastily transferred over to Dominic as each body took its perilous fall. The now former senators, whom lay there deceased after spewing their own publicized political voice, became a statement to the American people. Who was crazy enough to stand in his way? It was so bizarre and unheard of for a President to subside from traditional presidential behavior and become an individual that had divulged his mentality driven by his past criminal ways by publicly using his power to murder other human beings and do so blatantly in front of witnesses that felt incapable to stand up and say or do anything.

Dominic made his way over to one of the senators' bodies and sat down beside him as he was gurgling blood in his mouth, while gasping for air and awaiting his last breath. The president leaned his head over, whispering something so demented into his ear as it became the last words that he would hear before his life had been fully taken. "Just so you know, I thought about having the soldiers of mine brutally cut out your tongue from your disgusting mouth instead of death by gunfire as punishment for your defiance, but this way is quick and less painful. But know that I originally wanted you to suffer!"

confirmed Dominic as most of his eerie comments were not heard. By this point the senator had already passed away. His eyes lids slowly closed and his chin slumped over into Dominic's chest.

One man soon afterwards began to argue with the soldiers that stood at the front of the crowd while trying to restrain him from rushing the stage. "You can't do this. It is in the Constitution that we have the right to bear arms and that you can't come into our homes to seize our weapons. I would love to see you try to take our guns from us. It better be by force and we will fight back! I know our rights and I know the Constitution," denounced the angry civilian. Dominic got up off the ground immediately and heading back over to the podium and pulled out a rolled up document that he had stashed behind the staging area. The man looked on as he was curious to what the President had in his hand. It remained hidden till it had been brought into view for all to see.

"Do you mean this Constitution?" Dominic acknowledged before setting the Constitution on fire in front of the many people in attendance. The flames tore away at the fragile document with ashes and smoke floating through the air. People gasped at the horrific site that was taking place as a U.S. sitting President heartlessly burned the American constitution. "Treason!" one women screamed out waving her clinched fist in the air Dominic picked back up the microphone and demanded that the soldiers in the audience bring the woman to the front of the stage. She tried to push her way through the mass amount of people, but was cornered and apprehended. The soldiers escorted her to the front as President Harvey had them restrain her arm, still with her fist clinched, across the top of the podium. Jarvis brought out a large machete and handed it to Dominic.

"Treason you say? I can't do this because of the constitution you say? I can do it if the military supports it. You all need this tough love. I had been given that kind of love when I was five years old in the basement of my own home. Consider this that same kind of tough love," the President voiced before slinging the machete down on top of the podium and slicing off the woman's arm. One could hear the cracking of her bone as it separated from her body. She screamed in agony as Dominic was gracious enough to put her out of her misery by slicing her throat wide open in front of everyone. Could this really be happening by a President that we put in office? Why is no one doing anything? It is obvious that if we allow them to have this power, then they will take it, do what they want with it and eventually want more. This was the point of our own demise. It is no longer a nation built on those three little words, 'We the People!'

A few military officials walked into the room after the assault on the woman with assault rifles drawn. They walked towards the two Senators in the back of the auditorium and pointed their guns in their direction. They placed their hands up and shouted out for help, but before they were able to get out a few words the military executed them on the spot. People began to scream and panic as they ran out of the auditorium. Upon exiting the building, they noticed armored trucks and tanks roving the streets. Thousands on top of thousands of heavily armed military officials with assault rifles walked the streets searching people's homes nearby and collecting all firearms.

A man ran out of his home wearing a t-shirt with the confederate flag on it and his boxers, shouting out various things at the tanks that passed him by. He shot off a couple rounds at the tanks and trucks passing by. "You fuckers want some! Come get some of this! I have my rights! I don't care if you burned up our constitution" he yelled out. One of the tanks turned its cannon towards the man and fired off a deadly blow that killed man and blew half of the front of his house away. Pieces of his home were scattered everywhere and a baby could be heard crying inside that laid there covered in debris.

As some soldiers rushed into multiple houses in groups, they were seen bringing out several handguns or shotguns and placing them into an armored truck after a thorough search of the grounds. The soldiers left one house nearby as they quickly moved off to raiding the next. It seemed as if our rights had been stripped and things had gotten worse than ever. A group of soldiers were walking out of one house with a few weapons in hand, as they notice a neighbor close by within his backyard burying something. The soldiers stampeded into his yard with their weapons aimed at him. They forced the man to the ground as one soldier begins pushing some of the dirt away to find a nine millimeter handgun stashed securely in a clear plastic bag. The soldier that was holding the man down took a pistol out of a holster from his boot and executed the man on his own property. The group of military soldiers packed up their things and left him where he was in cold blood, bleeding out next to his patio.

They walked across the grass trampling many of the flowers along the way while heading towards the next home to knock on the door. No one answered when they arrived as they pounded even harder with their closed fist. A voice was heard eventually on the other side telling them to hold on. When the door opened, one soldier looked at the man and asked if his name was Jesse Dean. "Yes, I am Jesse Dean," he replied. The brute soldier pushed Jesse aside and forced his way past. Several other soldiers rushed in behind him and began searching the house. Jessed wasn't going to just let them men come into his home. He hadn't been watching the news to know what was going on, however, he did know his rights as a citizen and decided to voice what was on his mind to the soldier.

"I am a federal agent," he retorted. The soldier turned the other cheek and continued searching around. "Did you hear me? You do not have the right!" Jesse shouted even louder. The soldier turned around in pure frustration to the remark and shoved Jesse against the wall by his throat, as he explained that government officials are being overthrown as well. "There is nothing you can do about it?" he mentioned.

A few military soldiers came down the stairs of Jesse's home with several handguns as they passed Jesse and other soldiers. One soldier patted Jesse on the cheek and told him to have a good day before exiting the home, leaving the door wide open behind him. Jesse picked up a vase that was nearby and stepped out a few steps from his front door as he threw the vase at them. It smashed against the soldiers' head and sent him plummeting to one knee. The soldier turned around enraged, as he began to bleed from the back of his head. He stood up and began walking with his assault rifle aimed towards Jesse. Blood poured down his back, drenching his uniform, with visible pieces protruding out from his skull. Another soldier who was of higher ranked screamed out to the soldier that he should let him be because they had other houses to raid before the late curfew shift was to begin. "It just isn't worth it. We will get you to medical to have that looked at," he added in response in order to calm the situation between Jesse and the now infuriated soldier.

The exchange of facial expressions and body composure could raise hairs on any mans' arm. There was a tension between the two that was like a ticking time bomb waiting to explode. The time constraint was easily recognized when the soldier looked down at his watch. He holstered his weapon, but not before glaring into Jesse's eyes and expressing to him that he had dodged a tremendously fatal bullet today. Jesse rolled his eyes and stood his ground, so not to be intimidated by the remark. The soldier then turned around and walked back to the camouflaged military jeep, as all of the other soldiers piled in with him and rode off to the next street around the corner.

Jesse ran into the house and picked up the phone and began dialing a particular number. The phone rang and rang until someone answered. "John, there are soldiers everywhere, they are confiscating weapons. This is all President Harvey's doing!" he remarked. John tried to calm Jesse down and implored him to stay inside while things brushed over. He continued to explain to his friend how knew about everything going on because he had been glued to watching the news every hour and was up to speed on everything happening. "Its way worst that you can imagine!" John added. He informed Jesse that there were soldiers roaming around the motel complex where he was staying and taking lives of those that didn't comply or were in possession of any fire arms.

A knock at the door was heard in the background. John told Jesse he had to go and that he would call him back later. He quickly hung up the phone and ran to the door to open it. When he did, a few soldiers walked in past him and began searching John's room. When they were unable to find anything, they packed up their belongings and swiftly left without an exchange of a single word to him. He casually complied and wasn't confrontational with them, so not to set off any triggers that would cause them to stay longer than expected. They came in and did what they had to do and left with little conversation or interaction. As the door shut behind them, John rushed over to the air vent and took off the front panel. He stuck his hand towards the back as far as he could and pulled out two silver plated Beretta 92FS handguns. John checks the ammo on both handguns and places the safety back on both weapons, before putting them both back into the air vent where he was hiding them. He closed the vent and puts back two screws loosely into the vents pre-drilled holes.

The phone rang again as it startled John. He rushed over to the phone and answers it. When he picks up, he recognizes it to be his close friend calling back still enraged at what was going on. Jesse had begun talking before John even got a chance to greet him, asking him if everything was alright. He tried to calm Jesse down while asking him what the noise that he could hear in the background was. His friend explained that he is in his car on his way over to the motel that John was staying in because he was worried. John assured him that things were fine and that there was no need to be concerned. There was a pause of brief silence on the other end before John called out Jesse's name. Jesse stammers to respond back but told John that he will call him back in a minute and swiftly hung up the call.

When Jesse set the phone down, he had then pulled over to the side of the road and notices hundreds of convicted felons that were wearing orange jumpsuits rushing out of the gated front entrance of the local Washington D.C. prison. While the prisoners scammer around in large groups, Jesse opened up his car door and stepped out of his vehicle. Everyone was running as fast as they could, as they crossed the street causing the flow of traffic to slow down tremendously. Jesse even notices an older man around the age of seventy pacing around amongst other inmates that were seen running out of the jail, The man gingerly walked behind the mass hysteria that was ensuing behind him almost like a lost puppy. Jesse calls out to the elderly man, "Sir...Sir, do you need some help?" The man appears to be wearing a prisoner gown as well. It was obvious that he has been locked up for a long time at this particular prison from his scruffy appearance and noticeable scars on his body. There were also several tattoos visible, some of which stood out as being very dark themed. He had many covering his neck and arms of very satanic looking images and even more alarming phrases. One that caught Jesse off guard was a tattoo on this mans' arm that appeared to be of a deteriorating human heart that was slightly cut open and sitting in a pool of blood with a phrase beneath it that read, 'till my last heartbeat.'

It was just as the man had heard Jesse calling out to him, that the fragile looking senior citizen scampered over to greet him but not before acknowledging that he has no clue what was happening. Jesse then demands that the gentleman get into his car and they drive away from all the madness so they can talk in private. When inside of the vehicle, Jesse got straight to the questions he needed answers to by asking him what his name is. "Huh?" he responds while steadily distracted from several other convicts pushing their way by one another in sheer happiness to have been set free. They were aggressively pounding on several car windows along the way, including Jesse's vehicle, as they passed by in a disorderly fashion.

Jesse didn't want to lose sight of finding out more about the mysterious individual that he knew nothing about, so he asked him a second time as to what his name was. The man softly replied that his name is Samuel and he had been incarcerated at that penitentiary for over forty years now. "I was actually serving a life sentence on death row!" he added as Jesse becomes a little alarmed and even more curious. Samuel then tells Jesse as to how his day had gone up to this very point where the two of them had crossed paths. His words were jumbled and sometimes were received with much confusion by Jesse as he tried hard to remain attentive and focused while listening to Samuel tell his story. "I woke up late and continued reading parts of the Bible. I had finished up several versus and headed to lunch. After that I sat in my cell pondering to myself about life. My life and others that I have affected with choices I made within my life. Soon, an announcement was made over the telecom that the all prisoners will be released immediately with little information to follow that announcement as to why," Samuel mentions.

Jesse nods his head when listening to Samuel vent about what he had been through and explains to him that the President had just announced today that he was placing the nation in a State of Emergency and enforcing martial law. He did this as a means to exchange conversation and tell Samuel how the day went for him. As Jesse explains most of what happened during the town hall meeting in detail, he adds that one of the President's first acts was to pardon all current criminals of the United States. This was enough to have caught Samuel up to speed with what was going on with the government, considering how he spent most of his days behind bars. Samuel, still confused, asks why the President would do such an unthinkable action. From what he had watched on the television within the last most recent days, the President seemed to be about helping people to him and trying to make this world a more free society and safer place.

Jesse sarcastically laughs and points out that he feels this may be the level of freedom that the President was going for. "Some knew about his dark past and tried to point it out that we shouldn't elect this monster, but people are too blinded voting for either their political party or the person that tells them the most that they want to hear that they overlook the kind of person they are actually voting for. We got what we wanted or so we thought," denounced Jesse. As the two drove back towards Jesse's house, he realizes that the local diner near his house was on the way and asks Samuel if he was hungry. The prudent old man nodded and agreed to how stopping for a bite to eat wasn't such a bad idea suggested. Jesse pulled in and parks the car. Throughout all the mass hysteria, this local diner seemed to be the most normal place around within miles at that time. They walked in and saw the television on, with many people standing around watching, as they continued to eat their lunch while glued to the screen.

Margaret then comes up and asks Jesse if he can believe what is going on. "This is some insane stuff we are dealing with. And no one is going to say anything or challenge the President," noted Margaret. Jesses shakes his head and tells her that he feels this is only the beginning. Margaret realizes that Jesse is with someone that she has never met before and most importantly that he has on a prisoner gown. She immediately asks him who his friend is. The older man with him was noticeably out of place by the attire he was wearing. Jesse smirks and replies to his friend, Margaret, that he picked him up from the local penitentiary a few miles back. She gives Jesse a look of confusion before asking if they are staying to eat anything and also to watch on as things begin to lavishly unfold. The two nod in agreement and begin to order some food with Samuel giving his order first. Margaret jots down their requests and walks away to go and put it in on the computer.

The fond waitress casually walks away and Jesse sees this as a great opportunity to ask Samuel what he went to jail for. The curiosity had seemed to be surrounding him since they both first met. Samuel gave a weird look considering how he figured that sort of question was bound to come up at some point. "I didn't mean to be nosey or pry. I was just curious what you were in prison for on death row," Jesse noted after asking. Samuel takes a sip of water as it was expected for such a question to come up. He wasn't happy about his past and knew that he was young and made bad choices back then. "Murder!" he responds.

Jesse had chills rise up his spine hearing that word. He was casually sitting in a diner having lunch with a convicted murderer. Samuel didn't want to be seen as a monster from a choice he made long ago that is reflective of five minutes of his life or even shorter as one to define every waking minute of his life and become incumbent around what kind of person he was. "I hate to be viewed as some sort of aging dog whose years are dwindling down and needs to be taken out behind the shed and put down. My story is more than that one moment that I regret. We all make mistakes, my fuck up just happened to be bigger than what most make, but this is my story," he continued.

Samuel lays out the whole situation in detail about everything that had taken place over forty years ago. He told Jesse that he had a friend named Marcus about that he had got into some dirty dealings with. He explained to Jesse that they both had made a gamble for a lot of money they won, totaling around fifty thousand dollars. "That's a lot of money in my eyes!" he added. Most of the money was supposed to be invested in a startup company the two had planned and the rest was supposed to help his friend, Marcus, pay off a debt he owed so they were squared away before going into business with one another.

Samuel's friend, Marcus, ended up taking all the money and skipping town with it without him knowing. This kind of betrayal had enraged Samuel without a doubt. He continued with his story explaining how he began to search for Marcus by interrogating some of his known friends and accomplices about his whereabouts. Some stayed loyal to Marcus and gave Samuel no information to go on until he had come across a former ex-girlfriend of his that he had contacted for a late night booty call. She proclaimed that she was so turned off by the gesture, especially after not hearing from Marcus for over four and a half years. Marcus' ex-girlfriend stated that he flossed much of the money her way and asked her to meet him at a hotel he was staying at to which she had declined. She gave Samuel the address and he was on the hunt for his former friend that had blatantly stabbed him in the back.

Samuel stated that when he found his friend, he was so upset that he had reacted foolishly. The intent was to just confront him about the money and get his full share back, but Marcus had already spent a significant amount of it. Samuel was carrying a gun on him that day as he had assumed that Marcus would be carrying protection on him as well while lugging around that kind of cash. When the news was spilled to Samuel about the amount of money he had already spent, they got into a heated argument that led up to Samuel shooting his former friend in the head within broad daylight. He was tried, convicted and sentence to prison for life for pre-meditated murder in the first degree.

"This isn't the ideal direction I saw my life headed towards, but I was young with goals, yet still making immature decisions. I got involved with drugs, alcohol and gangs. Many called me a bitch for not confronting Marcus and getting the money that was rightfully discussed as mine. It was some of those people's words that had me conflicted to a point where I had ignorantly gone out and killed my closest friend. It was like I had no remorse. I ran from the cops for a while, but they caught up with me and well I already told you the rest of the story and how it ended. After my first decade spent in prison, I found myself through God's teaching and started to become more religious. I also saw my mistakes and asked for forgiveness. I changed around who I was and how I saw life. I also think that spending three years in solitary confinement at one bad for some savage attacks on a few other inmates had a huge role in that. You can't imagine the wear and tear that does on ones' mind. Can you picture sitting in a small cell with just a toilet and mattress? Nowhere to go! No one to talk to! I saw demons enter my cell at night as they tried to coax me over to their side. They would suggest I end my life and they would assist with the rest of the healing. A stronger power that be intervened and had convinced me to a different path though," Samuel continued. Jesse was shocked by the story considering how innocent looking Samuel appeared to be, though he knew that looks could be deceiving. Samuel told Jesse that that was a long time ago and he regrets it all now. "Some things you do are things you can't go back and fix. You spend the rest of your life trying to figure out how to make up for the past. That is where I was!" Samuel dually contested.

Jesse asked Samuel if he believed in fate, considering all prisoners that were let go, for him to have a second chance to fix things. "Don't you want to turn things around?" he added. Samuel shook his head in disagreement as he remarked that he is too old to spark a change in someone else's life or to make things right within his own. "I have faith that things may happen for a reason, but what is the reason I killed my friend," he criticized himself. Jesse completely understood where Samuel was coming from, as he did his best to explain how he too messed things up in his own life. Jesse made it no secret as to how he had made many mistakes within his marriage that ended up causing her to leave him. Marie and Jesse were once madly in love and that love had dwindled down in their final months together. He remarked to Samuel that he wants to fix it, but hc knows that it is too late. Their marriage had surpassed the final stages of divorce and all the paperwork has been sent his way to be signed. "Why didn't I listen to her more? Why didn't I show more love and affection? I was going through such a troubling time where I was caught between trying to help my best friend that had lost his family and the woman I vowed to spend eternity with," muttered Jesse.

Samuel cuts him off in the middle of his sentence and tells him that he has plenty of time because he is still alive. He insisted that Jesse could always change someone else's life so they don't make the same mistakes that he initially did. "You are still young, unlike me. I have more years behind me now than what I can physically see in front of me," Samuel added. Jesse smiled and told Samuel that he is still alive and that he has the same opportunity and just doesn't even know it. "What do you mean?" he asked. Jesse smirked as if he had something on his mind to share but didn't know if he fully trusted someone he had just met today. "Don't you ever think about fighting back? Look at how things are going down right now. The world needs people that are willing to stand up and fight back. It needs a group of people that will stand up and take back the country they live in instead of letting a mad man call all of the shots," profoundly voiced Jesse.

Samuels' head slumped over as the inspirational comments whisked by him unheard. "I am not the young man I used to be. Fighting isn't an option for me. I am fighting just to see tomorrow and I wake up thanking God for allowing me to see another day. This isn't the Wild Wild West, Jesse, and you're not Robert Conrad. Why is that we, as people, feel obligated to fight back at every injustice we feel has been placed in front of us? Sometimes helping another person goes a long way is all I am saying. You can show up to protest with a gun in your hand, but in my hand I can only lift a walking cane at this point. No one wants to allow that kind of man to be heard," Samuel contested. It was almost as if he had given up or maybe he was thinking clearly after spending so much time behind bars. "My intent isn't to fight you on the topic. I just realize that my time is almost over here and the mark I want to make has to be a positive one!" he continued.

Margaret returned to the table and placed two hot plates of food in front of them with steam rising from atop. She looked at Jesse and told him that she didn't forget about him and she will be back with a cup of coffee on the house that would be freshly brewed. She then walks away as Jesse gives her a small grin. There was obviously some sort of connection the two of them shared. "I have seen that look before," Samuel stated even though Jesse denied that anything was going on between the two. Samuel rolled his eyes as he wasn't thoroughly convinced. "I have seen that look before and that is only given to another person that someone has an interest in. I been around a long time and I have seen her looking your way every few minutes since we got here. Sometimes it even feels her attention is set on you more that her other tables," added Samuel.

Jesse was now beginning to blush. "I don't know what you mean. She and I are just friends. I highly doubt she has any interest in me and I am just getting out of a divorce soon. I love Marie," Jesse mentioned. There was little confidence in his voice when he stated that. It wasn't just that Marie fell out of love with him, but maybe he was falling out of love with her. Samuel simply agreed with him, but remained unconvinced that there was no spark of love interest between him and the beautiful waitress. The two sat there for a few hours talking and learning more about each other. Jesse knew that Samuel had just got out of prison and probably had no immediate family to stay with. So he offered a place to stay at his home until he got things together within his life. Clearly, the kind of heart Jesse had was proudly worn on his sleeve in plain view for all to see. He was always willing to do for others at the cost of missing out and losing things himself that were important to him. Samuel kindly thanked him for the courteous offer and accepted before promising that he would not stay long.

"I will stick around just till I get back on my feet, I promise!" he noted. Jesse demanded that he stay as long as he wanted because of how things were getting right now. The two guys finished up their food and Jesse placed two twenty down on the table, which was more than enough to cover the tip on top of a generous tip. He waved goodbye to Margaret, whom waved back in response as they both tried to walk through the mass of people in the diner watching the newscast.

They both exited the diner, when Jesse's phone suddenly rang. He looked down to notice that it was his friend,

John, calling. When he picked up, John immediately asked why Jesse didn't call him back. "I thought something may have happened to you!" addressed John in concern. Jesse apologized for not returning the phone call as he knew how he was seen as the only family John had left. He asked where he was so they could meet up and chat considering that he didn't want to be alone during these trying times. It would be devastating for John to lose Jesse after having lost his family. "Calm down, everything is alright. I have just been a little busy," Jesse mentioned.

John told him of how he was worried after a few hours so he drove over to Jesse's house, where he realized that he wasn't home and became concerned. Jesse reassured his friend that things were alright and that he was right down the street at the diner and would meet him back at his house shortly. John was bewildered by the fact that Jesse decided to go grab some food during a situation like this. Jesse hesitated a little but came right out and told him about how he met Samuel from the prison. John began to ask questions, but the two got off the phone when John saw Jesse riding down the street and vastly approaching his home. He pulled into the driveway and both Jesse and Samuel got out of the car. "John, this is Samuel," Jesse stated. John greeted Samuel as they all walked into the house. "Nice to meet you," he responded in kind.

When Jesse opened the front door, they all walked into the living room and sat down around the class coffee table that sat in the middle of the room. John wasted no time and began to immediately ask Samuel questions that were weighing heavily on his mind. The first question he asked was what he went to prison for. Jesse quickly intervened and said that it was a long story as he began to change the topic by asking John what happened when the soldiers came to the motel. John explained to Jesse what happened and how he hid two handguns in the vent that they were unable to find. "Why would you do that, versus give up the weapons? It could have ended badly for you if they found that you were stashing them," here marked.

John was unfazed on the account of them finding the guns and possibly even taking his life. This was a weird time they all were going through and John was a firm believer against giving up his right to bear arms. Jesse restates to John how by him doing that may not have been the smartest idea. This was a confession that didn't sit well with Jesse. He reminds his good friend about the consequences as well as what the world is becoming. How could the President of the United States gain so much power? He had a military that backed him. He killed people that opposed him and even those running against him. This was unbelievable to happen, but it was truly happening. Jesse turns on the television and witnesses all the chaos taking place in the neighboring streets that once were silent and calm.

Within the newscast, the reporters cut from the chaos back to the President speaking. The police were in awe about the blatant shooting that took place and dismembering of a person's arm on national television, but recognized the chain of command and did nothing about it. America was placed under martial law and it is unclear if people really understood what that really entailed. Dominic was the only person with the authority to place the United States under martial law with many that stood firmly in support of his decision. Many governors complied with the insanity of such a harsh call. They were the only ones that had the authority to invoke the conditions of martial law put in place within their respective states but were fearful as to how taking a stand could lead to their own demise. Since President Harvey wasn't part of the Republican or Democratic Party, it was easy for a side NOT to be taken. Of course, there was one or two that were in attendance during the announcement made that were in disagreement, but sided with the President and his decision for fear of their own life being taken. People will subside to any commands when a gun is placed up to their heads. Samuel asks Jesse to turn up the television as he is intrigued about what craziness was next to occur following the presidents' order. Jesse picks back up the remote and turns up the volume as they all listen intuitively to what Dominic states in his next publicized declaration.

"This is just the beginning. We approach an election day that begins a legacy worth remembering. My legacy! This...my friends...is a day of reckoning. I have been viewed as weak and incapable of delivering said justice and freedom. However, I am not weak and my strength isn't just defined by the role as your President or Commander in Chief, but yet by the decision made today to do what I feel is best for your well-being. I placed this country under martial law because the death of our people has to stop, and so for that to happen I have taken away your guns. People have to stop being jailed like caged animals under a system we all say is a failing us but have done nothing to fix it sufficiently over the many years. For this reason, I took away the courts and granted pardons to all prisoners. I have always hated the labels we place on each other. Someone with the branding of Republican or Democrat is no more of a derogatory insult that that of calling someone a spick or nigger. These separations categorize us all with no empowering qualities. Where is the equality in that? Now you shed your hatred and spit my way in disgust because you hate my politics and proposals. You tell me that the decisions I make aren't right and argue over these political views, when your decisions have done nothing for the greater good of the people. How ignorant of you to question what choices I made in eight years and not evaluate what any of you have yet done for this country to help within the last eighteen years. I challenge anyone to ask themselves what they did today that changed the world. Go ahead. Ask yourself! What about yesterday? How about within the last, month....year...DECADE! I made one decision that catapulted this world into a new direction and I see no weakness behind it. The only decision you made was to put me in power and you did this with the hopes that I would made all the right decisions that every single person will agree with and complained about along the way. It's easier to be the sheep than wake up with the responsibilities of being the sheep herder. I did it out of love for this country, under the belief that you will support me and become the same change that is desperately needed. A change where that said equality I preached before and during my presidency has become one that we all deserve. I was not born into luxury, but I damn sure was bred and groomed for it. This is what lets me know I am not one to show weakness. A wise woman once told me something that stuck with me my entire life and I share with you all today. She said that I will NEVER know how strong I truly am; until the day comes that I forced to be strong. That day is here! That day is NOW!" Dominic states with a coldhearted tone. Audience members try to move in closely for questions. Military soldiers with guns start to violently force everyone back from the stage. Dominic quickly leaves through the back entrance of the staging area as he walks by Sky and signals him and Jarvis to follow behind him. They all get into a long black stretch limousine and drive off down the boulevard to avoid confrontation amid his historic proclamation.

While passing by the beautiful city landscape, the president sees this time as a moment to relax and reflect. He just made history with his speech and did what no other president had done in history after committing a crime on television as the most powerful person in the country, but yet with no consequence to follow and no one to question his decision. Jarvis, Sky and the president sat in silence for a brief instance while composing themselves about the briefing they had just left. Jarvis grabbed a drink from the mini bar inside the limousine, while Sky did his best not to make any eye contact. One could tell by the young boys' body gestures that he was placed in an uncomfortable position and much was on his mind. Dominic takes out a long cigar and clips the end as his lights it up and takes a huge puff. Sky looks over to Dominic and asks him why he did what he did to those people. "Did you have to hurt them, Dad?" he questioned. Stunned by the innocent remark, Dominic puts out his cigar that he was just beginning to enjoy and leans forward towards Sky with his breath steaming down the side of his neck. As the squeamish young boy waits for an answer from Dominic, his hands began to nervously sweat.

Dominic swings his hand back and strikes Sky with the back of his hand. The crazed Dominic pulls at his own hair and apologizes repeatedly to himself for hitting the inquisitive child. "I'm sorry son to have hurt you. I hurt you like your mother!" banters Dominic with such a crazed comment that made no sense to Sky, nor followed by an action that wasn't justified. The boy cries and whimpers in fear as he flinches at every small movement Dominic makes, even by the slightest twitch of his fingers. Jarvis had no choice but to watch young Sky be taught a lesson, no matter how absurd the actions may seem to him. There was nothing he could do to help him at this point to protect Sky after he had spoken up without creating more problems for him. Dominic demands that the driver pull the car over to the side of the road, tossing out blatant and absurd obscenities. Jarvis looks on terrified, knowing what things Dominic has done in his past and even more so what he is capable of now with such high power and authority.

"People have fear about what could happen in a more un- controlled society. I have placed a sense of control and security in their grasps. I am the man who possesses the power. I, as the President, shouldn't be scared and neither should someone in this nation. Though I accept the fact that I have the power and I will prove to you the level of security I provide!" Dominic states with a firm voice. He reaches over next to Sky and opens the car door. He then demands that Sky get out and step onto the sidewalk. Sky does what he is told, still holding the side of his face, in scarce fear for his life. His cheek was red, with a cemented imprint of the president's hand on it. Dominic gets out behind him as they see several people rushing by trying to get in doors just in time to beat the eight o'clock curfew. They stood under a large oak tree, while watching people run around in a huge panic.

A loud siren sounds in the distance as the time reaches eight o'clock in the evening. The loud siren echoed throughout the neighborhood, emitted from the carefully placed horns on almost every corner. Dominic takes out a handgun and shoots a passing pedestrian in the street as they try and scurry pass him into a nearby building. He slowly crosses, before stopping in the middle of the street and lets off two more shots as the pedestrian was crawling towards the stairwell of the apartment complex he lived in.

Military soldiers looked over and noticed a gun being fired, as they raised their weapons towards Dominic. The sinister president turned his head, only to reveal to the soldiers his identity, which in turn caused them to all lower their weapons and turn their attention away. Dominic holstered his weapon and moved in closer to the intimidated young boy. "Would he have not been killed if he followed the rules and been in the house by the designated time I ordered? It is the same question one would ask if they got a speeding ticket. One would ask if only they would have left the first destination that they were at earlier or even gone a different direction, would they not be pulled over by this police officer or any one for that matter at that given time. Sometimes we have to live in a world of consequence by the choices we make. Each choice we make spirals us into a direction that never would have happened if we had chosen a different path. I indeed gunned down that poor individual, and who is running out of their house to handcuff me? I have provided security with the same kind of conformed laws that were provided before my presidency. You follow the rules, or consequence will be met," he states with authority.

"But why? Why is the punishment death?" Sky asks just before flinching, under the assumption he would be struck for asking a question. Just as Dominic was about to answer his question, a baby bird fell from the tree behind him. Its loud thud against the concrete caused both Dominic and Sky to run around. The baby bird had a broken wing and couldn't fly. It wasn't clear on if the bird had broken its wing from the fall or had already had suffered the injury prior to the fall. Dominic placed his arm around Sky and guided him over a few steps to where the bird flapped its one wing in an attempt to fly away and escape the approaching humans it saw. The more the bird flapped its wings, the more it exhausted itself and then stood still in one place panting nervously as if it was playing dead. Dominic quickly lifted his foot and slammed the heel of his boot onto the skull and body of the helpless bird. Blood and guts gushed out onto the sidewalk as Sky tried to turn his head away from the horrific aftermath. Dominic didn't want him to miss a thing, so he sternly held Sky head in the direction of the lifeless birds' body and screamed at him to keep his eyes open.

"This is a lesson that must be learned. You asked me why I killed those people and I am sure that you have the same question about this helpless bird. I saw that the bird was suffering. Is it right for me to continue to allow it to suffer? The better option was to put it out of its misery. You do understand, don't you?" asks Dominic.

Sky shakes his head, still in pure confusion by the message he was trying to convey. "NO! I don't. Naturally humans and this bird will die. What makes you the decider behind whether they live or perish? It's all crazy to me?" responds the aggravated adolescent. Sky had mustered up enough courage to speak his mind to Dominic, but not out of defiance more so than from a genuine confusion. The president grabbed Sky by the throat, with his fingers and nails digging their way into the flesh around his neck. "What the fuck did you just say to me, you fucking cock sucking pussy? Have you lost your goddamn mind? You are just a prince, living in a kings' kingdom. I did that bird fair justice by putting it out of its misery. You better be careful with your words or you will find out that 'misery' loves 'company'," Dominic dictated. Sky was turning red at this point in the face as he tried to get out a few words pleading for Dominic to release his hold. Once the deranged president was done speaking and teaching what lesson he thought needed to be taught, he released his grasp and Sky had gasped for air. The lesson he gained from this wasn't the one that Dominic had cryptically proposed, yet one where he understood that it was best to not speak his mind when in the presence of this delusional madmen.

Dominic orders Sky to get back in the vehicle so they could continue to drive off down the street back to a home they were staying at every so often that wasn't far from the White House. Dominic remained in power within the presidential office after his insane announcement inflicting martial law and enforcing this new way of living for at least the next two years. He then decided that he wanted to allow even more freedom and enforce a new law he had devised. Dominic made a public statement that he would be soon releasing this new law, where crime of any kind would be allowed without consequence. Those that commit crimes would have to pay an affordable tax to the nation for being allowed to commit any heinous acts. He explained to the media that it will take some time to write up the guidelines to this new law and will start to be in effect within just a few years' worth of time. This announcement had sent the world into instant uproar. Even though most senators backed up a lot of what Dominic said, they did so either because they were scared of him or because they supported him. Many were entrusting that what he was doing was beneficial and that those new laws truly protected the nation. It is also assumed that they decision to back him may have had something to do with the assassination of those running against him from his last briefing. The crime and murder rate dropped significantly since the abolishment of guns. Though many questioned if those statistics would stay the same when the new 'crime tax' was set into motion.

There was a concern from the American people how these off the wall laws and changes within the government would affect people of all sorts moving forward. Many showed up at rallies and town halls to try and gain insight from state elected officials and anyone that showed up with some sort of response to these new changes, but the people were never able to get any clarity on the matter. The only information that was deemed to have come from a reliable source was whatever information that had come from the President. Well, whenever he took a moment to speak to the people. Dominic would occasionally make a televised appearance to go over vague details of this new crime tax that didn't seem to be so cut and dry. He had recently made an appearance that past weekend to ensure that everyone has the equal right to protect their investment as long as they paid the tax to protect it at any cost they deem necessary without the use of guns, considering they were being banned all across the country. He felt like if someone was gutsy enough to try and commit a crime, they were taking a chance that the other person is willing to do the same to protect themselves or their investment.

The appearance Dominic made lasted a little over an hour, but ended with his final message to the people about some of the drawn out details to what was allowed. "Many people committed crimes because they could get away with it. They were fearless and many did not commit crimes, because they were scared of theconsequence. These individuals were cowards. Oh how the tables have turned! Those cowards don't have anything to fear now. They are no longer weak. I came from a rough neighborhood and was a victim to an even rougher childhood. I have seen it from both sides of the fence. That is the problem with many out there. We don't understand each other. The rich can't fathom why the poor takes advantage of the system and the poor don't understand how to not become a statistic in the system but only how to use it to their advantage. So they grind and they scratch and claw their way to the surface as if the rich are holding them underwater. I changed the system now. Now both sides have reversed their roles. The poor people amongst us take what they want without any complications and the rich are now the ones scratching and clawing to survive. Every day is a struggle to stay alive! It was different when their only weapons used to be a check book and a lawyer. For the poor, our weapons were our streets smarts and sometimes a weapon. We made bad choices, but that is because we wanted what others had. Don't tell me that they can have the same luxuries if they work hard. Some were born and as soon as they came out the womb, they were met by two loving parents holding one silver spoon for them. If everyone can achieve the same thing then be accepting that the pathways to get there may not always be the same, and better yet understand that it's possible that not everyone will even make it there to the top. There are more deaths by poor people trying to reach that goal that death by rich that are handed everything. The new crime tax law will propose that anyone can commit a crime as long as they pay this tax. Anyone found committing a crime without valid proof that they paid this monthly tax will be punished by the military by any means necessary. The tax will be affordable to all and that is the best part. Now we get to see what happens in this food chain. Remember, you can't starve a bear! At the end of the day, they will always find a way to eat," noted Dominic within his closing statement.

Over the next few months Dominic met with many world leaders as they discussed his current way of doing things within the U.S. government. Considering Dominic had an intriguing way of explaining things, many political world leaders began to see the positive side behind his decisions he made. Some of the world leaders asked Dominic to be a personal political advisor for them, to which he agreed. He would take phone calls all the time from world leaders asking him for his thoughts on how to control the violence or hunger situations they were initially dealing with. The world leaders jumped right aboard to whatever was suggested, no matter how insane or insensitive the people of that country sought it to be. Dominic would even fly over to other countries to either be beside certain leaders when they were speaking publicly to the people or even televised. Many of those times, Dominic would be asked to speak a few words or even take it upon himself. He was becoming not just the voice heard by many America citizens, but yet by people all around the world.

Three years had passed now as the martial law and State of Emergency orders had continued well within over that time frame. Within those three years, as Dominic consulted other world leaders, their politics and laws began to slowly resemble things that Dominic had set in motion for the United States, specifically within banning firearms everywhere. Even though Dominic was an advisor to the leaders around the world, he seemed to possess more power than them as he was seen more by the people than the leaders running their own country. He was able to make certain laws in other countries that many leaders of those countries backed him up on. They even allowed him to place his signatures on documents when things were passed into law within their country. Other world leaders found loopholes to placing Dominic as their second in command or Vice President.

Needless to say, eventually most of those world leaders were assassinated or ended up disappearing with no investigations to be had. By the end of these troubling three years, Dominic was considered the overall World Leader. This became his more formal title outside of still being called the President. A large majority of the world was run by or delegated by Dominic and his laws. It then came around to the moment where Dominic was set to begin enforcing the new crime tax across the globe. He called another press conference, where he made the official announcement that every citizen in the United States and around the world would be allowed to commit heinous crimes as long as they pay a monthly crime tax. The tax remained as something that everyone could afford, even if you had to steal the money to be able to pay it. The past laws still were in effect where no person that isn't a military official under Dominic's command could possess a gun of any kind and were continued to be taken from the households of those that possessed them. People began to sell knives and pepper spray for large amounts of money. Some people became creative, as they could be seen walking down the streets carrying machetes, axes, swords, chains and baseball bats. The only outlined weapon that was considered banned was guns.

A few days after the announcement of the new global crime tax, Dominic decided to take Sky out for a walk in public to show him what he had created the world to be and his new vision. Sky, the adventurous teenager, though still frightened by Dominic walked with a bold stride next to the crazed individual he knew to be as his father. Dominic kept Sky very sequestered from the world, so this was something that the young teenager appreciated for various reasons. He was never privy to what was delivered by the news and the violence shown in the streets. He was sheltered from it all, aside from the violence inflicted upon him by Dominic within their household. These harsh punishments or tough love was something that became second nature to the teenage and no different in his eyes from another child being scorned for bad or unruly behavior.

Time flew by while taking a casual stroll down the street with Jarvis and secret service security when Dominic decided to bond some more with Sky with impromptu conversation, which almost never happens. Very little words are exchanged between Dominic and Sky. Especially ones that don't lead to him being abused or assaulted. Today seemed to be different. It was a day where Dominic tried to implement a little fathering connection.

"Which is better? The world we used to live in or the world we live in now?" Dominic asked Sky with adamancy. Sky sincerely responded, "The world we used to live in was like being confined in a prison jail cell. The world we live in now is one where we at least are able to roam the courtyard of the prison even though we are still caged like animals. I see your vision and understand its purpose. More people do for themselves in order to have the same things as others, without being detoured or detained by a broken system that was intertwined with multiple imperfections. Yes, both versions had its issues, but who is to say that one is better. That only means that one is worse!"

Dominic gives Sky a resentful look, even though the young teenager appeared to be in agreement with him, but doesn't read too much into what Sky was trying to imply by his statement. Sky, still frightened by Dominic, reassures him that no ill-will was intended by his comments. A small pause emits between the two as they stop in front of an electronics store. Several televisions are sitting behind barred windows as the news report can be heard playing in the background. Dominic looks at Sky, reminding him that he has power that no one else has. When he looks over to Jarvis to ask him for his pistol, a man can be seen walking on the other side of the street. Jarvis hands Dominic his firearm, which he then quickly passes over to Sky. "We live for power and die powerless, "Dominic remarks.

Sky holds the pistol in his hand. The metal feels cold and causes goosebumps to pop up on his arm. He was holding one of many things that could easily take another persons' life. Dominic called out to the man crossing the street and asks him to come over to them because he has a question for him. The gentleman recognizes Dominic and decides to go over to see what he wanted. The man was very muscular with short black hair. He crossed the street and approached the President greeting him with a smile as he extends his hand for a friendly handshake. Dominic ignores the gentleman's greeting and with an inquisitive tone asks him for his opinion on if having a gun gives someone power. The man looked at Dominic and the several bodyguards surrounding him with pure confusion as he responded to Dominic stating that he didn't feel that it would. "It doesn't give you power. What if you deal with someone that isn't fearful of dying or a gun someone wields," he rants back.

Dominic turned back to Sky, "he is saying you are powerless, my son," Dominic sarcastically noted. As Sky began to breathe heavily while still glancing at the pistol, his palms began to sweat and shake. He looked over at the muscle bound man and lifted the pistol towards him firing a shot into his chest. The man dropped to his knees as he then toppled over onto his back. Sky walked over to the gentleman as he bled onto the sidewalk and he placed his foot onto his throat. The man began to choke, gasping for air, as he begged for the teenager to have mercy on his life. Looking down at the cowering individual, Sky lifted the pistol towards the man's face. "Who is powerless now, motherfucker?" Sky says with anger in his eyes as he fires a deadly shot into the man's head followed by several more shots afterwards. Dominic smiled as he was pleased to see the growth of Sky. "People complain about how I put an end to hospitals around the world, but I placed more money in the pockets of a mortician. How is that valued, you ask? It isn't. Nothing I do is valued and appreciated. I just make choices like the rest of you people. A person isn't a murderer when I place a gun in their hands. That category that they are placed in is based on the choices they made with the weapon provided. I took away the said weapon and still left people with choices. That's real power, my son!" Dominic deemed while standing over the corpse, beside Sky.

The man's face was completely unidentifiable and covered with bloody bullet holes. It was a ghastly sight, as one could see directly through the man's skull to the concrete beneath him. Blood flowed out from the man's head like the Nile River Red straight into a nearby sewer drain. Dominic grins at the teenager's actions as he reaches out and takes the pistol from his hand to return it to Jarvis' possession. Dominic told Sky that this is why they are considered to have power and what it feels like to be in control. The two turned side by side as they walked towards the sunset. The televisions continued to play in the background in the nearby shops as Adriana Hart gave her daily news report.

CHAPTER 8
A GODDAMN SHIT SHOW

"No one can understand why the world has gone from shit to shitty. We have a President who is doing things to supposedly be within our best interest, and is only creating more chaos! He is already putting in executive orders to close down all police departments and hospitals world-wide that remained constantly busy during the state of emergency and martial law due to the overwhelming amount of violence ensued by crime taxpayers. Patients are now being forced out of every medical establishment and police are being ordered to turn over their firearms and stand down, because the military is the acting authority during these times.

The thing we have to ask ourselves is if he is truly leading our country into a better direction? No President has ever enforced martial law or put a hit out on those that run against him! Politicians will hold a town hall meeting on the situation scheduled for next week to discuss some of the Presidents' actions within leading this country. The President needs to realize that you lead by example, and you learn by mistake. He is leading with mistakes and making us the example.

The nation feels that President Dominic Harvey has made a lot of mistakes within building or even rebuilding this country. Then again, we also have a lot of people in this world that back him up on the things that he is doing. People seem to actually enjoy being able to commit crimes without consequence. They are more responsible for the way the world is than the actual President whom put us in this current state. How do we judge a President for how he leads a nation and just disregard the people and how they have chosen to live in it? Who truly made this world mad? Is it the people or the President?

I feel like the people are the ammunition to the weapon, but it is forever and always the President pulling the trigger. His politics has become deleterious to our society, while he finds this to be inconsequential to fixing the issue at hand. We are trapped in a cage behind bars made of hatred! We need to excogitate how to move forward and not sit silently, becoming heedless. We are not unencumbered by Dominic's reign, but have become remunerative to his power and success. We are the penultimate puppets poising the least importance within his propaganda of proficuous gain. Either way, this is turning into a GODDAMN SHIT SHOW!"

CHAPTER 9
A RESISTANCE BORN

It was late one Saturday night that Jesse sat on the edge of his bed looking through a collection of photos. A soft knock was heard at his bedroom door. "Come in!" Jesse replies. Samuel walks through the bedroom door and sees him try to secretly wipe away a few tears. "Everything alright?" he asked with Jesse replying that he was fine. Samuel knew that this couldn't be true, so he dug deeper to try and find out what was wrong and how he could help.

"I know that look. Something is on your mind and holding it in isn't the best solution. I can't say that talking to me will fix it all, but I know that it will make you feel better. So talk to me, my friend. What's wrong?" Samuel continued. His voice to Jesse was calming, so much so, to a point where he felt comfortable. He hadn't known Samuel long; though his comradery was a noticeable badge he wore on his sleeve throughout his life or in this case, his prisoners' gown

"The thing is that I miss people in my life and these pictures remind me of them. I don't see any of them with all this craziness going on. I barely see my closest friend, as he is dealing with his own issues and I miss my wife. I see people around the world hurting from all of this, and the pain they are enduring and that makes me want to help them too," acknowledged Jesse. The regret was heard in his voice. "I just wish I would have made better choices. I wish I could have been there to help everyone instead of the choices I made that has led me to this point in my life," he continued. Samuel didn't want to yet interrupt Jesse as he wanted him to vent as much as he wanted and get many of the things that bothered him off his chest. Just as he was about to continue, he became speechless being at a loss for words. It was as if he was about to cry, but he didn't know what else to say. The memories were haunting to him and he expressed how he just wanted his old life back. He wanted things to be normal again.

Samuel took the photos from him and tossed them onto the floor. "I understand where you are coming from, but these are memories of the past. Crying and being sad won't change any of those things. There is no time machine that will allow you to go back in time and do things differently. You have to snap out of it and go create new memories and new photographs instead of dwelling on the old ones. You are steadily trying to fix things with your wife, but she has to want to fix them too. Otherwise, move on and find some-one else. You want to help your closest friend, but his pain can only be healed by him. And everyone else isn't your concern. What do you owe them?" asked Samuel.

Jesse heard everything that Samuel had said when he put it like that and even the question he ended with became one that lingered in his mind. Jesse had a kind heart and it showed within the field of work he did as agent within the Federal Bureau of Investigation. "What do I owe them? Well, nothing!" he responded. That was exactly the answer Samuel was looking for as he knew that it wasn't

Jesse's responsibility, so he replied in kind, "then why do you feel like you owe them everything!" The words spoken by Samuel were food for thought, but it was unlikely that it would change Jesse's mind as he was just that type of people that wanted to help others.

It took a second to process everything being said, but Jesse saw the same kind of love for others in Samuel's eyes. He had lived with regret behind bars and also wished he had done things differently. This was something that couldn't be in question and couldn't be overlooked. "I completely understand what you are saying, but I know that if someone could have stopped you when you killed your friend then he would still be here and you wouldn't have been imprisoned, only to live with that regret. You are right that I may not owe them anything, but should I overlook a person and give them nothing when it comes to an outreached hand in need?" Jesse delivered as a retort to Samuel. His point was received by the formerly imprisoned inmate.

"You have no arguments from me. You are such a great speaker. You should have done that instead of FBI work," Samuel joked with an apparent sense of seriousness behind his statement. Jesse walked over and picked up the photos and placed them into a shoe box that he had on his nightstand that was filled with other important pieces of papers and slipped the box back under his bed. He told Samuel that he also had agreed with the things that were said to him and he was going to make an effort to go out and make new memories as proposed.

"I am glad to hear that. Pain is temporary. That means for you and everyone else. Handle you first and then you can look to help others. Remember, you can't save them all, Jesse!" remarked Samuel just as he stood up to make one last comment. He tells Jesse that he was about to make a late night trip to get a cup of coffee and asked if he would like to grab one with him. Jesse declined the generous offer as he explained to Samuel that he was going to finish up a few things around the house and maybe just go to bed if it got too late. "Thanks for the offer!" he added.

Just as Samuel was about to exit the bedroom, a loud thud that was followed by glass breaking was heard downstairs in the living room. Samuel rushes over to turn off the bedroom light and peeks through the window shade out to the front yard. Jesse quickly makes his way over to the closet and grabs a metal baseball bat. "What was that?" Samuel whispers to Jesse. The two creep towards the door trying to make as little noise as possible along their way. Jesse then opens the bedroom door and leans out into the hallway.

Another sound of glass shattering onto the floor is heard and two men begin arguing at the bottom of the stairs. As Jesse peers back into the room he bumps in the dresser near the door and knocks over a book that was on the top of it and hanging off the edge. The book hit the floor making a loud noise that caught the intruders' attention and stunned both Jessa and Samuel. The two men stop arguing downstairs, directing their focus towards the noise that they heard and began slowly ascending up the stairwell with their guns poking around each corner along the way. Jesse makes an effort to hide behind the door with the baseball bat in hand as Samuel picks up a glass vase and waits behind him frightened. As the two men reach the top of the stairwell they walk towards Jesse's bedroom door and slowly open it up. The hinges creak ever so softly, but loud enough that anyone in the room would hear someone entering.

The first robber peaks into the room, not noticing Jesse lurking behind the door, anxiously waiting for the intruder to flick on a light switch. Just before the robber had the chance to turn on the light to illuminate the room, Jesse swung back the bat and struck it against the intruder's head. The bat collides with his skull and sends him crashing down to the ground with blood gushing out as he laid there on the floor unconscious. The second robber then rushes in and pushes Jesse away from his partner in crime. Jesse falls backwards over a small footstool into a dresser as Samuel raises his hand with the glass vase and slams is across the back of the other robber's head.

The man plummeted to one knee, not showing signs that he was out of this fight just yet. He picks up a piece of glass that was on the floor from the broken vase to use as a weapon. Without thinking, he swung his arm towards Samuel with the broken piece of glass barely slicing open his leg. Samuel then also fell backwards over the corner of the bed. The robber stood up and rushed towards Samuel, still holding the shard of glass in his hand. Jesse saw the assault occurring, while steadily tried to snap out of his brief black out. He rose to his feet and quickly jumped over the stool, tackling the robber to the ground before he had a chance to take another possibly deadly stab at Samuel who was on the floor bleeding from his right leg.

Jesse twists the man's arm as the intruder gave in and released the broken piece of glass, dropping in beside him. Samuel limped over and picked up the baseball bat. His leg was bleeding profusely as he tore off the arm of a t-shirt nearby and tied it around his leg to slow the bleeding. Jesse slowly released the robber telling him to take his friend and to leave his house. The robber stood up as Samuel prepared himself for another possible tussle if the intruders weren't willing to comply with leaving the household. The robber then helped pick his friend up from the ground as he was beginning to now regain consciousness and helped guide him down the stairs out the front door. As the two men left the house, Jesse turned to Samuel and told him that things were probably going to get worse in this chaotic world where crime is rapidly becoming a necessity to survive. Samuel nodded in agreement and explained how they may need to find somewhere else to stay that was more secretly confined to which Jesse agreed. "We need something so secret that it would be the last place anyone would ever look," he added.

An idea popped into Samuel's head just shortly after he had made the statement to Jesse. He suggested a spot that a prior cellmate of his had told him of several years back. "Oh yeah! Tell me more. Where is it at?" Jesse inquired. Samuel verbally laid out the brainstormed thoughts he remembered having while he was in prison. He said he remembered meeting a guy named Kenneth Romero that was also doing time for armed robbery and he had told Samuelabout this underground subway station that had been closed for about fifteen years.

Samuel continued to point out how Kenneth went into detail about how he had used to lay low there for a while after robbing several liquor stores in the area till the police had lost a tail on him. Jesse was pleased to know that they had a secondary place to hide out, but he was more concerned that Samuel's friend Kenneth would be there as well at some point to lay low from the nation's madness as well. "Kenneth was gunned down in a drive-by shooting about a month after he got out because he owed a lot of people money. I know where the place is and it isn't too far from here. He told me all about it when he asked me about being his wingman. I told him I was in prison on a life sentence so that wasn't even a possibility," Samuel dually noted.

Jesse pondered back and forth, trying to think of other 'what if' scenarios. He didn't want any surprises headed over to some place that was foreign to him and deal with another likely attack similar to what they had endured tonight. He brought up the idea to Samuel how they could stop by there in the morning and check out the place, but considering how late it was it was recommended that the two get some rest soon. Samuel agreed with him as he questioned Jesse on whether or not he had a first aid kit somewhere in the house for his leg. "Come upstairs! I have one in the bathroom cabinet, let's get you bandaged up before we call it a night," he mentioned to Samuel. The two then headed upstairs and Jesse grabbed the first aid kit and began stitching and wrapping Samuel's leg up. As soon as he finished almost a half hour later, the two headed straight to bed afterwards. Samuel had slept upstairs in a guest bedroom and Jesse slept downstairs beside the broken out window with his metal bat in hand.

When the morning came, the two friends packed a few suitcases and drove over to the closed down subway station. The entrance was completely fenced up with metal bars and chains covering it. It looked as if there was no way inside. Jesse looked at Samuel and asked him if he knew of another way in or was that the only entrance he had heard about. "Of course. The subway has been closed for a while, but there is a back way into the underground subway station that he told me about," Samuel mentioned. He directed Jesse to the back of the building where there was a small alley that one could tell had been abandoned for years. There was scattered trash all over the place, rats crawling around, and graffiti on the walls that one could tell had been there a while as it was losing its color. The stench in the air reeked of molded food and feces. Samuel explained how his former cell mate used to tell him about

114

how there was a sewer entrance to get down into the sub-way behind the building. "We aren't going to have to crawl through a nasty sewer, are we?" asked Jesse.

With them unable to go through the front entrance, it wasn't sounding like a reputable home to Jesse when the front entrance appeared to covered in other people's shit "Don't worry, the sewer has been drained and it is no longer in use. We will be fine!" Samuel voiced as a means to create less of a concern for his new friend. The two began searching around looking for any sewer caps that were within the alley. Jesse turned towards Samuel after the two had searched everywhere to tell him that he couldn't find anything. As he turned towards Samuel, he noticed a piece of paper blowing out towards the middle of the alley due to a gust of wind that was emitted from a nearby trash dumpster. Jesse asked Samuel to help him push the dumpster to the side. The two lined up on the side on the dumpster and pushed it as far as they could until a sewer cap was revealed. They reached in and grabbed the handles and lifted the heavy steel cap off, before slinging it to the side. Samuel notices a ladder and tells Jesse that this is probably the entrance that Kenneth had spoken about. He took out two flashlights that he had stashed away in one of the duffle bags and handed one to Jesse. "Ready for this shit!" joked Samuel with the perfectly timed pun. They both climb down the ladder to the bottom and trudged through an empty sewage drain of a nold abandoned sub-way tunnel. The smell of feces wasn't something that faded over time. It still lingered in the air with many dung beetles and flies scouring around the surrounding walls.

As they walked a few steps into the waiting portion of the tunnel, they noticed a few old dismantled subway carts that were broken down and rusted away. Jesse told Samuel that this may be the perfect place for us to call home just to avoid all the mayhem happening above. He told Samuel that he was going to go up above and grab some of the suitcases and bring them down. "No problem. I will scout the area and see what is all down here," Samuel stated while pushing many cobwebs out the way before entering one of the carts. Jesse made his way back to the ground level to grab a few suitcases and other belongings they had all brought across town to make the subway a little more home-like. He lowered most of the suitcases down by a long rope and stacked everything against the wall until began to bring the things into the main staging area. He knew that if this was to be known as his new home, he had to start dressing the subway carts over with items from his home to give it a homier feeling. Samuel was steadily searching around for a power switch to gain some sort of electricity in the lower station. He finally ended up locating an electric box near the conductors' operations booth. When he flipped the switch, the lights flickered several times as if they were in a horror movie, as it took a minute for them to warm up.

Jesse brought down the last suitcase from the end of the tunnel and saw how Samuel had successfully found the power switch, "Let there be light!" he sarcastically proclaims. It took a few days for them to get things somewhat set up and they even made a few trips back to Jesse's home to grab some other belongings and small furniture. It was clearly nowhere close to the home that Jesse lived in, but he started to grow some attachment to it as being a close resemblance to the real thing just with the added smell that they got used to. Things were definitely quieter down within the subway tunnels than that of the everyday reoccurrences of crime that they were exposed to above ground. One night while they were finishing the final touches, they decided to take a step back to admire their work. "It's looking more like home each and every day," Samuel noted after looking around to admire their work. Jesse nods his head in response while sitting at a desk writing in a journal of his. As he turned towards one of the nearby carts he spots a shadow moving in the distance of the tunnel. He assumed that it was nothing and continues on with what he was doing. To him, they were the only two people residing down within the depths of the subway station and he assumed it was his eyes deceiving him.

Meanwhile, beside him Samuel turns on the television to see how the signal is being received below considering the old cable lines that was withered away some. Jesse becomes distracted when he sees the shadow move again as clear confirmation, but this time behind one of the nearby subway carts. "I think this calls for a celebration drink. Stay here!" Jesse pointed out. He tells Samuel that he will grab a drink from one of the subway carts and he would be right back so they could celebrate. He steps away for a moment as Samuel uses the remote to flip through the various stations to try and find something more entertaining than a newscast covering the crimes being committing throughout the city and around the world.

Jesse crept through the back door of the subway cart to head towards the rear end of the line of carts. He gets to the back and comes up behind a young boy who is peaking around the corner watching Samuel, unaware of Jesse now standing directly behind him. The boy had on a baseball cap and a torn jacket. Jesse grabs the boy from behind, placing him in a headlock as he begins to scream out that he be let go. Samuel rushes out of his cart and looks over to sees Jesse coming from the tunnel with a young boy around the age of thirteen carrying a backpack on his shoulders. Jesse releases the boy as Samuel picks up a baseball bat. "Why are you down here spying on us?" Jesse yelled out towards the teenage boy. He acknowledged that he noticed them coming into the sewer and was only seeking shelter from the crime and killings he had been running from above. He told Jesse and Samuel of how he doesn't know his parents and has always been a homeless orphan. His story was brief, but he was detailed in expressing how he had never known who his real parents were and that he never had a real solidified family. "What is your name?" Samuel hastily interrogated while brashly demanding an instant response. "My name is Justin," he replied. Jesse notices the backpack that Justin was wearing and asks him what is in it. Justin empties the contents of the backpack.

The contents are dumped out onto the floor to where Jesse sees a hunting knife, a taser, a few snacks and a few comic books. Jesse grabs the knife before he makes a remark as to how that could come in handy. "Especially in a world with no guns," he denotes and then places it inside his back pocket. Jesse confiscates all of the other weapons he found before acknowledging that Justin could stay with them in their humble abode. A smile grew upon Justin's face as he felt the warm sense of comradery. He hadn't had a family like this before, especially one so welcoming after he had invaded their space. Samuel states that he has an epiphany. He turns to Jesse and reminds him of what happened between him and his friend, Marcus, whom he had murdered. "I know that I can't bring him back or go back and change what happened, but I feel like this is my chance to do something bigger to help change someone else's life in a time of need. When you are born, you have the chance to change something on this earth. Several decades later, someone else will be born and have the opportunity to live in the change you made. We call that being a part of history. I want to make a difference and this is how I can do it," Samuel jeered.

The idea, sounded phenomenal, but there needed to be some clarity to what was actually being suggested. Jesse asked him what he is contemplating as a concept. Samuel smiled and turns to Justin before speaking. "There are so many others above who need shelter away from the mayhem. I propose we start a resistance where we help others. We have the room down here and could gain more supplies to survive. Think of how many people's lives we could save from the crime and murder taking place above," he proclaimed. The two listen to Samuel speak with such logical wisdom as to how the world needs this very change and of a way that he wants to be the one that brings that change to them. Jesse agrees to help Samuel make a difference based on his vision.

"I think it's a great idea. Maybe we can take down the military and liberate the people. We could fight back and show them that we can't be controlled or bulled. We can grow this resistance to something that could truly be unstoppable," Jesse raved. He was so passionate behind the idea. It was as if he had already been sitting on the idea or something, but Samuel didn't take a liking to the version that was being described by Jesse.

"Fight back? Oh no no no. That isn't what I am proposing. Fighting back and even fighting in general is how people end up getting killed like my friend Marcus. If we do this, I want to do it a more peaceful way. I propose we secretly bring people to this safe haven that has been created to be a world of peace away from the world of hate. Absolutely NO fighting!" Samuel voiced. He had been through so much, and it showed the growth he had gained from his time in prison. Jesse was begrudged to the idea, but it wasn't his idea proposed and still saw the good behind the task at hand. There were definitely others above like themselves and Justin that needed a place to feel more comfortable and not scared that they might become a victim for not being in by the 8 o'clock curfew or to someone that may pay the crime tax and decide to make them a statistic to the crime rate. Samuel saw this as an opportunity to make peace with himself as well as the mistakes he made in the past. It was also a chance to help others and give them a place to live away from a place they could end up dying in. He tells both Justin and Jesse of how he nominates himself to be the leader of this resistance and hopefully get to a brighter day where things will go back to normal. They were all excited to begin recruiting others in need of help the following night. "I want to lead us to a better world. We don't need a President to be the dictator to how we live our lives. Create our own world that we live in with good people. We can achieve world peace within the tunnels of this subway station," he added in closing.

The look painted on Jesse's face was strongly overlaid with much disagreement. There were things that he sought as being possible issues if they moved forward with this plan and remained highly vocal behind stating his thoughts on the matter. "What if we are discovered? Dominic and the military will not be happy about us being here. I understand it is still a world where we can live here behind closed doors, unbeknownst to the rest of the world, but if he knew that the purpose is to form a rebellion, he would have us all killed without a care in the world. You say that you don't want to fight back, but what is the plan if they come knocking on our doorstep?" Jesse questioned within having all good points that were brought to the table. Samuel rubbed his fingers through his scruffy beard as he scratched his chin to think on all the things Jesse had just brought up. Right now, there was only the three of them and who knows what number this resistance could grow to. It seemed as if a thought out response had come to him when he grabbed a remote and turned off the television.

"You're right. But there may be a term for us at that point if it led to that. We would be referred to as martyrs. I still don't advocate for fighting against the military. Sometimes, sadly, a life or many lives must be lost for others to recognize the importance a life holds. It's a stupid idea and I know what you will say. You will say that if we fight then no lives can be at risk of being taken before their time, but whether they kill us or we kill them protecting our own lives, ultimately lives still will be lost. The thing is that when they die, no lesson is learned, they just go get more soldiers to selflessly take more lives. We must become the hope that we will preach to others, so if a day comes where we are possibly made martyrs, we are looked at differently by the heart we possess and not the weapons we wield," Samuel compassionately explained.

There was no sense of time based upon sunlight being emitted beneath the tunnels, but Samuel was able to look over to a clock that was brought to the underground subway from Jesse's house and he saw that it was getting late. It was past two in the morning and they had spent most of the day dressing the station up to their liking. With a new plan in mind with this resistance that was born, they had to get some sleep before starting their new day following this hellacious one. Everyone headed to their own carts and propped themselves up on a few mattresses before being knocked out from exhaustion while the sound of their television or radios were a noise to help coax them to sleep.

CHAPTER 10

THE FUCKING HATRED WITHIN

I know what most of you are thinking, while tuning into this broadcast. You see all the bad stuff happening in the world and one question keeps pounding over and over in your head. You see others forking up hatred and think that you, yourself, are not a contributor to it all. This becomes difficult because you have to find a way to separate them from you to answer this daunting question. Sometimes with this kind of evaluation, one realizes that they, themselves, are also a part of the problem. The question is; WHAT IS HATE?

I can't stand people of color. Everything about them bothers me. Black people are out here destroying the environment and bringing down neighborhoods, while immigrants are illegally coming into the United States and taking up our jobs, not paying their taxes and fair dues like the rest of us. These people cheat the system, while I work hard every day to make ends meet. They are loud, violent and unruly people that don't make me or my family feel safe.

Come to think about it, I also can't stand others with differing religions outside my own. These people really get under my skin when they preach to me about of the God or Gods of theirs I don't care about or also about the rules to their religion. Who are they to say they know the truth about God, how many there are or what color of skin he or she had. I also don't understand them covering up their face, praying on rugs, or not eating certain types of food.

Don't get me started on those Democrats. They are a bunch of soft ass snowflakes. They want to take away many of our rights to help make it better for those to continue cheating the system. Bunch of fucking dumbass liberals! Or what about those Republicans? All they do is lie and steal so the rich stay rich and the poor stay poor. They are the main reasons why wars are started. They don't like people that aren't like them; people that are rich and wealthy well-off individuals. Bunch of fucking dumbass conservatives!

Is it not a heard concept to understand? One man for one woman. All these people walking around as a man that in turn wants to be a woman or a woman trying to become a man. What about people that can't decide what they want to be? You were born one way! Just be yourself and by that, I mean the gender you were born as.

These aren't my words. They are yours. They aren't my beliefs. They are yours! If you have said anything similar to these comments, then you are part of the problem and not the solution. Do you think it is hard to answer my previous question? You don't know how to determine if someone applies to the said quality. You don't have to look any further for the answer. The comments, the point of views, the beliefs and anything that resembles it; THIS IS HATE!

CHAPTER 11

THE NEWEST EDITION

The following day came and the itinerary was filled with preparations. Things had to be put in order and all affairs met before this resistance was set to expand. The space was available and the only thing missing was the population. Jesse sat around and made plans for safe extractions and a list of things needed within the underground subway that weren't available or brought to the station because Jesse didn't own certain items. Samuel had started sewing together some clothes that would become the known symbol for the resistance. The color associated with the faction was a dark brown with a clinched fist stitched onto the upper right chest side of each shirt or jacket. Samuel had spent many of his years repairing prison gowns while incarcerated. This talent came into use for not only creating the outfits for the resistance, but also for any repairs needed along the way. Justin worked hard as he cleaned up many of the remaining subway carts, clearing out much of the junk inside of them and sweeping away the cobwebs. He even took out many of the benches inside to make more room for the potential inhabitants.

It took them all day until they had completed their task and the time had come to start recruiting. They all gathered up a few weapons, packing them away in some book bags they had and headed above to the chaotic world. Justin had come out ready to go, but was stopped immediately. "Whoa there! Not so fast. You are only thirteen. No child that young should be out there on this kind of dangerous mission. We need someone to stay here and watch over the place if you know what I mean," acknowledged Samuel. Justin had been so excited to come help, but his assistance wasn't turned down. Jesse and Samuel demanded Justin remain at the subway so he wouldn't get hurt and could stay out of harm's way. He was just a teenager and they took a liking to him very quickly as if he was their own flesh and blood. It was now a few hours after the eight o'clock curfew that the two snuck around town searching for others in need of shelter. They knew there had to be homeless people hiding out who didn't have a roof over their head and maybe even runaways or people who lost their homes for whatever reasons that could desperately be in need of the assistance and shelter. It was very difficult to walk around un-noticed, considering how many military soldiers and tanks were patrolling the streets.

Around eleven o'clock in the evening, they had decided to call it a night after not coming across a soul that needed help and began creeping back towards where the underground subway station was located. It was a ghost town within the streets even shortly before the curfew had started, but they had stayed hopeful that if not this night that they would have any luck recuing someone that maybe one of the following nights they would come across someone in need. Just as they were about to call it a night, they walked past the entrance to a well-recognized alley that they used to avoid blatant detection by the military patrolling the streets when all of a sudden they heard a woman scream out. Jesse jumped back behind the corner and peeked around the brick wall only to spot two soldiers in an alley with two civilians holding their hands in the air at gun point. One soldier was steadily pointing a rifle at a man who was on his knees with his hands snugly placed behind his back. The other soldier was pacing around a woman on the ground that sat there weeping with her mascara running down her face. Her purse was next to her with the belongings spilled over onto the ground beside her. The soldier came behind her as he grabbed her shirt, ripping it off her body and leaving her almost topless in just her bra.

Jesse instructed Samuel to sneak around to the other side of the alley and that he would distract the soldiers. Samuel did not want to carelessly leave Jesse up to being the distraction, but knew since he was younger and more in shape than what he was that it was the better decision. He crept quietly avoiding the several troops patrolling the area towards the other side of the alley. When Samuel got there, he gestured to Jesse that he was in position displaying his thumb up in the air as the given signal.

Jesse then picked a nearby rock and threw it at one of the soldiers, striking him in the back of the head. "Fuck Dominic and those that support him!" Jesse screamed out down the alley as he scurried away. The two soldiers immediately chased Jesse, while they radio in back up to assist them as they pursued their target. Samuel quickly rushes to the aid of the solemn couple. He tells them his name and that he is here to help. "Don't be afraid!" he added. Samuel takes off his jacket and gives it to the woman so she can cover up and begins directing them safely towards the subway station. They walked about seven blocks down, avoiding patrol units, before reaching the subway's sewer entrance. Samuel quickly leads them down below, but not before closing the sewer cap behind him.

"Come this way!" he remarks. Justin was relaxing when he heard a commotion outside his sleeping quarters. He rushes out and meets Samuel halfway, whom asks the young boy to go grab some food and clothes for them. Justin speeds away to see what he can find as he returns with a couple choices of women's shirts that Jesse had of Marie's and some snacks in case they were hungry. Samuel gave them a moment to settle in and get dressed in more fitting clothing. The questions at this point, alongside a more formal introduction, seemed fitting and began to roll out of Samuel's mouth. He started by asking them what their names were. "Stacy Parks! And this is my husband Carter," the woman replied in thc friendliest way.

"What are you doing out after curfew?" Samuel asks as he continues to toss more questions out to the couple. The man informs the resilient leader of how his sister is pregnant and also to the notion that she had gone into labor. He added that they were both heading over to lend a helping hand, but it didn't look like they made it all the way there seeing as how they were stopped by soldiers along the way before the resistance managed to rescue them. "I just wanted to be by her side as my little nephew was about to be born into this world. She needed me. I mean, she is my sister and I love her to death," voiced Carter with such a loving sibling endearment.

Justin had stepped away for a minute and returned shortly afterward, only to recognize that Jesse hadn't arrived with the group. He asked with an urgent concern as he assumed the worst case scenario. At first, he assumed that maybe Jesse was just bringing up the rear or checking to make sure the coast was clear, but too much time had gone by and there was no mention of his whereabouts. "Oh my God, where is Jesse? What happened to him? Is he still alive?" Justin spouted off, hoping for a positive response. Samuel turned and placed his hand on Justin's shoulder, while trying to calm him down.

"Take it easy! Relax! He was a distraction within helping me rescue this couple and was chased off by a few soldiers. He is alright!" Samuel responded with an unreassuringly reassurance. Stacy suggested that they all go look for him, considering how he risked his life to save them, though Samuel disagreed because of the risk already put forth by them to rescue the couple. "Jesse is a smart man. I know that he will be alright. He can take care of himself. Trust me! There is no need to worry!" Samuel continued.

The sewer cap door could be heard opening and quickly grinding against the concrete with it was closing behind whoever was coming their way. Everyone saw a figure walking at a fast pace down the poorly lit tunnel, but didn't recognize who it was until the person got closer. When the person exited the tunnel into the main staging area, everyone saw that it was Jesse covered in dirt with several rips in his clothing. He broke down his story to them how he was chased for a few blocks until he lost them. He stopped mid-sentence to introduce himself so not to seem rude.

"Oh I'm sorry! Hello. My name is Jesse Dean," he kindly states. The couple greets him in return as he continues his story of his fine heroics. "They almost caught me and I can guarantee that they would have executed me without any remorse. There were some other people out during this time that distracted them. I believe that they didn't realize I was alone and thought that those people were with me. They ultimately saved my life. I hope they are okay! But I am here and luckily with not a scratch on me. That is all that matters, right?" asked Jesse as everyone nodded their heads with smiles lingering from ear to ear.

Upon finishing the story, Jesse noted how he wants to just relax and then asks Justin to get him a glass of water. Justin runs into the subway cart again and comes out with a glass of ice cold water. "What is this place? Stacy gestures. "This is our home. We are a resistance against Dominic's day of reckoning. I am the leader of the resistance!" Samuel explained. Stacy continues on with several questions curious of what they do exactly as a resistance faction, especially one that isn't large within its given members.

Samuel goes into further detail about how they had realized that there were people that are going through rough times above and assumed that they would need an escape from the madness. It was clearly expressed that they weren't a resistance meant to fight back against the military carrying guns, but yet a resistance that would rather shelter others and build a safe environment for people to live there down below. He also notes that he wants to give those that join a sense of shelter as well as assistance towards building a brighter day in this nation and around the world. "I just want what is best for others!" he adamantly voiced.

Carter interrupts him to remark on how wonderful it is that they are standing up to the President and everything that is going on currently in the world. He offers to help in any way possible when they can down the road. "My wife and I are here and alive because of you putting your lives at risk to help us, but I think we need to get back to tend to my sister. She is in need of me being their right now. Times are rough and that is where we would be if it wasn't for the encounter we had with the military," Carter expressed.

Stacy realized that they didn't have to put their lives on the line and couldn't even imagine what would have happened if they weren't there to help. "I think that we should stay here and help. We needed their help and I am sure they could use ours," she mentioned as Carter begrudgingly gives in to the request of his wife. Samuel thanks her for the kind offer and accepts it as he knows that they will need more people to build this resistance once they get a larger team of people behind them. He hands them both a few articles of clothing that are branded with the resistance symbol stitched on it. "Welcome to the team! You are now considered part of the family and always welcomed here. It will be an impossible mission that we will make possible each night by sneaking out after the curfew to help these people in need," stated Samuel. Carter knew the risks at hand and remained a little skeptical, but felt the urge to help without knowing what would be fully asked of him. Stacy had no problem with the idea as she indicated how she was on board with everything.

"If it wasn't you for you courageous act, I would have been raped or even worse by being murdered. I like the thought that we can help save others and prevent lives from being taken. There was too much hate in this world before the martial law was announced and I see it growing even more now. People need to realize that peaceful world cannot be created by hateful minds," acknowledged Stacy as Carter threw his arm around her. Carter saw the passion his wife had behind wanting to help, but deep down inside of him he didn't want to put her at a further risk. They got lucky tonight within his eyes considering how Jesse and Samuel showed up just at the right time. It just didn't seem like a good idea to him at the time. Carter realized that Samuel is an older man out of all the men living below and that considering he is the leader of the resistance, it was proposed that he should stay at the underground hideout and watch over his wife and Justin due to his age.

Carter had made this suggestion to Jesse in front of everyone that they both be the primary ones to go out every night looking for other civilians in need until they acquire several other younger men willing to put that life at stake to help save others from above. Samuel paced back and forth pondering the idea and responded as to how that was a great idea. "I don't think these old bones could run as fast as the two of you anyway, even if I needed to. I also may not be so lucky to have others wandering the streets as distractions to assist me within a successful escape. For now, I think we all need to get some rest because there will be a busy day ahead of us tomorrow.

In the evening the next day Stacy came out of her subway cart and saw Carter playing catch with Justin as the two tossed around the pigskin. She begins to cry when Jesse approaches behind her and places his hand on her shoulder. "Is there something wrong?" he asked. Stacy wipes the few tears from her cheeks and replies back by expressing how she and her husband hadn't been able to have kids for a while. It was an emotional thing for her seeing her husband right now having so much fun with Justin. She could only imagine how he would be as the same loving and caring father figure. Samuel abruptly walks out from his cart and asks for everyone's attention. They all gathered around to hear what he had to say. His face was filled will so much happiness while speaking from his heart about what was on his mind.

"Tonight is the night we bring back something to this underground subway. Tonight...we bring back hope. Someone is out there in need of our help and we must all have faith that we were sent to help those individuals. I wanted to hold a prayer for lives are on the line for what we are doing. They will be lives saved throughout this journey and that bring me to complete happiness. The realization is that there will also be live lost along the way. We must all realize that this is the sacrifice that we make and understand these risks. We start here with the five of us and I hope you all remember this day as it grows to five hundred or even five thousand plus Everyone is deserving of this place we have made our home away from the one that is being overrun by government and military with the intent to control how we live our everyday lives We will fill this subway to capacity and then we will be face with finding more shelter to hide more people that we save from above. No person should be left behind and no kind soul should be forgotten. We are all family, so let's go out there and help grow our family tree," Samuel preaches with a tone of vibrant inspiration.

Carter casually interrupts him to ask a question. "Great speech Samuel and I think about the point you bring up about family. This is something that has been on my mind and I wanted to share. Considering we are here to help people in need and grow this family tree, can I make a suggestion that we go out to try and help my sister? I mean, she is one of those people that essentially needs help, right?" Carter questioned. The hope was to have them understand the relationship he had for his family and the willingness to want to protect her. It was obvious that Carter was very concerned for his sister's safety after giving birth to her son. Stacy spoke up in agreeance that it was a good idea to be considered if everyone else saw the value in keeping the family together and helping it grow in numbers. Jesse asked out of curiosity as to how far it would be to get to where she lived.

"I don't see it as being that far away," he acknowledged. Carter then told Samuel it was about five miles away, which didn't sound that bad seeing as how they were currently traveling by foot. He knew that it may be a long way to walk after curfew and avoid so many soldiers but Jesse felt that it was the right thing to do. "Yea that isn't far of a walk, but what if we have to run back? Can your sister keep up carrying a baby? We could bring them here during the day, couldn't we?" Jesse suggested. It wasn't bad of an idea, but Carter was opposed to the concept, because most of the crime occurred during the day. They were safer in their home during that time of day, which made it not only a better idea, but also more of a risk to retrieve her and his nephew after hours when people were sleep or just inside after the curfew had begun.

"That is very true. I see your point. It seems like the best time to go then is after the curfew so not to be travelling across town with your sister and a newborn baby in this kind of environment. Let us waste no time as it is nearing the time where the sirens will sound and people will be inside," Jesse urgently suggested. The two gathered their belongings that they intended to take on their endeavor and were about to head up until Samuel stopped them both. "If you leave together, you come back together!" he commanded. The two nodded in agreement and Carter kissed his wife as the two headed down the tunnel towards the subway's alley entrance. They came up from the tunnel and walked towards the street, only to peer around the corner to see if the coast was clear. Jesse and Carter noticed way more soldiers than usually patrolling the streets. "What is going on?" Carter remarks. "I don't know but try to keep a low profile and stay close," he responded.

The two traveled around town for a few miles as spotlights turned on and military jeeps and trucks began patrolling before the first warning siren was about to sound.

They approached Carters' sisters' house just in time, a few minutes before the final siren had sounded. When they arrived, they noticed a light on in the living room and suggested that it would safer to go to the back door of the house as his sister was used to answering that door to trusted visitors, like himself. The military would more than likely knock on the front door, plus they didn't want to be spotted entering the home through the front door so close to the curfew time as if they were trying to get inside before being shot and killed as the presumed punishment. They crept towards the back and both took turns hopping the fence trying not to make noise or be detected by soldier on the streets as the final siren was now roaring through the streets.

They approached the back door of the house and Carter then tells Jesse to wait a moment because he knew that his sister stashes an extra key in case she gets locked out of the house. He tells him to search under some of the garden pots in the back near the door. He didn't know which one, but he knew for sure that she kept one under one of the pots switching it to different spots every time. It was a better plan to find the key that to pound on the door, since Carter knew that the doorbell didn't work anyway. They both began rigorously checking under the pots until Jesse found a small rusty key under one of them. He whispers over to Carter that he might have found the key he was looking for. Carter takes the key from him to unlock the door and inspects it for a minute after wiping off some of the mud. "That's it!" states Carter. They open the door and both walk in, but don't see anyone in the kitchen area of the house. They are startled to hear a baby crying upstairs. "Denise!" Carter yells out in concern.

An older man comes into the kitchen and shocked by the two unknown strangers he begins to scream out for them to take whatever they want. Denise rushes into the kitchen only to try to calm the older man as she explains to him that there was no problem and that it was just her brother. Carter walks over and hugs his sister and asks if she is alright. She reassures him that everything is alright and that the man standing next to her is one of her neighbor's relatives in town from Florence, Kentucky. She tells him that he happens to be a medical doctor and how he helped delivered her baby boy. Carter cordially introduces Jesse to the doctor and his sister. Jesse shakes her hand and tells her how it is nice to meet her as they both exchange the same pleasantries.

Carter apologizes for interrupting the two as they greet each other and he requests to see his nephew. "Of course, come on upstairs to meet him," she responds. Denise then guides them upstairs and enters an all blue bedroom as she tells them to come closer to the crib, but quietly so not to startle him. Carter moves in closer and looks into the crib and notices a very small baby boy with tears on his face. He asks if it was alright to pick the baby up. His sister nods with a smile. "Of course!" she proclaims. Carter picks the baby up and begins to rock him back and forth. "What is his name?" Carter asks. "Jordan!" she replies. Jesse interrupts them and apologizes for having to cut short. He reminds them that they have to get back to the hideout, but was not going to leave empty handed. Denise asks him what they are in such a rush for and what he meant by not leaving emptyhanded. Jesse begins to tell her about the resistance and their plans to take Carters' sister and his nephew back to the hideout with them.

"It will be a place full of safety and security and the best part is that no one knows about it," Jesse adds. Denise tells them that she is fine here and doesn't want to relocate to some underground subway station to where her new born baby would be exposed to the dust and possible insects or rodents living within the underground hideout. Carter tells his sister that things are not safe now in the world.

"Would you rather worry about dust or someone coming in here to rob and kill you because you put up a fight or being struck by stray bullets meant for others by soldiers trying to gun down someone else who isn't in their home by the time the curfew begins?" Carter proposes as a few options that could happen and end badly for his sister and nephew if hi advice wasn't taken. He has seen things on the news as to how crazy people are getting and how much the crime rate is beginning to grow versus decrease. His sister mentions that she feels safe in the house and that the military will do their job within enforcing the safety of the citizens. She sided with the government even though she didn't like the crime tax and how that playedout. Denise felt like the government and the President were doing what was best for the people and wouldn't let anyone intentionally get harmed.

"What the hell are you talking about? Dominic is a madman! He killed people on national television and nothing happened to him. Are you even watching the news and seeing what is going on out here?" screamed Jesse in pure frustration. His intent wasn't to yell at Carter's sister but he didn't think she was thinking clearly. Carter was a little bothered by the tone Jesse was using and asked him to refrain from yelling, especially in the presence of his new born nephew. Jesse apologized and reworded within a more calming tone by reminding her that the soldiers are only doing what President Harvey tells them to do. "The military will not protect you against someone that pays the ridiculous crime tax," Jesse adds.

Denise still doesn't seem convinced that going to an underground subway station is any better than the mayhem above. She also expressed that she didn't agree and gave more valid points as to how it wasn't the best environment to raise her son. She kindly offers them to stay the night until the morning time when the curfew is over, but that states that they would have to leave without her and her son. Jesse accepts the offer to stay the night but wanted to leave first thing to get back so no one started to worry about them. He gives Denise the night to think over about his offer and to think about the future and safety of her newborn son. Carter sets his nephew back down into his crib as they all leave to allow the baby to get some rest. Denise grabs some blankets and pillows and shows them to where they could sleep for the night. The morning came as everyone awoke preparing for the day. Denise had prepared breakfast for everyone. Carter and Jesse walked into the kitchen to the smell of fresh bacon and eggs being cooked.

"I made breakfast for everyone," Denise gestured. "It sure smells good...Did you think about our offer?" Jesse asks. Denise tells him that she did in fact think it over, but she still didn't want to leave her home as she stood by her original statements. She deeply believes that things will get better eventually. Carter walks over to her and places his hand on her shoulder. This was his big sister and there was no telling her what to do. He knew that she had always been hard- headed growing up. Denise could tell that her brother had something on his mind though when he approached her and was going to be very vocal about him not wanting her to stay there alone.

Before he even spoke, she cuts him off to give him the reassurance that she and her son would be okay. "I already know what you are going to say baby brother, but my mind is made up. Now come get some breakfast before it gets cold as ice. I know you are all hungry," she retorts. Jesse doesn't want to make an argument of it, so he grabs a plate and hands one over to Carter. They all sit down to eat as Jesse says grace to bless the food. Denise then looked over to her baby brother and smiles as she mouths to him that everything will be alright. They all sat at the table conversing and laughing at the stories Denise told about her childhood growing up with Carter. When they finished eating, Jesse grabs everyone's plate and takes them to the kitchen and places them in the sink since she had done all of the cooking. Carter says his farewells to his sister as Jesse mentioned how nice it was meeting her. "Same to you, Jesse!" she replied

The two left the house and began walking back towards the hideout. Jesse had stopped halfway to their destination and told Carter that he had to make a stop real quick and for him to continue on without him. "Is everything alright?" Carter asked, to which Jesse replied that things were fine. He seemed as if he was hiding something, but Carter had no choice but to take his response as being the honest truth. Sweat started to drip from Jesse's forehead, implying that he was nervous so Carter asked once more if things were fine. "Of course! I just have to make a stop and talk to someone. Head on back! I am fine!" Jesse voiced to try and diminish any further concern. Carter reminded Jesse what Samuel had said about how he had wanted them to come back together and not split up. Jesse was very hard- headed and insisted that he was going to be right behind him. "My stop is on the way and it is day time anyway. What could go wrong? Just head back and tell Samuel that I am right behind you and will be there soon!"

Jesse added. Carter and Jesse then parted ways as Jesse headed a few blocks over to a nearby motel. He walked up to the second floor and knocked on the door of one of the motel rooms.

John opened the door and greeted his friend with a hug. "I haven't seen you in a while, where have you been?" John asked. Jesse started to run down the list, starting with the home invasion that took place at his house and how the situation caused him and Samuel to move to an abandoned subway station to get away from everything taking place and especially the martial law being invoked. John looks at him with confusion and offers his friend and Samuel a place to stay with him at his motel room. Jesse declines the offer before telling him of how they have started a resistance that is trying to help others get away from all of the mayhem. "A resistance?" stated John. Jesse went into a little more detail about their plan to save others and build a society of people that are against the craziness going on in the world. He even goes as far to offer John a chance to come and live with them instead as well as for his help building this resistance that believes in fighting for a good cause by helping others.

Jesse begins to tell John about the few members of the resistance that he helped save. John cuts him off, explaining that he doesn't fight anymore. "I didn't get to this point after my family was murdered, to kill others just because I disagree with their politics or how they are running this country. My family is dead and so is the old John that would go out trying to save and help others. I have to focus on finding myself and my own happiness," John declared as his viewpoint about everything going on and what he had been through. Jesse reminded his friend about the family he lost and how someone could have been there to help them and they weren't. "Imagine if someone had been there to help, just how things could be different. Your family could still be alive but they aren't here, because no one was there to do anything about it. This is your chance to do something and help so no one else has to lose someone they love like you lost Julie, Jennifer and Sky," Jesse mentions. The words spoken by him hit hard with his friend, but one could see how the truth started to make John's blood boil. Jesse asked him if he wanted the same thing to happen to someone else less fortunate or capable of defending themselves. John scoffs at Jesse's comment, only to tell him that he refuses to fight because fighting will only make him more like the heartless people responsible for killing his family.

"What the fuck does it matter if I help someone else? It isn't going to bring back the wife I married or my two loving kids. Someone shot them and burned their fucking bodies to cover their tracks. What kind of heartless person does that over stealing a few valuables? You steadily stay committed to investing your time and energy into others and maybe if you gave that time to Marie, she wouldn't have left you!" screamed out John in anger. The words spewed out from John's mouth may have been out of utter frustration, but Jesse replied carelessly in response as he now was angered by the comments made in response.

"Marie didn't leave me because of me. She left me because of you! There, I said it! You were always there and I spent more fucking time caring for you than her and she saw that. I stood by your side in your time of loss until you could get back on your feet and it costed me my marriage," rumbled Jesse. Things weren't going as planned. The visit to see John was supposed to be a friendly one with an even friendlier offer to join his resistance and help build the family that he and Samuel were building.

"FUCK YOU, JESSE!" yelled out John. It was a moment of tenseness between the two and someone had to be the voice of reason. Jesse cared about John, but didn't want to continue screaming out hateful things to each other that they would regret later. He persisted that he didn't mean anything by the comment as he saw the level of anger his friend had reached by his statement that he thought to be harmless truth that needed to be heard, but he also knew that John could be a great asset to the resistance.

"I am sorry you feel that way. I honestly didn't mean anything by it. I am just trying to create new memories and moments. Such moments and memories that we will look back on in twenty years and think about how we changed this bad situation into a good one. We risked our lives everyday as police officers and then federal agents. When did we stop caring about each other? We both lost people we love, but we still have each other and our friendship. I didn't come here to tarnish that!" muttered Jesse. John realized how riled up he got over Jesse's comment and found a way to calm down a little. They both had possible said some things that got under each other's skin, but neither were willing to allow the friendship to be demolished over it. John declined the offer and tells his friend that he is about to go out running and asks if he wanted to come with him. "I would love to, but I have to get back so no one begins to worry about me," Jesse kindly responds.

The two say their goodbyes and John closes the door as Jesse leaves. The friendship between them both seemingly appeared to be growing apart with it being made clear about the opposing visions they had on how they should live their new lifestyles. John remained frustrated by the conversation he just had. He reached over and opened a drawer, pulling out the bible that had been given to him by Jesse and opened it up to a spot that became seemingly ironic within the book of Exodus. It was a particular part where the commandments were discussed and most specifically the one about thou shall not kill. It was then that John thought to himself how some unknown person to him had broken that commandment and killed him family and that he would never kill again for the fear of seeing himself within that same vial image.

Jesse walked back to the subway station with his chin slumped into his chest and the first thing he did when arriving back was apologize to Samuel for not returning with Carter. He tried to explain that he had to go talk with John because they hadn't spoken in a few weeks and he was highly worried about him. Samuel understood his reasoning, but tells him that next time he needs to still stay together because anything could happen when they split apart like that. He asks if Jesse suggested to John the idea about being a part of the resistance as he was curious within trying to expand their population within their secret faction and also was aware that John definitely could be a huge addition. Jesse responded stating how John wasn't interested and gave him excuses of how he didn't fight anymore and doesn't want to be a part of this so-called war.

Carter walked up to Samuel and Jesse while they were talking to ask a question. His mind still stuck on trying to help give his sister a better life than living in the dystopia created by President Harvey. "I know the resistance is known for helping people. I know my sister says she is happy where she is at, but sometimes people do things thinking they are good for them and they are not. I am asking the resistance to still try and help. If anything, maybe I can just go now and be by her side. She has been raising this kid by herself after her last husband skipped town!" Carter pleads. Jesse looked at Carter and promises that he would do whatever it takes to help his sister and nephew. Stacy had entered, awoken by the commotion, catching the tail end of the conversation and even through in her two cents about the idea. "Carter, you have to know that that is your big sister. She is an adult and will be fine. I think we need to stay here where it is safe. I think she will realize it is getting bad in the world and will eventually change her mind. She will be running back to her baby brother asking to be a part of this resistance. You are worrying too much!" Stacy deemed as her opinion. Carter subsided once again with his wife's thoughts and decided that she was right and that the two of them would stay and help.

For roughly the next year, Jesse skipped out with other newly recruited resistance members during the day and sometimes after curfew hours bringing in more people that were victims of the chaotic world. He would return with men, women and even children of all ages. The resistance began to grow vastly in numbers to where many slept in carts together or outside the subway station on tattered mattresses. Eventually by this point, there were now hundreds of people, maybe even totaling a thousand, that were living in the lower subway hideout and this was more than what they had envisioned within such a short amount of time that had passed.

Samuel would hold daily meetings where he would talk to all of the resistance members about hope and faith. One night after Jesse had brought back a family in need a shelter, Samuel stood at the front of the crowd talking to the resistance members trying to inspire them about how change is coming.

"For a long time now I have brought you faith and today I bring you hope. I want everyone to understand the difference between the two... Faith is a trust or confidence that has... no proof. However Hope, is the proof... that something is possible. I am giving you all proof that it's highly possible for things in this world to change. I look around this room and see men, women and children that believe in a brighter day. A brighter future! As you walk through life, people will try and discourage you. They will try and make you unhappy when they see your face is bright. They will scheme, lie and deceive to make themselves happy. They try to take what they can to bring you down to their level, because it hurts them to see anyone at a higher point than them. You must be strong. You must have faith. You must have hope!" Samuel concludes as the crowd begins to cheer for him.

A resistance member rushes in, side by side with a man wearing glasses, as he calls out for Jesse. Everyone turns around as the two hurried into the main staging area from the tunnel. Carter also turns around and recognizes the man. It is the doctor whom he met when he was at his sister's house. The doctor calls out again for Jesse. As he gets closer to where Samuel is holding the meeting, Jesse yells back to the doctor that he is here, curious to what the commotion was about.

He approaches Jesse and notices Carter with him. "I am glad to find you both, I have some troubling news. Soldiers came to the house and found a handgun stashed away when doing a random search. Denise didn't know about it because it belonged to her ex-husband. The soldier executed Denise and the baby. Shooting them both in cold blood! I was very fortunate to escape after the first deadly blow I heard that had killed Jordan," the doctor raved. Carter drops to one knee and begins to cry out. Tears began frolicking down his face as he receives the horrific news. Jesse walks over to him and places his arm around him as he tries to console him. Carter forces Jesse off of him and begins to scream at him. "This is your fucking fault! You fucking did this! You all are supposed to help people and you let my sister and an innocent baby be murdered! You promised you would help them!" Carter pointed out as he gave Jesse a cold stare.

Stacy walked over to her husband and places her hand on his shoulder as well and asks him to calm down. Carter hauls off and back hands his wife to the face. Stacy was sent tumbling to the ground. Jesse started to approach as Samuel held out his hand to hold him back while Carter continued his rant. "All of you fucking back away from me! Stacy, you aren't innocent from it all. You never gave a damn about me in my opinion. You couldn't even give me kids, like I wanted, so why stay with you? You're as useless as your ovaries! You thought it was a great idea to stay here. If only I would have gone with my gut feeling, then I would have been by their side to protect them and none of this would have happened. You are all selfish! But who am I to judge you! I won't judge you, but God will!" Carter adds with a spiteful voice. Samuel finally speaks up and yells at Carter, demanding that he leave. "Go now! Leave this resistance. You are filled with rage and hatred and that isn't needed here. It is not us who are responsible for your sister and nephew's death. Your sister made her choice and it is as if you are looking for someone to blame!" exclaimed Samuel standing strong behind his clash with Carter. He had one job and that was to protect the people at the resistance. Samuel had heard and had enough.

Carter clinched his fist in the air and his eyes were blood-shot red, ready to swing on Samuel, but Jesse stood by his side along with other resistance members that weren't going to allow Carter to take his anger out on anyone else. He was easily triggered by Samuels' words. "You all are fucking stupid! You follow blind leaders! This isn't a resistance. It's a barn full of sheep. I will kill all of those responsible for the murder of my sister and nephew! EVERYONE RESPONSIBLE! Mark my words you fucking goddamn cunts!" Carter raved as he knocked over several nearby items while storming out. Stacy stands up with her hand to the side of her face as she watches Carter walk away down the subway tunnel.

Many days came and went as Stacy waited for her husband to return, questioning what she had done wrong. She loved her husband, but maybe he was right. She wanted to stay at a point in time where he thought it was best to be with his family. Jesse tried his hardest to console her by relating his experience to when he had his wife walk out of his life. He didn't want her to feel alone and feel as if she couldn't protect herself. At one point, he had taken it upon himself to teach her hand-to-hand combat. A talent he picked up along the way throughout his lifetime. The two became close friends and the time spent together helped her feel more like a part of a new family and ease her pain about the separation between her and her husband. One night they had sat down after a long session Jesse held with Stacy to teach her about how to disarm an enemy holding a weapon when he asked her how she felt about losing Carter and what he had hatefully stated before walking out of her life forever.

"I don't know how to answer that, Jesse. Carter is someone I loved and still love. I don't know if I will ever find that kind of love again. I know how hurt he was about the loss he endured. He needs someone to blame and so he blamed up. In all honesty, I think he hasn't been happy for a while. The shape this nation is in and places around the world is getting to everyone. I pray every night that the world finds a great leader. They need someone that will spread a positive message; someone that will be an example of love and change. We, as people, need that right now more than ever. It is impossible for love to grow, if it is always surrounded by hate. It boggles my mind that people love their family, but can hate someone else because of the color of their skin, their religion, where they are from and their political standpoint. Are we not all children of God? It is almost as if some purposely go out of their own way to find some difference one has from their own views and opinions so they can have a reason to hate them. If you plant a seed, it is undebatable that it will grow, but only if you water it. That is a concept that is so hard for many to take in. Even a person like Carter! I will love again I am sure. I can't thank you enough, Jesse, for being there for me. You are like a brother and I treasure your friendship," she blithely uttered.

Life eventually went on for everyone, as the resistance continued to pull in survivors and other people looking for an escape from the madness created by the martial law. Every day that passed was difficult to get through. The resistance became popular as one of the most talked about topics on each news channel which progressively still growing in numbers. It was to a point where their rebellious presence could be felt. Even when walking down the streets, you could see the walls covered in graffiti messages and symbols from the resistance. Their trademark of an iron fists placed perfectly over all of the propaganda widely exposed to the world from President Dominic Harvey's reign.

Resistance members would help people and tag the walls with the words like "Freedom Fighters" and "Long Live the Resistance!" Jesse went out many nights looking for more members. Sometimes when he went out he would be gone for hours and not return with any people or news. Most times he would sneak out through several tunnels that ran throughout the whole station. Jesse appeared to be living a double life that no one knew about as most days he would return and be very tired, trying to keep himself awake while on many of their following runs. He did what he did for the goodness of helping people find a safe haven from the dystopian terror that was caused by the forceful tyranny of the President.

Samuel would preach every day that the people of the resistance must remain strong and focused. He sat in his subway cart many days hoping that things would change. One night that he had sat in his cart contemplating how things were as he watched the Channel 6 News broadcast in the background. He would watch on a daily basis as the resistance became the most wanted entity within the nation.

CHAPTER 12

RESISTANCE COVERGE

"I am Adriana Hart with your Channel 6 news. President Dominic Harvey is upset by the group that calls themselves "The Resistance." He feels as if they are creating a sovereign state that is separate from the way of current living conditions that he had put in place. No one has come forth with any leads as to who is responsible for the undermining heroic acts.

Dominic has stated in a press conference a few days ago declaring that anyone aiding or abetting any citizen of this nation will be an act punishable by death. Here I am live on air; outside a summit meeting, where the Presidents' second in command Jarvis Holden has just spoken a few words about the Resistance. As he walks away towards his vehicle, let's try and get a few answers to some questions.

Jarvis...Jarvis can we ask you a few questions? What will the President do as a reward for anyone that comes forth with any information? How could the Resistance hinder any plans the President has? Jarvis, Just a few moments of your time...Asshole!

The world may be torn between the feelings on President Harvey's reign, but what choice do they have? It is good to know there are people out there who are taking a stand for what they believe in. What happened to our government and humanity? We have all become a fucking mess with how we view the world and also how we choose to live in it. What makes this dystopia any better from what we believed used to be our utopia? You can argue which is better, though there is NO argument on which is worst. We, as people, are like a baby bird that has falling from its nest and lost its wings and voice. I cannot speak ill will about our President for the consequence could be fatal. I fear him!

I once stood by his side, while he destroyed MY world afterwards. I was once helpless in fighting back against him as you all are now. Need I complain to you, as this was the man we all thought was best for us! This was the man that said what we wanted to hear and did what we feared he would do. Are we shameful of the man we created or the world created by the man we elected? I have no fucking words for this damn nightmare! I didn't come on air to bitch about the fucking world and what it has become, but this is the goddamn news EXCUSE MY FUCKING FRENCH!

I report the news and President Dominic Harvey has created chaos to becoming the everyday news I present. I could come on air and feed you shit for breakfast, but by the time you digest it and defecate, it will still be shit. Shit is shit! And I am the son of a bitch that brings you these newscasts filled with shit! Well this is Adriana Hart reporting outside the Washington summit meeting, back to you Paul!"

CHAPTER 13

A WORLD GONE MAD

Jesse sat inside the local diner near his old residence, drinking a cup of coffee. He patiently waited for his friend John to show up. They had planned earlier within the week to meet and maybe continue their conversation, but yet in a more civilized manner than that of the last. Margaret comes over with a pot of coffee to ask Jesse if he wants anymore. He refrains from being topped off; proclaiming that he is fine for now, before inquires what was being talked about on the newscast as the screen across the room had caught his attention. The footage displayed seemed as if something big was going on in the world but he was unable to hear what was actually being said. Margaret turns her head towards a few customers that are crowded around the television.

"Dominic has fully moved all of his belongings out of the White House and into an abandoned ten-story building. He wanted more room to work out of, though he still using the Presidential address for certain confidential meetings. That's all!" she stated in a ginger voice. Margaret told Jesse that things are changing and that he needed to do something. Overwhelmed by it all Jesse was a little baffled at the comment because he was also drained from everything he had going on. Life for him wasn't some easy walk in the park and he felt that even with Margaret knowing his story, she was losing sight of the hardships he was enduring.

"Do something? You already know how hard I am working. I almost consider it overtime at this point. Most nights I don't get any sleep. The three of us are trying to lead this resistance and that has been the hardest struggle on top of dealing with this cancerous bullshit," Jesse openly vocalized. Margaret knew about so much more than anyone else, even John. She was one of the few people that had been told about the underground resistance, even though she didn't reside there and lived above with all the madness.

"I know. I haven't lost sight. You are a family man and I know that. You would do anything. Maybe I need suck it up and help fight the good fight!" Margaret suggested. Jesse snickers at her comment and asks her why she doesn't join the Resistance with him and Samuel. Margaret sneers with a spiteful voice, "Hell No! I was being sarcastic. You know me! I have seen some of the things that President Harvey is capable of. We have had this talk before. No resistances will help change my life, only make things more difficult for me right now! Plus I am in NO condition right now to be out there fighting the good fight and you know that. I would be at risk to hurting more than just myself in doing so. You should think about the same with you and how much you are doing!"

As they continue to converse, a young boy runs by and throws a large rock through the window. Margaret moves her head slightly to the left to avertedly dodge the rock. Jesse covers his face as the glass shatters over his table near the window to where he is sitting. The other customers in the restaurant turn around and then back to the television unfazed as if this is an everyday occurrence. Margaret picks herself up off the floor and runs towards a secret compartment behind a fire extinguisher. She pulls out an Uzi and storms off towards the entrance of the restaurant as she bumps into John along her way. "Hey John! Bye John!" she spouts off while whisking by him. Margaret turns the corner and runs down the street passing the window that was broken out as she unloads a half a clip from the Uzi. The echo rumbled throughout the streets, causing much unneeded attention to be directed her way.

John enters the diner and plops a seat down at the table that Jesse is at as he nonchalantly wipes away some of the broken pieces of glass. "I see much hasn't changed," John sarcastically remarks. "Same Shit, Different Day! Nothing has seemed to change out in this fucked up world," Jesse responds back. The two chuckle as if not a bad word had been spoken between them.

Noise outside the diner wasn't the sound of cars passing by and children playing. They both stare out the window to see chaos unfolding. This wasn't the world they remembered and it was getting worse. Many cars are seen intentionally running stop signs. A gang is spotted beating up an old lady across the street and stealing her purse as they take off running down the street. People were steadily looting at several strip stores. A woman screams out for help as she is raped during broad day light by a scruffy looking vigilante and others just walked by minding their own business. The soldiers continue down the street paying no mind to the enduring craziness. Some people were stopped occasionally by the soldiers and asked to show a current crime tax receipt before being allowed to continue their heinous acts after presenting that proof of purchase.

Aside from that small interaction with civilians and military officials, they weren't the most active group within that neighborhood that particular day. Of course, if most of them had physically seen Margaret with that Uzi, she would have been captured and/or worse by being killed on the spot. When she ran outside with it, she remained careful and sneaky about it by keeping the weapon somewhat concealed and only fired it if military weren't present and watching her way. It was very ballsy still of her on her part to take such a high risk, considering how she stated that she didn't want to be involved with the resistance or any violent retaliation of any sort. She was passionate about the restaurant that she worked in and took much pride in her work as she had worked there since she was old enough to see over the table tops. Someone coming in there and purposefully destroying the property had just set her off because of the spot that restaurant holds in her heart. Margaret knew that chasing the vigilante into the alley was almost an instinctive reaction towards his criminal acts and that couldn't be overlooked. She was willing to take the life of anyone who created harm to that business or the customers dining in it. The criminal had got away but not unscathed as she had grazed him with a few bullets fired during her pursuit.

Margaret returned shortly thereafter to the restaurant, passing by the broken window, and entered back through the front entrance. Her hair was in total disarray, with blood on her clothes as she inconspicuously hides the Uzi back behind the fire extinguisher. She approaches the table where Jesse and John were at to casually continue waitressing. John was in shock but Jesse knew her passion and loyalty to that diner. He was well aware to how important it was to her, but you could see the look of concern on his face. Margaret took out her notepad and turned to John and asked him if he needs anything, but Jesse intervened to speak what was on his mind.

"Guns are not permitted in the possession of civilians and you know that! You could have been killed if a soldier saw you in broad daylight with that. I know that you would give your life protecting this place, but I am worried about... you know what? Just don't do that again! I am begging you," Jesse boldly stated. Margaret fixes her hair and looks into Jesse's eyes. She could see the concern she had caused and even John could see a little flame flickering between the two, though he sat there and kept quiet. Margaret didn't want Jesse to be worried and helped put his mind at ease. "I know sugar! I hid that gun and keep it near for safety purposes. I doubt those soldiers would have noticed or cared anyway about little ole me out there firing bullets at some criminal. It seems like so much madness is going on, why pay attention to me running down the street with an Uzi? I get what you're saying though and understand why you are worried and for that I apologize!" she responded back. Jesse still warns her that it isn't a good idea to keep a firearm on the premises as she may have been lucky not being noticed now, but people are losing their lives for not obeying the laws that the President has set forth. "They will kill anyone with a weapon. Even 'little ole' you!" he stated.

The thought then hit Jesse about how she obtained a gun in the first place. She tells him of a guy who came into eat at the restaurant one day that supposedly runs a drug house a few blocks away. The man came in and told her that he sells weapons to people that he was able to illegally acquire. He gave me the address to the house and told me if I wanted to buy anything from him to stop by. Margaret takes a piece of paper out of her apron with an address written on it as she places it on the table and slides it towards Jesse. "I know you don't believe in disobeying the laws because it could be dangerous. Is it any different than having your resistance out here running around playing savior?" Margaret adds.

Jesse takes the piece of paper and places it into his pocket. "Would you rather the resistance play savior or the so called humanitarian President Harvey playing God? I think this is the start of something special. Guns are definitely needed for our protection. I am just worried about something happening to you if you were discovered to have one in your possession. The soldiers don't separate flowers based on how they look or what garden they are in. They would shoot any beautiful rose!" Jesse utters the cryptic message that only she would understand. He adds that he isn't considering buying any guns, but he will hold onto the address just in case it could come in handy. Margaret looks over to John and apologizes for not taking his order.

"I am not hungry, but I will take a water" John cordially responds. Margaret smiled and nodded her head so not to dismiss his request. The disassembled waitress headed over to the drink station to grab John a glass of water. "Did you think about joining the resistance?" Jesse hinted to his friend, John, in confidence after Margaret had stepped away. "I told you already that I don't fight crime anymore," John bantered back defensively. Jesse stated that he would back off from asking even though he wanted to run down the list of how having his friend as a part of the resistance could prove to be very useful. "I come in peace and am not looking to start an argument or war with you," he added. John sees Margaret over Jesse's shoulder making her way back to their table. She squeezes by a large group of people still gathered around the television. John looks to Jesse and tells him that he wasn't staying long because he was headed over to the cemetery.

Margaret sets down a tall glass of water in front of John and asks if he had changed his mind and wanted something to eat. John apologizes for having to cut short and explains to her that he wasn't staying long. He takes a few large sips of the water and wipes his mouth. Jesse candidly tells Margaret that he was going to walk with John and places a few dollars down upon the table to cover his bill and a tip. Margaret immediately picks it off the table and places it in her apron. "You can't trust anyone anymore! Money is too valuable to just be leaving on tables for all eyes to see," she pointed out.

The two exited and made their way towards a nearby parking lot. While walking, Jesse stops to ask John why he was still visiting the cemetery. It had been many years since the traumatic night that has still haunted him till this very day. Jesse knows that he loved her, but the one thing he hadn't seen from his friend is progress. He wanted to see John find love elsewhere. It was known that everyone grieves differently, but that night didn't just leave a scar. It was visibly still gushing blood from the wound and Jesse saw how draining this was to him.

John acknowledges to his friend that whether they are gone or not, they are still his family and for that reason alone, he will always love them. "I understand that and I am not saying to never stop loving them. I just want you to find love again and see if that brings you back to the John I once remember laughing with and joking around with," Jesse declared. He tries to hint to John that he should get out and find someone else as he even began listing suitable women from his life that may be of interest. John kept the conversation very brief as he quickly changed the topic. He was aware of what Jesse was trying to do, even though John felt the time wasn't right for him at this moment. The two approached a black motorcycle in the parking lot as John came to an immediate halt by its side. He then mounted the bike, placing a key into the ignition and started the engine. Jesse takes a step back, "Whoa, where did you get such a nice set of wheels?" heasks. John revs the engine a few times as it roars like a lion. Jesse took a few steps back and John puts on a motorcycle helmet and lifts the wind guard up to respond. "Who said crime doesn't pay?" John states as he skirts off down the street.

Jesse watches his friend ride off when something hit him. He reaches into his pocket and pulls out the piece of paper that Margaret gave him with the drug dealer's address on it. Many ideas started to flounder about inside his head. He quickly jogs back to the subway hideout. When he scurries inside, he sees Stacy sitting down watching television with Justin. Jesse walks up to her and asks her to go somewhere really quick with him. Unbeknownst to what reason he had to go out so late, Stacy trusted Jesse dearly. Even though they had known each other in what some may feel has been a short amount of time, he gave her no reason in the past to never not trust him. She points out that it is late and close to curfew, but he insists that he needs her help with something. She agrees and grabs a jacket as she was easily swayed by his charm before the two try and scurry out unnoticed.

Samuel sees them leaving in a hurry and stops them to ask where they were going. "Do you both know what time it is? It's getting late!" stated Samuel. Jesse explained that he had asked her to go check something out with him and that they would be back very soon, even before the alarm sound. Samuel demanded they hurry back as there was only an hour or so left before the curfew was to begin. Jesse and Stacy quickly jogged through town trying to at least get there before the curfew. They had eventually reached the neighborhood, where the house was located, that Margaret told him about. Stacy had no choice but to stop Jesse to inquire what this was all about. She wanted to know what she was initially getting into.

"Why did you bring me all the way out here?" she asked. Jesse couldn't tell her a lie. He knew that the truth would have caused her not to come with them, but they were at a point where turning back wasn't an option. They had come this far and he knew that not telling her could also create problems. He explained about how his friend, Margaret, gave him the address to look into purchasing guns for protection. She gasps for air in astonishment as she explained to him how being in possession of a gun was against the law. "Don't you know how Samuel feels about guns and fighting back? Why are you doing this?" she questioned. Jesse tried to calm her as he explained that sneaking around town without any sufficient protection was more to his concern. He reassures her that he was just going to find out how much they were asking and then they would be on their way.

"I promise you that this is just a safety measure. I would have come alone or with someone else, but there wasn't a better candidate that would go on such an insane mission. John doesn't want to help! Samuel is against guns and fighting back! Justin is too young! Of course I have other people I could have reached out to, but I was closest to your subway station cart making you the best person to ask. I believe that Samuel's vision to build a resistance while having a clinched fist is a good one to have, but I don't believe that an unclenched fist will fight back when we need to protect ourselves. I just need you to trust me. I know that we are the only ones that want to help others, but it feels like we are fighting this war with rubber bullets. I just didn't want to come here alone. I need you to be by my side on this one. Will you do this for me? For the Resistance?" Jesse voiced as being reasonable, but yet rhetorical questions stated, under the assumed implication in his mind that she really didn't have a choice.

Stacy knew how much it meant to Jesse to help others. It was becoming his life's work and she also didn't want him to go into this situation alone. She nodded, agreeing to help him. "Just this one time! Quick in and out! No one gets hurt!" she added as a compromise to the mission. Jesse then walked up onto the front porch and rang the doorbell. When no one answered right away, he rang it once more. Someone within the house yells out, "Just a fucking minute, goddammit!" The two bold resistance members stood patiently waiting, not knowing how things were going to end. They could hear rustling and whispering from the other side of the door as someone could be heard approaching. The door slowly opened to a scruffy looking older man. He had on a black and white bandana and a white tank top with blue jeans.

Jesse looked over the shoulder of the scruffy looking man and saw a very young teenager in the kitchen in tears as she appeared to be in fear for her life. "What do you want motherfucker?" the man stated in a stern voice. Jesse tells the man about how his friend, Margaret, who gave him the address and told him to stop by to inquire about purchasing guns. "I just want to know how much for them and maybe even see some of the goods," Jesse continued. A few men in the background pass by as one can be seen grabbing the neck of the teenager and forcing her to sniff a white powder on the kitchen table that was easily identified as being cocaine. The scruffy man does a double take and realizes that Jesse is being distracted by the other people in the house.

"Never mind them! My name is Snake. What kind of weapons are you looking for?" Snake questions before taking a puff of the joint he had in his hand. "Well price is everything, so let's start there," Jesse negotiates. He asks how much he would have to spend to get a hold of a berretta of any kind. Snake laughs, telling Jesse that he has a few different selections he could choose from and that it would cost him a few hundred dollars at least. "Could we enter the house so not to be completely outside visible after hour?" asks Jesse as a suggestion to be more inconspicuous. Snake denied them access as he pointed out that he doubts that anyone would have a problem with them being on the front porch a few minutes after the curfew. "Plus you are both strangers to me!" he adds. The warning siren sounds and some patrols cars start moving down the street shining spotlights around the neighborhood. Stacy looks at her watch and then over to Jesse. She states to Snake that she thinks they will need a few handguns and informs him that they may need some time to get together all the money before returning to finalize the deal.

Snake licks his lips, takes another puff of his joint as he looks at Stacy with a sensual gaze. "I am sure we could cut you a discount if you were willing to make other personal arrangements," Snake whispered to Stacy as he reached his hand out to touch hers. Stacy pulls back and states that she will have to think it over and that they would be back as soon as they have all of the money. She dodged every sexual attempt that Snake threw at her in hopes to get the information Jesse needed and get out of there. Jesse reached out to shake Snake's hand, however the gestured was not received. Snake snarled at Jesse's way to setting the deal between them. He took another puff of his joint and put it out on Jesse's jacket before tossing the rest aside. Jesse dusted the ashes off his jacket and patted himself down a few times to avoid the embers catching his jacket on fire. "I don't shake hands. You wouldn't be stupid enough to stiff me on a deal. My word is golden. Yours better be too, motha fucka. Now get the fuck out of here! I don't wanna see ya'll back till you have my fucking money," noted Snake.

The tone he used was disdainful. He had taken a few steps back to slam the door in Jesse and Stacy's face. Just as it was about to be closed shut, they both saw an everlasting final image of the teenage girl look up and make eye contact with them. There was a large trail of cocaine on her face as he mouthed the word 'HELP ME!' to them. They both stood on the porch for a brief moment in disbelief. So many thoughts were running their heads. The good news from it all was that they made it out of there alive with little confrontation. The final alarm sounded and both Jesse and Stacy were now at a point where fear ran up the back of their spines. They were completely exposed and still needed to get back to the underground subway station. What options did they have? How were the two of them to survive this all? They quickly turned around and began walking away from the house as Snake peeks out suspiciously through the blinds of the front window. They crept towards a nearby alley to get out of the street's lighting where many military cars were heavily patrolling.

Jesse's phone vibrated abruptly as he took it out from his pocket and sees that it was John calling. He answered the phone with a quiet whisper. "Hello?" he muttered. "I am at the cemetery and I just wanted to call you to say that I hope we are still cool. I don't want to lose you as my friend and regret I didn't fix things. It's just that I don't fight any-more. I know you want the old John to come back and I would say that that would take time, but I don't know how much time that will inevitably take. I am grieving, but I am also healing. I wanted to call to tell you that," John replied.

Jesse recognized that they had said things they didn't mean and he too wanted to make sure they were good. He stated that they will always be cool, but he will have to call him back because he is out with Stacy after curfew. "No problem. I just didn't want the last words spoken to be bad ones. I would ask why you are out after curfew, but I am sure there is reason and I would be a hypocrite any-way, since I am at the cemetery. Get back home safe!" de-manded John while glancing down at the three headstones which read his family member's names. They sat one next to the other in a row with Julie's tombstone in the middle. It was difficult for John to look at their graves and recog-nize the reality that his family was gone and never coming back. It began to bring back memories from that tragic night. He begins to have quick flashbacks of sirens and flames in the air passing him by as he remembered push-ing his way through spectators and police officers. John bends his head down and whispers a prayer above their grave. He finishes his profound benediction and stands up to say his last goodbyes before heading back to his motel room, which is only a few blocks away from the cemetery.

John purposely chose that motel to be closer to where they were entombed. He walks down a dark back road to head back to the motel as the safest route possible. When he gets closer to the motel, he turns into another alley that leads to the back part of his building. Two thugs jump out from behind a couple of dumpsters located in the back of a Chinese restaurant that were against the wall. "What are you doing out past curfew?" one of the thugs boldly screams out. The other thug circles behind John as they both begin to close in on him. John tells them both that he doesn't have anything of great value and how he doesn't want any problems, but it appeared that they weren't there for the purpose of money, more so than to just inflict pain on another person. They were thugs that had paid the crime tax and wanted to do harm to others in addition to robbing people at the high risk of doing so after curfew hours.

The thug that was standing behind John takes a metal bar out of the back of his pants and swings it towards the back of John's head. John forcefully plummets to the ground after the blatant strike. A loud ringing echoes throughout John's head as he fades in and out of consciousness. The thug in front of him begins kicking him in the face and the chest as hard as he could. As John was laid out on the concrete, the two men stood over him repeatedly stomping him and bashing things against his body. They used anything that they could get their hands on, such as; glass bottles, rocks and other metal pipes. They then searched his pockets looking for cash or something that had some sort of value to which they could sell for money on the streets.

Upon realizing that John wasn't carrying anything on him except for a key to his motel and a cell phone, they took the phone and ran off down the alley. John stood up and stumbled towards his motel room as he reaches into his pocket pulling out his key to unlock his door. He quickly hobbles over to the phone in his room and dials the first person that comes to mind while in need of help. Jesse picks up the phone to hear his helpless friend panting on the other end as he curiously asks what wrong. John explains what happened in detail. Jesse, enraged by the story, tells John that he is on the way over. John didn't want anyone else to get hurt, especially for his friend to risk being killed over being out after curfew. "No NO! NO! Don't do that!" John raved. He quickly calms down Jesse, reassuring that he is fine and tells him that is isn't safe to be out just to risk something bad happening to him. "I am fine. I just wanted to tell you what happened. We will talk soon and continue to our conversation about getting me back to the old me. The guy you remember laughing and joking with. I promise," noted John emphatically.

The conversation between them had remained brief before John explained how he wanted to place ice on his bruises and climb into bed to get some rest. Jesse had agreed to not leave out from the subway hideout until the morning as suggested by his friend. He had hung up the phone to focus on his travels back to the subway station. Stacy walks over to him after he finished up his call. The look on Jesse's face indicated that something was wrong. While beside him, she places her arm around him as she inquisitively asks him about his long face. He pulls away from her as she could spot that other things were on his mind. They continued making their way back through the various alleys until they had reached the sewer cap that led down below. Their conversation continued all throughout the tunnelway about the pros and cons to their plan. It was all so much to take in. Stacy declared how the priority is saving people but had to be done strategically so no one was to get hurt or die. Jesse heard what she was saying but reminded her about their mission as a Resistance member. He indicated that they put their lives on the line every time they go out to save someone and bring them back to the subway station.

"We need to gather up as much money as we have and go back to buy a few guns. Hell, I am at the point that we could go back and steal them all. They are a bunch of thugs and the world won't miss them. We are supposed to help people and that girl doesn't seem like she wants to be there. She was forced to sniff the drugs off the table. You saw her beg for help. We need to save her. We need the guns. The more time that passes by... the more people that are lost along the way! You of all people should know that. Your husband despises you and blames you and me for the loss of his family. We could have helped. This is the time to act now, so not to regret it later," Jesse states to her in a stern voice. He continues to explain what happened to his friend, John, and how he can't let people get hurt anymore by the madness that this world is coming to.

"All I am saying is that when we go back to get the guns, we need to grab that girl. She is obviously being held there against her will. That is a fact. If the resistance is going to stand by the motto of helping people, then in my opinion she needs help. OUR HELP! We need to stop being the resistance that hides and start being the resistance that fights back!" Jesse continues to rave. Stacy reminds Jesse that Snake has seen both of their faces and so it would be impossible for one of them to distract the drug dealers to a point that they could sneak in to help save the teenage girl. Samuel walks in as he had overheard most of the end of the conversation between the two. "It seems like you have a dilemma. How can I help?" Samuel calmly states to the two.

Stacy reminds Samuel that he is older and he may not be able to help if things went haywire. Samuel looks at them both, "I can bring a good fight with me. Don't under-estimate me!" he replies with a manly tone. Jesse doesn't see any better option. It was the only way for Samuel to not worry and know that they were safe by being right by their side. Jesse could see the desire he had to want to help and prove that the motto that he preached to the resistance had meant something. Jesse then suggests that Samuel pose as an elderly homeless person inquiring about their weapons, while they both sneak in through the back to grab the girl. The plan sounded perfect, damn near sound proof, though they didn't give much thought to what they would do if things didn't work out as they had hoped and planned. Stacy had to be the reasonable one that thought through all the possibilities. She reminds him that he will have to stall them as long as possible and also make a purchase on one of the handguns as well as some ammunition. "That will buy us enough time to do what we need to do. Just stall him as long as possible," Stacy expressed.

The three continue to plan out their devious plot in detail as they prepared for their courageous endeavor. They agreed that they will make haste on the plan the following day at night after Jesse returns from checking on his friend John. So the next day, when they all awoke, Stacy told Samuel that she was going to go out to find the perfect disguise for him to wear. She explained the she would be back by mid-day sometime. Jesse had just exited his subway cart as they were parting ways and says 'good morning' to them both. He was already dressed and on his way to head out for the day to visit John. Before he left, he wanted to finalize when they were to all meet back up to enact their plan to save the girl. That had seemed to be the goal in mind that was discussed and the mention of grabbing weapons had been left out. Samuel was not a fan on using firearms, especially in a world where they weren't allowed. This would bring too many more problems to the doorstep of the resistance for having them in their possession. Jesse still believed that they were need. It was as if he had other plans for them. He knew that protection was needed at some point and he rather have them on hand that not to have them at all. That all agreed to meet back at the hideout around six o'clock at night before parting ways.

"No problem. See everyone tonight at six!" Jesse remarked. He flings his hood over his head as he walks away with Stacy down the tunnel. The two reach the top surface and Jesse looks over to Stacy and tells her to be safe, to which she smiles. "Always! You too!" she responds back. Jesse turns the corner and begins walking away. He sees many people up early in the morning as they were up to no good, as usual. People were breaking windows of nearby businesses as they quickly rushed in and exited with whatever they could grab. Some of them ran out the stores right near Jesse as they bumped into him almost knocking him over during their rampage. Not so much as an 'excuse me' comes from the vigilantes' mouths, as they quickly rush down the street. Military trucks and soldiers still patrol through each neighborhood as the chaos ensues.

Jesse continues his path down the sidewalk and then crosses the street to the other side trying to keep a low profile and ignore what madness had surrounded him. It almost becomes two separate worlds to him. Jesse is so used to kind individuals in the resistance who are against the way the world. Everyone is kind-hearted and geared more towards helping each other and other people. Then he goes out into the streets of Washington D.C. and exposes himself to the other world that he is more akin to living in during the nightly parts of his days. A world that is more chaotic, where crime has become a necessity to survive.

Jesse approaches John's motel room door and knocks a few times as he waits for his friend to answer. John limps over to the door, battered and bruised, as he opens it to find his best friend Jesse standing before him. Jesse comes in and tells John to take a seat and rest, knowing the injuries he had sustained. "What is new with you, aside from being all banged up?" Jesse asks. "Same Shit, Different Day!" John replies jokingly before groaning in pain as they both chuckle. Jesse makes a comment about how he wouldn't be in this condition if he was in the resistance because of the fact that they stay together and protect each other. John shakes his head in frustration as Jesse states to him that he isn't trying to push him to join, though he wants him to understand that things could be different instead of always being the same shit on a different day.

"I hear what you saying!" John verbally notes. Jesse then reminds John of how he was there for him when Julie and the kids were killed as John was there for him when Marie left him. "We have been there for each other. I could use you here now more than ever. Well, maybe after you heal up! Samuel wants this resistance to help people and hide from the government and military. I think we should fight back and have been doing so since day one without telling Samuel or anyone about the risks I take each and every day. I can't do that without my good friend by my side," proclaims Jesse. It was obvious how strongly he felt about how things were going in the resistance. He knew that his friend appeared to feel alone after losing his wife and may even feel like he was losing his best friend, whom kept himself busy by always running the streets trying to save lives.

John asks Jesse if he heard from Marie or even tried to contact her. The thought had actually crossed his mind. Jesse explains how he felt that trying to contact her under the circumstances to how she left had led him to believe that she doesn't want anything to do with him anymore. He told his friend that he thinks about her every day, but he hadn't heard from her in almost twenty years. "Yes I will always love her, but I have learned how to move forward and make new memories with new people. I understand the importance. I have people that care about me and look up to me. I have people in my resistance that depend on me. I learned that you can buy moments, but not more time to purchase more moments. A wise little girl told me that. You believe that. I learned that from a child. Children see the hate that we are creating and we adults don't. We just keep creating hate and subject our kids to being injected by our own hate. It infuriates me talking about it all. I always get a little emotional," says Jesse. He quickly changes topic as he offers John to come and at least stay a little bit at the resistance's underground hideout until he gets his strength back.

"How am I supposed to get there? Do you want me to hobble a few miles?" John remarks sarcastically. The two laugh as Jesse realizes that it would be difficult for him at this given time. "Of course not! We'll figure something out though," he responds. The two laugh some more and converse about how things have been coming along for the resistance lately. "It has been growing every day and we have been helping a lot of people find that safe haven they were looking for. A world away from the world they all hated," Jesse indicated. He tells John that he has to make another stop before the curfew begins and then get back to the hide-out to tend to business he had planned with Stacy and Samuel. The two say their farewells as Jesse sees himself out.

The day was ramping up to be an eventful one for Jesse. He had gone to see his friend and now had one last stop on his itinerary before heading back to the Resistance hideout.

He wanted to stop by his old home that he had lived in with Marie. When he arrived at the address, there was a different feel to how it looked. The home stood there, mostly boarded up after many of the windows had been broken out. One was still open and easily accessible to gaining entry and Jesse saw this as the perfect time to enter the now foreclosed property. He walked up to window near the front entrance of his old home and chips away some of the broken glass. As he quickly climbs through the window, he sees his former house in complete disarray. The window shades were torn and most of the furniture was overturned. There was broken glass all over the floor next to small meaningless household items. Jesse had taken many of the expensive belongings and huge essentials to the resistances hideout. Many of the small things had been stolen by several criminals that had broken into the boarded up household ever since Jesse and Samuel had moved out.

Jesse went upstairs to his old bedroom, where he hoped to grab some things of importance that he had left behind. When he walked in, he saw various items scattered around the room. He walked over to an old dusty dresser and pushed it far to the right as he could. There was a floor panel that appeared to be loose as he immediately lifted the thin board piece and reached his hand into the dusty dark compartment. Jesse then pulled out a few photographs and a small jewelry box. He opened the box to find a silver bracelet with an inscription on it that read, "Once a guiding light!" It was a bracelet that he had bought for his wife, Marie, for their anniversary which was a few days after she had walked out on him. The backstory behind the bracelet made it priceless. Jesse and Marie had tried many times to have children and weren't able to able. It became of mystery as they repeatedly tried. Jesse had desperately wanted to have a child to raise and call his own. He bought that bracelet and had it inscribed as a reminder to Marie to how she had stuck by him. He had come so far and he didn't believe that he would have made it so far without the persistence of her steadily sticking behind him. She, herself, desperately wanted to have kids and was hurt by the notion that she had been unable to give him that gift of new life. He placed the jewelry box down and picked up the photos that were also stashed away. He began to look through them, as they consisted mostly of him and Marie. A few gunshots were heard outside of the home while he was inside. Jesse was startled by the commotion that he heard, dropping the items in his hand. He picked them up off the floor and slid them into the pocket of his jacket before rushing down the stairs to look out the broken-out window that he entered through only to be astounded by what he saw.

Sirens are heard echoing throughout the town as the mass numbers of soldiers begin entering the streets with assault rifles in their hands. A voice is also heard being projected through an intercom system that was coming from a large van that following behind the armored military vehicles, stating that the city is entering a strict lockdown one hour earlier than the intended curfew hour. Jesse looked at his watch, noticing how close it was till that start time and climbs back through the window. He begins racing down the street towards where the resistance hideout is located with his hair and jacket blowing in the wind. Everyone around him was also scampering around the streets crazier than ever as they tried to get into their homes quickly. Many others utilized the advantage to participate in last minute looting as they broke into several businesses and ran out with expensive items in hand. Gunshots could be heard in the distance, only to assume it was military force trying to gain order and control. Everyone was moving around as if they were completely insane with not a care for anyone else's well-being, stepping on or over anyone in their war path.

When Jesse got closer to the resistance hideout that was now only a few blocks away, he came across a few criminals that were dragging a gas station owner out of his business and begin beating him down in front of it. They continuously hit him with metal bats and chains, as he cried out for help. Jesse sees the senseless mugging going on as he contemplates the risks involved with helping by going over to assist the helpless man, but decides to continue on his way to avoid any conflict. This was by far from a decision that was able to be easily made by Jesse considering the nature of his heart and desire for helping other. He wanted him to stop and help the man but he knew that it was more dangerous than usual as he was alone and definitely out-numbered. He hears an argument behind him, while hurrying down the middle of the road only to spot Adriana Hart and her cameraman over his shoulder. They were heading towards the chaos, while crossing the street. Jesse rushed into the alley, headed down the sewer drain and through the tunnels to the safety and security of the Resistance followers.

Adriana remained above, amongst the commotion, pushing her hesitant cameraman aside. She takes the camera from his grasp as she sprints towards the madness ensuing at the local gas station to gain an interview and cover the villainous happenings. Her hair is placed in sloppy disarray as she negligently rushes behind a vehicle and places the camera on the back trunk and zooms in towards the action. She places the microphone that is connected to the camera up to her mouth and tries to regain her breathe as she begins covering the unfortunate madness.

CHAPTER 14

YOU GET WHAT YOU VOTED FOR

"What you are seeing is a few punk ass thugs beating down a local gas station manager. As he screams and begs for his fucking life, you can see a glimpse of truly what this world is slowly becoming. How in the hell can one call this madness freedom? The people of this world are showing that we don't give a damn about one another. The President has created an ant farm and is sitting back watching what we do. We're a world mixed of cheetahs and antelope. Everyone is out there for themselves. People need to fucking understand that HE didn't create this world of madness...WE DID!

I look onward to the chaos ensuing in front of me and want to reach out and help, though that will only bring me into being part of the brutal attack that is currently transpiring. As I look on and observe things from a distance, I notice a man with a baseball bat covered in barbed wire. He is repeatedly beating the helpless man with the bat, as he screams mercilessly. The barbed wire can clearly be seen ripping his flesh from his body, as the sharp points retract from his skin. You can see the other men kicking the owner while he is on the ground as a few other vigilantes carrying out some of the store items, while he is holding up a receipt to nearby soldiers indicating that he paid his crime tax.

This is the world as what we voted for and what we reluctantly received. This is the world today! Dominic is the asshole and the world has become the shitty feces spewed from that dirty anus! It seems that we are considered to be fucking free in this world to some, but the question I have is when did goddamn freedom become something you had to pay for?"

CHAPTER 15

THERE'S STILL A CHANCE

Jesse entered the lobby of the underground hideout and sees several people gathered around the television watching the news. Stacy is the first to run up and give him a huge hug. "I thought something happened to you!" she exclaimed. Jesse reassured her that he was alright and commented that he felt that they needed to still go through with tonight's plan. "I know that isn't ideal, but time is of the essence!" he retorted. Samuel walked over and stated that he wasn't sure if that was a good idea, suggesting waiting till tomorrow to lower the possibility of any causalities being accrued. "Things are not safe! It is crazier now more so than ever out there. We are NOT a resistance that fights, Jesse, we are one that protects! And I think it would be better if you guys stayed here," suggested Samuel again as being the smarter option. He just had a gut feeling about it.

The three of them went back and forth about why they should do it now or why they should wait till later. "I understand your point, Samuel, but this girl may not be alive tomorrow. I already passed a helpless man being beat to death to get back here and help on this mission," Jesse noted. Samuel was in utter disagreement with the idea; however he knew that he couldn't stop them and that the better idea was to go with them as planned to give the back-up needed. Stacy also agreed with Jesse, being the non-biased side that saw both points made by her two comrades. She knew that they shouldn't put it off and so the three decided to quickly get their things together and make haste on their mission.

Samuel put on some raggedy clothing as he wiped a cluster of dirt and dust off the side of one of the train carts' panels and pats it onto his beard to appear dirty and home-less. The three then left the hideout and jogged through the town and madness towards Snake's house with only thirty minutes left before the temporary scheduled curfew time was set to take effect. As they approached the front steps of the house and briefly regained their breath, Samuel told them both to make their way to the back of the house and find some way to gain entry silently. They all wished each other luck and were about to part ways just as one of the thugs had come around the side of the house out from the bushes after taking a piss. He had been assigned by Snake to stand guard outside the perimeter and was presumed to be armed. They all ducked down behind some bushes, but Samuel had been spotted by the thug. "Hey you, Come out from there. I fucking see you!" he stated with a knife pointed at the intruder. Samuel complied and stepped out with his hands raised in the air. "Who the fuck are you and what the fuck are you doing sneaking around this house? Do you know who the hell lives here and owns this prop-erty?" asked the thug. Samuel kept sliding to his left away from the bushes to distract the ruffian's attention so Jes-se and Stacy could sneak away. He was speechless and didn't know how to respond. "Didn't you fucking hear me, pussy?!" he exclaimed, while now approaching Samuel.

Just as the tip of the blade touched the forehead of the courageous Resistance leader, Jesse ran up and grabbed the thug by the throat using garrote wire. The man dropped his gun and tried grabbing the wire to stop it from cutting off the circulation of air to his lungs. It was too late by the time he had reached up, as the sharp thin wire grazed against his flesh underneath his adam's apple, digging into the skin against his esophagus. The thug was fading and Jesse had pulled backwards, using all of his weight to force the man down to the ground until he was no longer moving. Samuel could hear the final breathe slowly exit from the thug's mouth. "What the hell?" stated Samuel in a somewhat furious tone. Jesse started to stand up from the concrete walkway, but not yet before he had snapped the thug's neck to ensure that he was dead and would pose no threat to them all. He picked up the blade and placed it into his waistband and called out to Stacy for help, dragging the body around to the side of the house. This wasn't part of the plan and Samuel was not happy about how it all went down.

"I could have handled him without your taking his life. I said that we would do this without any violence. Do you not think that that was the pure definition of violence?" Samuel continued to voice, following Jesse and Stacy to the side of the house while they disposed of the body. Jesse had just about had enough though and was at his breaking point with Samuel about being scolded for his actions. "Are you kidding me? I call that saving your life. You define violence to me, because I am sure our definitions will differ," Jesse declared as a means to end the conversation.

Samuel was stunned to a point where he had no response to the comments made. "Just do your part and we will do ours! We don't have time to argue the semantics. You are alive and so are we. Let's keep it that way," Jesse added before he and Stacy jogged to the back of the house to look for any open windows they could climb through in order to obtain access to the drug house. Samuel continued on with the plan by stepping up onto the front porch and waiting for a signal from Jesse.

Stacy steadily looked around for a way in as her first instinct was to check the backdoor to see if it was locked, to which it was. "Dammit!" she whispered underneath her breathe. While pacing back and forth on the back porch she looked up and noticed that the window on the second floor was propped open. This was the best vantage point to gaining entry she thought to herself. Stacy tapped Jesse on the shoulder and uttered her plan for him to lift her up so she could reach the window sill. She climbs onto Jesse's shoulder as he raised her up and into the bedroom window of the two-story home. The room was junky and had a distasteful odor to it. As she approached the bedroom door, so she could get to the first floor in order to let Jesse in through the back door of the house, she hears the doorbell ring. Jesse had signaled Samuel shortly after he knew Stacy had got in safely. Stacy steps back and peeks through the doorway, as she sees Snake walk past the stairwell below to answer the door.

Snake opens the front door and Samuel greets him with a perfectly delivered performance as a drunken hobo. He played the character well as Snake tries to dismiss him. "Get the fuck outta here bitch!" Snake demanded. Samuel quickly explains before the door had been shut in his face how he has some money he wanted to spend and would like to purchase some weapons and drugs from him. This becomes an interest to Snake catching his attention as he calls out to one of the other men in the house. When the guy came around the corner, Snake asks him to come help him out with the deal by counting the money and checking to makes sure none of it was counterfeit. Another third man, wearing a blue bandana with a goatee, walks past the lower staircase and asks Samuel what kind of weapons he is looking for so he could go to the basement where they had the merchandise secretly stashed.

The three hold a conversation about what kind of weapons and drugs they had, as Samuel tries to stall them further by telling the thugs a made-up story why he was looking for the items and what he needed. "Whatever this amount of money will buy me. I need a pistol, two boxes of bullets, and a little heroine to get me through the next couple weeks," stated Samuel as his cover story. The men talked briefly amongst themselves, before Snake directed one of them to go get what was requested for their newly fond homeless customer.

Stacy opened the bedroom door and crept down the staircase as she swiftly moved around the corner, still keeping a close eye on the two thugs conversing with Samuel at the front door. As she came into the kitchen, she stops and notices the fourth man in the house sitting at a table with the teenager. His back is facing Stacy as she peeks around the corner. The teenager notices Stacy at the kitchen door that is parallel to the back door of the house that Jesse is patiently waiting at.

Stacy signals the teenager to keep quiet with her index finger up to her lips as she creeps past the doorway and slowly unlocks the backdoor of the house to let Jesse inside. The thug in the kitchen sniffed a line of cocaine and then forms another line for the teenager. "Can I do it when I get back? I have to use the bathroom," the teenager tried to negotiate as she gets up from the kitchen table. She does this as a distraction to help aid Jesse and Stacy within the attempt to saving her life. The young girl slowly starts to walk by the thug as he grabs her arms and tells her to hurry back, before smacking her on her ass.

"This nose candy won't sniff itself. Hurry back!" he added with a strong sense of authority. The teenager had then begun to walk toward the kitchen door where Jesse and Stacy were hiding. As the thug went down to sniff another line of cocaine, he saw Jesse and Stacy creeping into the house within the reflection of a clock that was mounted in the kitchen on the wall. He quickly turns around knocking most the powdered drugs onto the floor and screams out to Snake that there is an intruder in the house.

Snake tried to ignore the frantic alert given by one of his henchman, while staying focused on the deal he was making, but a second cry out for help was made shortly after his first. Samuel continues to tries to stall the two thugs at the front door, though they realized that he was a planted distraction. They grab Samuel by the back of the neck and drag him into the home, closing the door behind them as they draw their weapons at him. The other thug in the kitchen hurried to the back door to block and trap everyone in, also closing and locking the door so they had nowhere to go. He pulls out a forty- five caliber weapon and points in towards Jesse, Stacy and the young teenager. Snake came around the corner to the hallway that all three were standing in as he still sternly had a strong hold on Samuel by the back of his neck. He pushes the fragile built senior forward and tells them all to go into the kitchen and have a seat.

"I can see what is going on here! You think you can distract me and take this bitch away from me! I must be a dumb nigga that would just allow you motha fuckas to come into my kingdom playing Robin Hood. I should cut your fucking tongues out and make you swallow them whole!" Snake states while making direct eye contact. Jesse speaks up trying to convince the men to let Stacy go, indicating that she had nothing to do with this. One of the thugs punches Jesse in the jaw when he began to speak and tells him not to say a word unless spoken to.

"Shut your fucking mouth! You know what, I have an idea. I think I will actually let everyone go," Snake spouts off to Jesse, whom is at this point bleeding from the mouth. "Though I will only let three of you go. One has to stay and we will play a game to find out who that will be," Snake continues. Jesse looks around to his fellow comrades and courageously offers to be the one to stay. Snake denies his request to be able to choose who stays and leaves as he looks at the young female teenager and calls out her name. "Chance!" he screams to get her attention. She lifts her head slowly and looks over to him in fear.

"Grab my pistol out of the bread box behind you?" Snake commands as she whimpers and turns around to comply. Chance reaches into the breadbox and pulls out a silver six-shooter pistol and hands the non-loaded weapon to him. Snake reaches into his pocket and pulls out a few bullets. He picks out one bullet and places the rest back into his pocket. Samuel and Jesse starred at each other in confusion, though it was clear to them what the thuggish loose cannon had in mind. Snake then demands all four of them must pick two people to take part in a game of Russian Roulette in order to find out whose body will be the one that stays behind at a cost for the others to be able to leave freely.

Just as the gang leader was about to allow them time to decide whose lives were going to be put on stake in the grueling standoff, he had looked down and saw the Resistance patch stitched onto Jesse's jacket and the same patch on Stacy's sleeve. "Oh I see. You are all with that covert underground group. The bounty on your heads could be a pretty little penny, considering how wanted you all are. I could turn all three of you in, but I have to see some blood shed tonight. So who is it going to be? Whose life will be lost? I think any one of you Resistance members would be fine by me as payment!" Snake happily justified.

Samuel volunteered first to play the barbaric gun game. He was a genuine gentleman and also the eldest in the room amongst the four of them. Jesse didn't take too kindly to his adamant request and spoke up in hopes to change his friend's mind. "I can't let you do that. Someone will die from this and you have to lead everyone else. You have to continue to be the voice people hear and respect. This isn't you or who you are. Don't you see that? Don't you see that this is pure violence and that isn't what you are about!" stated Jesse. He was passionate within his words and his caring heart for Samuel was visibly worn on his sleeve, but one could look at Samuel and see that he had much to vent before placing himself into the game that was meant to end in bloodshed.

"Violent? You are one to tell me this is violent. This is just a friendly game. I feel you should look up the definition of violence for I am sure we both will have different meanings," Samuel announced with a small hint of plausible sarcasm. Stacy was next to step up and state that she would be the second participant, but Jesse wouldn't allow that either. He knew that she had just dealt with her husband walking out on her in rage and was now alone. It was almost as if she was looking for a reason to die. They both argued back in forth on who would face off against Samuel until the decision was made for them. Snake had intervened to inform them that Chance was selected to play the game. "I feel like she has given me enough trouble and she will be the wild card. Matter of fact I am adding that if she dies then one of you will take her place and we will have a round two. This game will be filled with endless twists and turns. Blood will be spilled and lessons will be learned by all you motha fuckas! That is the price you pay when you fuck with Snake!" he added.

The other thugs point their guns at the four sitting at the table as a precaution during the game. They huddle in towards the center of the table, surrounding everyone, with their fingers on the triggers. Jesse didn't feel Samuel was making the right choice. He could look into his eyes and see that he was taking on the role as the leader to stand up for his people with his life being at stake. Jesse asked him why he was doing this just before a single tear rolled down his face.

"I made a mistake and took my friend Marcus' life a while back and I need to live up to that decision. I need redemption and this is that moment. I don't have a choice but to face off against this young girl as so much is on the line. If she dies, one of you is next. You have to step up and be the leader if that is the case. Then you can sit across from me as we both put our lives on the live. It will become a domino effect, but remember that we all are doing this so everyone else can live in peace and harmony," Samuel calmly states. Jesse tries to talk Samuel out of it one final time but he was content with trying to set things right in his life to make up for the mistakes he had previously made. Snake placed the bullet in the six-shooter's chamber and spins it to conceal the random location of it. He then closes the chamber and places the six-shooter in the center of the table. Samuel speaks up to confirm to Snake that he has decided to play the game between the three of the Resistance members. Snake orders the thugs to remove the other two from their seated positions at the table so that only Samuel and Chance were face to face for the gruesome game.

The thugs have Jesse and Stacy stand back at a distance as they keep their weapons firmly pointed to the back of their heads. "Who is going to go first?" Snake asked with a smirk on his face. Samuel didn't hesitate, before announcing that he would initially go first. He picks up the gun and places it to the side of his head. Snake stops him and commands him to place the barrel of the gun into his mouth for a clearer sadistic enlightenment hoped to be brought on for his own personal enjoyment. Samuel slowly places the barrel of the gun in his mouth and pulls the trigger. A click is heard as it startles Samuel and Chance, though it was not a deathly blow that ended up being a fatal shot. Samuel places the gun back on the table and slides in towards Chance. She picks up the gun and places it in her mouth and pulls the trigger. Another click is heard, but she was relieved to still be alive.

The intensity continued to grow as she places the gun on the table and slides it back to Samuel, whom picks up the weapon and looks back to Jesse and Stacy. "If this is my time, remember my legacy," Samuel states as he pulls the trigger. The gun clicks but doesn't fire. Relieved by the clicking sound, he places the gun back onto the table and slides it back towards Chance. She picks up the gun and looks towards Snake and his thugs. "If I never get the opportunity to say it...FUCK YOU SNAKE!" she screams as she pulls the trigger on this fourth attempt between the two. The six-shooter clicks once more, as Chance's hands begin to shake from nervous relief surrounding her as she is reluctant to still see another few seconds.

She places the gun on the table and slides it back to Samuel as she reminds him that there are only two chances left. Samuel recognizes that if he survives this turn that Chance will have to place the gun in her mouth and pull the trigger knowing that it will be the death of her and the carnage will continue where another life will be lost. Samuel picks up the gun and places it into his mouth. He pauses and takes the gun out of his mouth for a moment. The thugs point the guns closer to the back of the heads of Jesse and Stacy to remind him that their lives would be taken if he didn't comply by playing this distasteful game.

"I gave the resistance hope and faith, and now I give them a Chance!" Samuel states as he quickly places the gun in his mouth and pulls the trigger. The gun fires the bullet through Samuel's head and out the back towards a picture hanging on the wall of the kitchen. His blood splatters over everyone and onto the kitchen table, while also continuously gushing out from the lethal hole in the back of his head. Some of the blood squirted out onto Chance's face as she looks at Samuel's lifeless body laid out in front of her.

Everyone was in disbelief as mixed emotions began to run rampart from the steaming adrenaline. Stacy was one of the first to react as she attacked one of the thugs, tackling him into the nearby wall. When the other thug saw this, he went to help and was attacked by Jesse. Bodies were flying everywhere as the brawl steadily unfolded. Chance saw this he opportunity to go after Snake. She ran up to try and sneak attack him from behind while his attention was more directed towards his fellow gang affiliates that were being mauled. Snake saw her coming and pushed her away from him as she fell into the chaos and was trampled by the various assaults ensuing.

The one fighting with Stacy, grabbed her by her hair and flung her into the wall and then into a counter before slinging her back into the same wall. Several appliances and dishes fell down on top of her after the harsh impact she had just sustained. The thug wasn't finished with her, tossing her body into another wall and then over the table to where she landed beside Samuels' deceased body. A couple of pit bulls, which were chained up in the next room, began barking out of control with foam and slobber coming from their mouths. Jesse continued to put up a fight against the thug he was wrestling around with as he was kicked away and rushed back to tussle with him over his gun.

Snake walked over to Chance, who was blacking in and out as she tried to regain her focus, but not before she was sucker punched, falling backwards into the kitchen counter that was in the next room. "For Samuel!" Stacy screamed out. Chance rose from the ground and ran at Snake, pushing him into the stove. "For Samuel!" she responded almost in unison. Stacy continued to hold her own, until she was blindly kicked in her stomach and smacked across the side of her skull with a metal toaster that the thug had picked up off the ground. "Long live the Resistance!" Jesse called out, just as Snake fired a warning shot into the ceiling, causing everyone to hold their position as he pointed his weapon wildly at the passionate resistance members.

"Today is your lucky day, though I should fucking kill you all," Snake says to Chance as she stands up away from the countertop. Snake told them all that they could go free, but he warned them to never come back to that neighborhood or he would kill them himself instead of giving them the opportunity for one person to play the hero. He picked the six-shooter off the floor that had fallen out of Samuel's hand after he had executed himself and hands it to Chance. "Keep this gun as a reminder of the chance it has given you in return!" Snake says with a heartless demeanor. He reaches back into his pocket and pulls out one bullet as he hands it to her. Snake demands that they leave now.

"Get the fuck outta here!" he yelled. They all start rushing out the front door with the thugs following behind them, surprised to have been let go. The thugs had their weapons still pointed towards them as they screamed and shouted at them to exit the drug house. Jesse looks back, while exiting the room, over at Samuel's body that laid hung slump against the kitchen table as several tears flowed from his eye ducts. The small group of now friends was lucky enough to escape with their lives intact. They all exited the home as Snake closes the door behind them, grinning from ear to ear with a smug look on his face.

Jesse saw that Chance was shivering when walking down the street. It was cold enough out where they were able to all see their breath when breathing. He takes off his jacket and places it around the shoulders of the half-dressed teenager that had left with only the clothes she had on her back. The three of them make it back to the Resistance hideout. As they walk in, Justin takes notice to them entering all covered in blood. He and a few other Resistance members run up to them and begin asking them all kinds of questions. "What happened? Where have you been? Where did all of that blood come from and whose is it? Are you okay?" they all spouted off, hoping to gain some sort of clarity. When they soon noticed that Samuel was not with them, they already begin to assume what happened, but had to hear it directly from them. Jesse begins to tell them the story of how brave Samuel was for playing the barbaric game of Russian Roulette with the newly recovered Resistance member, Chance, that the drug affiliate and heartless gang member known as Snake had forced them to take part in. He states in detail to them that Samuel didn't want them to forget his legacy and how he had sternly relayed that message before his untimely and unfortunate demise that he was doing what he felt was right so they all could live to see tomorrow. That was the important message he wanted conveyed by his actions.

"Who would be the new leader of the resistance?" Justin yells out in confusion. He felt lost as Samuel had always been the voice of reason. He was the leader of this Resistance that everyone looked up to and preached to them that there would be a better day. One by one they begin to scream out and chant Jesse's name as the agreed upon leader to take his place. In a short moment, everyone was chanting his name throughout the subway tunnels in unison. Chance walked over to Jesse and places her hand on his shoulder and tells him to help make a difference. The same kind of difference, if not stronger, than the one that Samuel had made. Initially the idea of this Resistance was Samuels' idea that Jesse had run with and helped grow, so to everyone there, he was the best fitting person for the position.

A tear rolls off her cheek and onto the sleeve of the jacket given to her by Jesse as she gives him a hug and thanks him for coming back to rescue her. "My life was in danger. I would have died there. My voice would have become deaf upon future ears. They pumped me full of all kinds of drugs, used by body however they pleased. I had good and bad days there, but all I can remember are the darker moments had. I may be new to this resistance, but I see the caring heart you have to make a difference. Something about you is clear to me that you are special and different. Be that voice! The voice I and all of these people need to hear! Chance phrased while advocating for Jesse taking on the new roll. He comes to grips with the reality that he needs to take a stand announces that he would step up as the new leader of the Resistance with his first order of business being to ensure that Samuel's memory isn't forgotten. He recommends that the people in the resistance make a memorial in Samuel's name.

"He had a voice and a message. That was different I believe to each of us as he affected our lives differently through what he said as well as his actions. I want to create something that we all can see that change in when we stop to look at it. I want a mural that is done in his honor. You all came from different places and we built this house into a home. You were hurting above and now feel safe below. Samuel gave all of us that. Let us give him something back as our appreciation to his idea and dream that we can be better than the hate we see delivered by people willing to hurt another human being. Let us be part of the change and not part of the problem!" denounced Jesse just before people started on the requested mural.

Several younger kids raised their hands, offering to spray paint Samuel's name on the biggest wall that was clear of debris and other sorts of things that they had inside the subway station. The grabbed a few cans of spray paint from a maintenance storage space and got straight to work. They spray painted Samuel's name as big as they could in the center of the wall in various colors. Others grabbed spray paint and began tagging the names of resistance members that had died over the tenure of time that this resistance had be formed. They wanted names of people that died trying to help create a better future for them and those that would come after them. It was a memorial meant to symbolize that Samuel was the centerpiece, but also to keep a memory of all the others that had risked their lives trying to help someone else out in this cruel chaotic world.

Many resistance members came and laid flowers and candles in front of the wall in memory of Samuel and the other fallen resistance members. The next day everyone held a memorial service to honor Samuel. Jesse approached the stage to make an opening statement and allow others to come up and pay their last respects. As Jesse approached the stage, everyone gave him their attention as they turned towards the stage to hear what he had to say. He looked around to the hundreds of people as they awaited his speech.

"Things are changing, even though it may not seem like it. We all are messengers to those that want to have hope and faith. We are all guardian angels to those whom have given up. We do not live in a world of hate and crime because of corrupt people, murderers, selfish people, scared people, angry people or any of the above. We live in the crime infested place where everyone is filled with hate because of one thing and one thing only...POLITICS. Let me explain! Politics doesn't always have to follow government and presidential affairs. There is politics in everything we say in do. The color of our skin, the God we choose to pray to, the sexual identity we prefer, where we work, how we dress, how we talk, who we associate ourselves with. The list goes on and on and there is politics in it all! Samuel's death was a result of politics, but we cannot let what he has done become meaningless. You may have chosen me as your new leader, but we can all be leaders. We can all create a brighter future for this world and help lead the people that are lost to a vision that doesn't include the politics of President Harvey and the world he forcefully created," Jesse stated with a bold demeanor. He looked around and asked anyone if they wanted to come up and speak on behalf of Samuel or anything on their mind. Justin raised his hand and yelled out that he had something to say. The young boy walked up to the stage as he stood in frontof the podium unable to see over it. He looked around, with his eyes peering barely over the top of it, as he took a deep breath before addressing the people of the resistance.

"You never realize how much you miss someone until they are gone. You treat them with disrespect, lie to them, talk about them behind their back and then ask for forgiveness when they are gone or want them back. At some point, you need to realize that asking for forgiveness and treating them better as a person was the best option while they were living. Samuel made a mistake that he regretted. He knew he couldn't go back and change what he had done, but he believed in beginning a resistance that could help direct people away from the dark path he felt subjected to himself. The one thing I learned from him is that you don't have to be a Samaritan to be a savior," Justin spoke freely with a face wet from a pool of tears.

The resistance members all turned to the wall, which was to the left of the stage that had Samuel's name spray painted on it and bowed their heads for a moment of silence and reflection. The service ended shortly after a few others had come up to speak and many people began chatting amongst themselves. The night passed, bringing in a new day. Many people stayed up all night putting final touches on Samuel's memorial. Chance walked over to Jesse and tapped him on the shoulder. He turned around and greeted the young teenager. He complimented her by telling her that he almost didn't recognize her because she looked like one of the adults. "How old are you Chance?" he asked. "Seventeen, almost eighteen!" she responded with a smirk. Jesse complimented her more by telling her that she looked older from how mature she acted and carried herself. Chance interrupts him while he continues to try compliment the seventeen-year old girl after realizing the growth and maturity he had taken notice to.

"I don't mean to be rude, but I was thinking about things that were said tonight and I think that we shouldn't live in this unwelcoming fear," she added in a soft tone. Jesse looked at her with confusion and asked her what she meant by her remark. She continued to tell Jesse that she thought they should go back to Snake's house and kill him. "I know it isn't what Samuel would want, but you are a man that agrees that this is a fight worth fighting for!" Chance continued. Jesse quickly pulls her aside to avoid from other Resistance members hearing their conversation so not to scare anyone or create panic. He reminds her of what happened to Samuel and that the fact that he, himself, doesn't think it's a good idea considering how young she is and the many risks involved.

Jesse continues on proclaiming to her how she should just let it go and be happy that she is alive and safe from that deranged maniac. This isn't what Chance wanted to hear, nor what she expected coming from Jesse. She insisted that they go and take care of the problem, so no other poor soul would become a victim of Snakes' like she was. "You don't understand what he did to me and I am confused as to how he was able to just let us go. Snake was a despicable person. He used me for sexual pleasure. I was a toy to him for his felching fantasies. He was sick and twisted and I wasn't the only one. There were other older women that were considered loyal veterans to his every command that he has control over and even then without me in his corner, he will find other younger ones to take my place that will grow to be used and abused as I was. I thought we are about saving people here and giving a safe solitude that can appreciate. Snake is a monster that won't stop till we stand up and stop him ourselves!" voiced Chance in hopes to be the voice of logical reason to the newly appointed Resistance leader. Jesse persisted within telling her that it wasn't a good idea. She became upset with the fact that Jesse didn't seek revenge against the maniac that took his friend's life and want to help make the situation better for those that were in danger by Snake still walking the earth by creating harm to everyone he came in contact with.

"If you're not going to do anything about it, then I will," Chance prominently demanded in frustration. Jesse looked at her with a small pause. "You need to just stay out of it. Mind your own business and be thankful that you are free from Snake. We took on a huge risk going in there to pull you out and the result was that we all didn't walk away unharmed. A life was lost in the process and you are talking about going back and placing you and anyone else that goes with you in harms' way. You remind me of myself when I was younger. So willing to do what is right regardless of what others say," he noted with refutable sarcasm. Chance pulled at her hair. She felt as if her voice wasn't being heard, though it was. The response just wasn't one she wanted to hear. Jesse was doing what he felt was right by what would have been the same approach by Samuel. Filled with anger by the decision not to help, the now mouthy teenager ranted off how she really felt.

"Then why don't you stand up and do what is right. It is what we all need right now. You said we were all leaders. I guess only most of us are then..." Chance added as she turned and walked away, exiting the resistance hideout. She made it to the top of the hideout and made her way through the dangerous streets towards Snakes' house alone with no one by her side, leaving Jesse behind to ponder what message she left him with. He plopped down on the bed of his subway cart and watched a little television. Contemplating!

CHAPTER 16

I VOTED

Today would have marked another election day. A day that is no longer existent in the United States of America. President Dominic Harvey is our World Leader and that is that. We used out last time voting to put him in office and now we will never see change. He has always said that even in death the world will be what he molded it to be.

I look at today and say that today has been treated just like every other election day before his reign as president. I say this people of our ignorance towards voting. I get it though. Many feel like their vote doesn't matter. They feel that they had to subside with whoever is affiliated with the party they are affiliated with. They feel like other candidates should be best and let's vote third party.

It is this foolish mentality that inevitably got us to this point. I also know that there are many people that like this world the way it is. Let me be the one though that tells you that your vote did count as it was symbolized as your voice. You many think that it is small as it represents such a small change or not understand how it affects you, but when you allow your voice to be taken away or skewed, is just another way to take away your voice, and make no mistake about it that even when you may not have anything to say, that you should speak up for those that can't.

Let me explain how important your vote was and still is. Imagine it as simplistic as I can make it. Picture it like making lemonade. Your two ingredients are sugar and drops of juice from lemons into a cup on water. See the cup of water as being the foundation to our structure. Obviously the world is split into two sides. Call it Democrats and Republicans. I call it sugar and lemon juice. Do your part, because if you don't vote and put it your speck of sugar or your drop of lemon juice, then the structure and formula won't be right. It will never taste like lemonade. And to those third party votes made. I won't knock you, as your vote is yours, do with it what you want, but know that when you add other ingredients that aren't listed, then that's how we got to this awful tasting drink we call Dominic Harvey.

Your vote still matters even without an election day. It matters because it is still your voice. It wasn't taken away. One person can't take on millions in a fight, let alone thousands. I know that they combat your voice with excessive rounds of deadly ammunition and lives are lost at the cost of one speaking up, but don't be fooled. One's voice is more powerful than you think. If you feel your voice isn't heard, then find a way to speak louder. Voting is one option, it isn't the only option. Today is a day to remember. I voted....DID YOU?

CHAPTER 17

THE OPTION OF ADOPTION

Chance continued steadily on her path to complete her mission by taking down Snake. It was mid-day and getting closer to dark. Chance arrived at the drug house and hid behind a bush nearby to scope out the area. She noticed the lights were on in the living room. The front door then abruptly opens and one of the thugs comes out to the porch to light up a cigarette. Chance takes the six-shooter out of her jacket that Snake gave to her and loaded the single bullet that she had into the chamber. As she crept towards the porch, she noticed that the thug was carrying a weapon on him as well. She jumped out of the bushes with the six-shooter pointed towards the thug. He was startled by her actions and quickly placed his hands in the air, dropping the cigarette straight onto the ground. The thug realizes it was Chance after a second gander that was directing the gun towards him, for her face was unforgettable to him after many times he had abused or sexually assaulted her. He acknowledges that she had huge balls for coming back and that Snake is going to kill her when he finds out she had returned.

"Shut the fuck up and take your gun out slowly and place it on the porch," she snarled, while still waving the gun in his direction. The man reaches into his pants and pulls out a slightly concealed handgun and slowly places it on steps. He kicks it off onto the cement walkway towards Chance as she reaches down and picks it up. She places the six-shooter back into her jacket as she pointed the thugs' handgun towards him. Chances fires off the weapon and kills the man instantly as she runs up the stairs of the porch and busts through the front door of the house.

A second thug looks over and notices someone barging through as he reaches for his weapon. Chance directs the gun towards him and fires off several shots into his chest as he falls backwards over the living room couch through a glass table. She runs towards him and peers over the couch as she sees the thug on the ground bleeding profusely, although he seems to still be alive and conscious. Chance raises the gun towards his head and fires a final deathly shot into his skull. She drops the handgun next to the dead drug dealer as she hears Snake running down the stairs. "What the fuck is going on down here?" he yells out. She takes out the six-shooter and points it towards the bottom of the stairs as he comes around the corner with a pistol of his own. He notices that both of his men are murdered in cold blood and standing in his living room is the young teenager that he held captive in his house for several months, holding one of his favorite six-shooters.

Before he could speak, she orders him to drop his weapon and walk into the living room closer to where she was able to better see him. Snake chuckles at the courageous teenager. "What ammo do you have for that gun? You have just the bullet that I gave you? I hope not, as you will need more than that to stop me!" Snake states with a slight hint of sarcasm before chuckling in front of her to agitate her more. Chance raises the gun towards Snake's head and cocks the gun following Snake's smarmy comment.

"I actually came back to this shit hole to give you a message," she comments to Snake as he snickers some more at her response. "What's that?" he asks. "Tell the devil that I sent you!" she exclaims as she fires the single bullet at Snake. It collides with his skull sending him crashing backwards to the ground. Several military soldiers walk through the door with their weapons drawn at Chance, as they order her to drop her gun. She places the six-shooter on the ground as two soldiers quickly go over to her and place her into handcuffs. They escort her out of the front door and down the driveway. A black limousine cruises down the street as it begins to slow down and comes to a complete stop in front of the drug house.

Chance glances up to the limousine and notices a Presidential seal on the side door. The back tinted window rolls down as Dominic peeks his head out and asks the soldier restraining her about what she was being arrested for. The soldier tells Dominic that she was caught in possession of a firearm and had murdered three drug dealers without a receipt as proof to paying the crime tax. Dominic orders the soldier to un-cuff the teenager as he opened his car door and invites her to get in.

The soldier was slightly baffled but did what he was ordered to do. He took off the handcuffs as Chance nervously walked towards the vehicle. She got into the limousine and saw Jarvis and Sky sitting in the vehicle with Dominic. Jarvis reached over and closes the door behind her as they pull off down the road. Dominic takes out a bottle of very expensive vodka with two glasses. He pours himself a large shot and offers Chance a drink as well. "I am seventeen!"

she states. Dominic looks over to her as he stares into her eyes, while he pours a second shot in the other glass for her. "I am the law. I don't care about your age!" he gestures back to her and hands her over the shot of liquor.

Chance accepts the glass from Dominic and downs the shot she was given as if she had being drinking moonshine at many a bars her entire life. A different side of her is seen when she request the bottle and pours herself several more shots, knocking them back one after the other. Dominic sat there impressed by the teenagers' wild side that she had presented. He takes out a few more glasses for Jarvis and Sky and fills everyone's' shot glass to the brim as he begins to question Chance about her prior actions made at Snake's house.

"Apparently you don't know who I am and what happens to people that are caught in possession of a firearm that is not a confirmed military official. Should I allow you to continue on breathing in the air you breathe or should your last breath be within the confines of this luxury presidential stretched limo?" Dominic rhetorically asks as he does another shot of vodka. Chance was speechless. How she would respond, could be something that works in her favor or end up being the reason for her cause of death. Dominic continues on with his various questions, adding to his list, by asking Chance where she got the fire arm and why she went to the house to kill those men in the first place. She finally speaks up and explains to him that she had been held captive by the men and forced to be their slave for several months, possibly even over a years' worth of time.

"You don't understand what I been through with them. They were rule breakers and criminals before it was even allowed by you. I fought back and I won. I won't apologize for my actions, but I am woman enough to accept the consequences. If this becomes the moment where I draw my last breath, I do so with zero regrets after knowing I was responsible for that maniac drawing his last breath!" noted Chance. She had little fear in her tone and even less fear in her proposed stance towards the President. Nothing was left off the table within explaining what she had been through to present a clear understanding behind her actions. She proceeds to tell Dominic of how they sold drugs and firearms to whoever paid them and the ring leader of the operation is the one responsible for giving her the gun

"Guns are still out there and threatening to kill anyone that possesses them though that isn't going to stop them from harboring them. In some sense, I did you a goddamn favor. You're welcome! Though I do have a question for you, now that I think about it! Here I sit in the presence of the most powerful person on the planet. Many refer to you as a monster. I want to know how you got here. What happened to you?" Chance inquired. Dominic poured another shot, but yet an even larger one and took a few sips. Jarvis and Sky both looked over in curiosity to how he would reply. Sky was more shaken by the question as he had hoped to learn more about someone he grew up knowing as his father yet knew so little about.

"You want to know about me and why they call me a monster. You would have to ask them. I am the peacemaker, contrary to belief. People view me as some common career-like criminal, but I once had a soul. Why I don't talk like a common thug with all the slag accompanied like 'motha fucka this' and 'pussy ass bitch that!' But you have to know that that side of me is still there but this world wouldn't have elected me if I showed them my true colors. This world took from me and when everyone else turned their head the other way to go on with their own life, no one looked back at my pain and misery. Now they hurt and have no one to look back to. This pain came from their doing and yet I am blamed. We hurt together now and I don't have any remorse about it. Now I sit here contemplating why I am explaining this to some cunty kid that I owe nothing to," denounced Dominic. Just as he was about to continue, Sky boldly interrupts with what on his mind. An act like this would be frowned upon followed by fatal repercussions, but his stance on what was being said was prevalent.

"Dad, this fucking kid doesn't get it and she was skating around your question. I mean, why did you go there to kill him in the first place? Was that really answered? So he treated you unfair and you wanted revenge. Is that it?" Sky asked. Chance turns towards him to explain her side in more detail. She let them all know how she had escaped and went back to the house to finish the job so he didn't hurt anyone else like he did her. She told him that she did what she did so she would be less fearful of what the men would do if they crossed paths with her again. Dominic comments on how much he likes Chance because of her edgy persona, also ignoring how Sky had interrupted him. It was almost as if their relationship was growing and Dominic was beginning to favor the young boy that he kidnapped and started seeing him as more like an heir. Sky was viewed now more so as the teenager he truly was and no longer a kid, moving gradually into adulthood. This respect allowed him to voice his opinion with no brutal backlash, but Dominic still had things on his mind to express to this mouthy teenager.

"I hear what you are saying, although if you want to continue disobeying the rules that I have set forth at least do it legitimately and pay the crime tax I am asking for," he added. Chance tries to explain how she doesn't commit crimes and how that was a once in a lifetime kind of situation. Dominic slams down his glass in anger at her remark. "Before I was President, things were different, but could be compared to the same kind of way the world is run now. Would you tell a police officer that you usually stop at a light you just ran, and then explain that it was a once in a lifetime ordeal? I let you live, even though you were in possession of a firearm, as a civilian. Let me show you what I do to people that don't follow the law. It's time I collect the payment for your crimes by having a lesson taught to you," Dominic voiced as he presses the nearby intercom button and directs the driver to stop over at the orphanage on Lancashire near Fifth Avenue.

The limousine drives a few more miles further down the road before pulling up to a tattered building in a rough poverty stricken neighborhood. Dominic tells Chance to get out of the car. She opens the door and steps out of the limousine as Dominic, Sky and Jarvis get out behind her. They all begin walking up to the front door of the orphanage with the President leading the way. Dominic knocks on the front door, as it appears that no one is immediately answering. He pounds on the front door harder and takes out his pistol, ready for confrontation.

An elderly woman opens the door as she appears crutched over using a walking cane to keep balance. "How can I help you?" she mutters to Dominic. She recognizes that the man standing in front of her is the President of the United States, as she kindly greets him and asks him as to what brings him to that part of the neighborhood. Dominic asks the elderly woman her name. "Carol," she states followed by an ill cough. Dominic questions her on if she pays the nation's crime tax. The woman tells him that she doesn't pay the crime tax because she and the children housed there at the foster home have no need to commit crimes. She then opens the door a little further and points to a large group of children playing in the living room near a fireplace. Dominic fires a shot into the elderly woman's leg, wounding her. He fires two more shots into her chest as she falls to the ground and he steps over her body into the living room while she lay on the ground coughing up blood and exhaling her last few breaths.

Smoke flows from the barrel of the gun, as the children scattered into a corner shaking in fear for their lives with their caretaker lifeless now before them. Dominic glances over to the group of children and slowly approaches them. "There is a new law that all orphanages must pay a crime tax in order to foster kids. Anyone caught disobeying this law could be subject to death by military discretion!" he proclaims as he holsters his weapon. Jarvis takes out a notebook and begin writing the verbally stated law down. He tells Dominic that he will schedule a press conference meeting to inform the media and nation of the newly en-forced law to be publicly announced at a televised event. Dominic gets close enough to the children to where he could reach out his arm and place his hand on the shoul-der of one them while kneeling down in front of her. "What is your name?" he questions. "Sarah," she responds to the deranged man that she only recognized from TV. Dominic tells her that she is now going to be the new orphanage owner and that he is going to give her three weeks to come up with this current months' and last months' crime tax payment. "Not a day more than that!" he adds.

Another kid yells out to Dominic that the girl is only six-years old. The President stands up and takes his gun back out of his holster. The kid puts his head down and steps back in fear, now regretting his courageous act to voice his thoughts. Dominic looks around as one could hear a needle drop. The child realized that his presence was scary enough and knew he would not have any more interruptions while holding the conversation with Sarah. Dominic kneeled back down in front of her, but this time placing his arm around her. "If you don't have the money in three weeks exactly, I will come back and set you and all of your fucking little friends on fire. I will take great enjoyment out of listening to your non-pubescent screams, while the flames burn through your vial and disgusting flesh," he verbally created the heinous visual for the frightened six-year old. Tears begin to roll down young Sarah's face as she begins sobbing and hyperventilating. She was steadily crying but wipes her face while trying to compose herself. "Are we clear?" Dominic calmly asks for confirmation from her.

Sarah has no choice but to agree to his conditions as she wipes several more tears away with each arm. Dominic stands up and walks back towards Chance as she looked on towards the horrific encounter between Dominic and Sarah. He stops in front of her and gives Chance a distasteful look. "I hope I made my point Chance. I cannot take you home to wherever you stay and there is about ten-minutes left before the curfew begins. So get the fuck out of here and try not to break anymore laws, bitch!" he sternly informs Chance. Jarvis places his notebook back into his pocket and opens the door as Sky and Dominic follow out behind him. They get into the limousine and it takes off down the road.

Chance turns to the children and quickly tells them to grab all of their belongings, because she is going to take them somewhere safe that is far away from Dominic's rampage.

"Where will we go? How will you keep us safe? This is Dominic's world and he will kill us if we don't do what he says," one orphan questions. Chance tells him that she is a part of the resistance and she will give them all shelter away from everything. The children's faces light up with joy as they begin to grab as much as they could carry. Most kids grabbed suitcases and filled them with clothes and toys. Some kids grabbed groceries bags and filled them with food and medicine. All of the children finished packing their things up as they stopped dead in their tracks. They glanced over to a nearby clock and noticed it was nearing the curfew. Sarah asks Chance how she intends to sneak twenty children through the dangerous streets and past hundreds of military officials without anyone knowing.

"You are right! It's maybe not the best idea right now. We can wait!" Chance acknowledged. She mentions to Sarah and the other orphans that they should get some rest and they would make the journey tomorrow during the day. The children were skeptical on if that was a better plan, but it was a safer plan than the one they were going to go with. Many people that pay the crime tax usually commit the most crimes during the day, considering that they too still have to abide by the enforced curfew time. Chance figured that that would be the best idea to avoid further problems with Dominic or the military, while also leading so many kids around town. She told all of the children to get in bed and get some sleep. Chance, took on the motherly role by tucking them all in, one by one, and reading a children's book to them. Her voice was so soft and calming to them that they felt so safe and most had fell fast asleep before she even finished the story.

The next day in the afternoon, Chance and all of the children grabbed their belongings and headed out towards the resistance hideout. They took several back alleys routes to avoid being spotted on the streets by other criminals or military officials. When they reached the hideout and were walking down the tunnel, Chance noticed that Jesse was just finishing a phenomenal speech to all of the Resistance members. He turned around and saw Chance walking towards him with many kids he didn't know. He immediately ran over to her and began questioning where she had been and where all the kids had come from. As she began to tell him the story about everything that had happened to her, Jesse's phone abruptly rang and he told her to pause her thoughts. He answered it to find that John was on the other line. The conversation was very brief as he hung up the phone and told Chance to hold on to her story for a minute longer for he had news to share with the person he put second in command.

Jesse called Stacy over and told her that John was stopping by the resistance to just see the place. "Maybe he is coming around," noted Jesse. He was so overjoyed that it appeared his good friend had possibly come to his senses finally. Stacy was very adamant within wanting to meet John for so long, considering she had heard so much about him. Jesse asked a nearby resistance member to go up to the alley and direct his good friend in when he arrived. Jesse then apologized to Chance for interrupting her story, but told that he would hear all about it later.

Jesse turned to the orphans and graciously told them to unpack and make themselves at home. The children's faces lit up with happiness and no sense of distilled fear as they hurried in and began to make friends with some of the other younger resistance members. Stacy looked on and smiled at the happiness emanating from the young orphans. Jesse turned around and saw John walking down the tunnel eventually with a few resistance members that had been sent up to retrieve him. He signaled his friend to come over and meet some of his other closer friends within the resistance. As soon as John got closer, Jesse shakes his hand and asks how he is doing. John acknowledges that he is doing better, as he notices Stacy and Chance standing by him.

"This is a close friend of mine, who is the first resistance member that Samuel and I had helped and also my second in command," Jesse mentions as John greets her. "Nice to meet you!" he states. The two shook hands as they exchanged pleasantries. Stacy adds that she has heard a lot about him and that it was good to finally meet him.

Jesse turns to Chance, "And this young lady is another member, whom we helped just recently. She has been an inspiration to me and many other Resistance members. She even brought us new recruits prior to you getting here. I see so much of myself in her. I know you two will get along," he remarks. John shakes her hand, as well, as he turns around and looks at the hundreds of people talking and having a good time. It was a completely different world down below than the one that John has been used to since Dominic's reign as President. People appeared to be happy and care-free. They all stood around smiling, singing and conversing with no apparent fear or pain in their eyes.

John looked over and sees the spray painted wall with Samuel's name on it and other resistance member's names tagged around it. He asks Jesse what was the sentimental purpose behind the artistic wall he took notice to. Jesse's head hung low with obvious sadness written all over his face. He sadly explained how recently when they went to rescue Chance that Samuel had risked his life for hers. Stacy intervened, while Jesse tried to compose himself. She added that everyone in the resistance felt the need to honor Samuel and his heroic act in some way by creating something they could remember him by.

Just as Jesse began to continue his story of what happened that night with Samuel, Justin runs over to greet John. He inquired if John was someone from above that was also rescued by the resistance. "No, this is my friend, John. He has been my friend for a very long time," Jesse responded back. John shakes the teenage boys hand and greets him with a smile. Justin cordially greets him back and runs off to play with the other kids. Stacy blatantly questions John on if he had given thought to joining the Resistance. John sneers at her gesture and boldly responds. "I am NOT here to join the resistance. I told my friend I would come here to check out the place and that is all I am here to do. God doesn't beckon me to be here to fight or take lives. He wants me to shed love even when those above committing crimes will not," he retorted.

Jesse immediately sees that their brief interaction could quite possibly lead to an argument, so he decided to jump in and offer to show John around as a means to defuse the situation. The two walked throughout the subway station as Jesse introduced John to several other resistance members and showed him how things were operated down below. He then pulled John aside and told him that he had something to share with him. Jesse reached into his pocket and pulled out a small jewelry box. "You're not proposing to me, are you?" John joked. Jesse laughed at John's comment. "No, I bought this bracelet for Marie as an anniversary gift. She helped me get through everything, which is why I had 'once a guiding light' inscribed on it," Jesse stated as he handed the jewelry box over to John. He took the silver bracelet out of box and glanced at it. "You bought your wife a collar?" John joked some more. The two laughed at Jesse's witty comment.

"No, I wanted to give it to her, because she was so furious that we couldn't have children at the time. We had tried many times and just never had any luck. I wanted to be her guiding light that reminded her that there was someone holding her hand through all of that We struggled having kids, just as did Stacy. Be patient with her as well. She has been through a lot," he continued to explain to John. Jesse asks his friend to hold onto the bracelet and to keep it safe. "Maybe it will bring you closure as I see you as my guiding light as well," affirmed Jesse. John couldn't understand why he would want him to take it, considering the sentimental value it held and to also ask for him to keep it safe from up above in the crime infested world, when he had this utopia down below that appeared a lot safer. He asked him why he would do such a thing. "I trust you the most and know that you will keep it safe," Jesse expressed. John agreed to do so as he apologized for having to leave early because he wanted to stop by the cemetery where his family had been laid to rest years ago.

Jesse looked into his friend's eyes as he saw nothing but a hurt soul. He wanted to help his friend, but didn't know how to. John placed the jewelry box in his pocket as Jesse walked him towards the exit of the hideout, being directed out by himself and a couple of fellow resistance members. The two parted ways as John climbed the ladder to the surface and closed the sewer cap behind him. Jesse walked back towards his subway cart as Justin ran up to him and asked him why John didn't stay.

He explained to the young boy of how John had unfortunately lost his family twenty years ago and how that pain had diminished the urge to fight for a good cause. Justin asked how John had lost his family. "A few thugs broke into his house over in Merlgrove Park and murdered his family before they had set them and the house on fire," Jesse explained.

Justin's eyes lit up as he pulled on Jesse's sleeve forcing him into the subway cart. "What's wrong?" Jesse inquired. Justin immediately asked Jesse if John's neighbor was gunned down and run over in the street. Jesse and Justin's eyes bolted open in unison. He asked the young boy how he would know information like that about an event that took place so long ago. "I used to work for this guy, breaking into people's houses before I was in the resistance. He used to tell me stories of jobs he used to pull over in Merlgrove Park a long time ago. He always made comments about this one specific job he pulled in that area where they had killed a family and set the house on fire. Though he never went into specifics, he would say that it was the day he got kicked out of the group by some guy name Dee," Justin clamored. Jesse asked if Justin remembered the guy's full name and address. "Yeah, his name was Drake Matthews and he stays on Vine Street over on the east part of town!" he replied to Jesse.

Justin then reaches over to grab a nearby piece of paper and a pen to write down the address and hands to Jesse. "You're not going to kill him, are you?" Justin questioned. "No! I am just going to ask him a few more questions," he replies in short. Jesse picks up his jacket that was hanging over a nearby chair and looks down at his watch. He realizes that there was about four hours left till the curfew. Jesse hastily exited the subway cart and walked towards the exit of the Resistance hideout before being stopped by Chance. "Where are you going?" she asked. "I got some information on a lead suspect within John's family's murderers that I am going to check up on," he acknowledges. Chance hinted that she didn't think it was a good idea for him to go and look into the matter further because John doesn't seem like he is completely over the loss of his family.

"John is my best friend, and I want him to have a peace of mind about the situation," Jesse voiced. Chance appeared bothered at the fact that Jesse wouldn't allow John to find his own peace. "You wanted me to mind my own business, as it had pertained to Snake and here you are all up in John's business. Let him figure things out on his own. Let him find God and happiness," she expressed. Jesse smirked at her comment and tried to explain that it was different than her situation, considering she had set out for revenge. He tried to convey the difference to Chance, but didn't have time to talk about the matter and noted that they would talk about it later. Jesse exited the subway station and made his way towards the eastern part of town. Chance could do nothing to stop him. She knew that he was going to be just as stubborn as she was.

Chance stepped into one of the subway carts and when she entered, she grabbed the television remote to turn on the TV and laid back on one of the tattered couches as she watched the live newscast play. She turned up the volume and tossed the remote to the side. The news reporter happened to be reviewing the earlier situation that took place at the orphanage that Chance was at the prior day, so this quickly caught her attention.

CHAPTER 18

NO CHANCE IN HELL

"The President made a brief comment at a press confer-ence today regarding a newly enforced law by military offi-cials. There was a situation apparently yesterday when a civilian was caught carrying a firearm. The laws set forth by the President state that anyone caught carrying a firearm, which isn't military authorized, could be punished by death. The civilian wasn't scolded in any way for possession of the firearm. This sparked an idea with the President to make an example that there would be zero tolerance for civilians not following any of the enforced laws.

The press conference was very brief explaining that all orphanages must pay the crime tax in order to house or-phaned children. Anyone caught not abiding by these laws may be subject to any punishable measure, including death. The name of the civilian responsible for the President feeling that this new law should be placed in effect has yet to be released. Many complain about the new law, considering that the punishment could involve another human deciding whether or not a person lives or dies based on if they follow the enforced laws or not.

I don't think it's any different than when jails and court-rooms where around before Dominic's election. The court system allowed the public to decide someone else's fate based on evidence obtained. These people were your everyday citizens, known as jurors. Evidence obtained could make the person look guilty and people served the death penalty because of what the evidence looked like. I don't find this any different from what the current President is doing. Humans are born unknowledgeable of the difference from right and wrong, though they would grow up to become the future that would judge and decide another human's fate. Imperfect in every way, people make mistakes! At the cost of their life, President Harvey has distilled a fear amongst people instead of the freedom he had once promised. I pray for God to be there the day when those that blindly follow Dominic come face to face with their creator and God judgest hem..."

CHAPTER 19

A DYING FLAME

Several cars raced through the streets on the eastern part of town. Jesse approached an apartment complex in an urban neighborhood. Many of the windows were broken out or boarded up. He looked down at the paper Justin had written on to see what apartment number Drake lived in. As Jesse walked towards the building, he spotted a few kids nearby tagging gang symbols on the building. The kids were between the ages of ten and seventeen. Jesse passed them and entered the building as an indescribable stench passed through the air. He walked down the hallway towards the stairwell as a completely naked woman stumbled out of nearby apartment room with track marks visible on her arm. A man runs out and grabs her by the wrist, forcefully pulling her back into the room. Jesse pulls his hoodie over his head and walks by the two people into the entrance of the stairwell, so to come off as one that was minding his own business. He goes up two stories and walks down towards the end of the hallway to the last door on the left. He stood in front of the exact apartment number that was written on the piece of paper and knocks a few times. Jesse hears someone approaching the door as they unlock several locks. The door opens as a stocky man with a full grown beard on crutches greets him.

"What do you want?" he snarls at Jesse. "Are you Drake Matthews?" Jesse asks. Drake takes a close look at Jesse to see if he recognizes him from anywhere. "Yeah, who are you?" Drake responds. Jesse confirms that he means no harm and explains to Drake that he had gotten his information from Justin, whom used to work for him. He continues to tell Drake that he had just a few questions about a job that he had pulled about twenty years ago. Jesse reaches into his pocket and pulls out a couple of photos he had on him of John's family from many years ago. He handed the photos to Drake and asks him if he had ever seen that family before. Drake's eyes got big like a deer in headlights when soon recognizing some most of the people in the photo. He quickly asked for confirmation on if Jesse was there to kill him for what he and Dee did a long time ago.

"No, Like I told you I just want to know what happened," Jesse remarked. "Well that's a shame! I was hoping someone would want to get revenge on Dee for doing what he did to that poor family. I didn't know anything about going in there or about killing anyone," Drake retorted in a distinct voice. Jesse broke down the relationship he had to John by stating that he was a friend of the family and he just wanted to gain some information to set his mind at ease about what had really happened. "All I want to know is who killed my friend's family, and I will leave it up to my friend to decide if revenge is the best decision," Jesse confirmed.

Drake handed Jesse back the photos. He was shaken up after his brain felt like it was on overload from visually reliving that night his crew turned on him as it had created a rush of memories. "I don't think that revenge is even an option, even though it was what I wanted for years! You'll never get close enough to the man responsible for your friend's family being murdered. Dee is one crazy motherfucker and

I wouldn't even use the word 'crazy' in front of him! It's a trigger word," Drake mentioned. Jesse asks him who Dee is and where he could find him. He wanted the pain to end for his friend and help him gain that needed closure. Drake looks at Jesse and snickers. "He isn't hard to find; you could begin your search at the White House on Pennsylvania Ave or even his new building he operates out of! His name is Dominic Harvey!" Drake responded.

"The President of the United States!" Jesse jeered. Shocked by what Drake had just told him, he inquisitively asked him to recap the events of that night that John's family was murdered. "Tell me in detail!" he stated. Drake begins by breaking down how him, Dominic and Jarvis were on a mission initially to gain entry into houses within local neighborhoods and steal items of value they could pawn or sell on the streets for some quick cash. They all soon afterwards decided that those neighborhoods didn't have anything of great value that was worth stealing, so they branched out to nicer neighborhoods, which is how they came across the neighborhood John and his family had lived in.

"When we came got to that house, it seemed like the perfect one that had a lot of valuable stuff! Man, was I wrong. It was nice on the outside and bare of valuables on the inside. We had seen a pizza delivery man getting out of his car, and it seemed like the perfect way we could use to get inside without sounding any alarms or raising any eyebrows about our crimes we were out committing," Drake explained. He continued to tell Jesse about how they murdered John's family and set the house on fire, but that it wasn't his idea. He gave descriptive details on how that night played out, although for some reason he didn't include the part about how Dominic took Sky. Drake felt awkward to tell that part as he felt like enough had been said in his opinion to someone he knew nothing about. He thought that things could get worse if John knew his son was alive, so much so, to a point where he might exact revenge on him, himself. It seemed like important information, but at that time not the kind of information that he thought was important enough to share at the cost of his own risk. Drake also didn't want to be seen as someone that was connected with Dominic taking Johns' child in any fashion.

Drake could already see a hint of anger in Jesse's eyes from the things that he was telling him, so why make it any worse he thought. He felt it was in the best interest to withhold that information and so he did. He began to babble on about how Dominic had kicked him out of the group for not stealing items of great value and had tried to frame him. Jesse quickly cut him off and thanked him for his time as he turned around to leave. He stopped and turned back towards Drake to ask one last question that popped into his mind. "Why didn't you come forth earlier and tell someone about this?" Jesse questioned. He knew that once he told John how that would be the first question he would ask.

Drake took a minute to ponder his answer. So much time had passed and it was now water under the bridge in his eyes as well as a moment in his life that he had tried to steadily forget. "I did a lot of time in jail for the shit that Dominic framed me for when they caught me weeks later! But I wouldn't turn in someone that became the President of the United States. How patriotic would I look, especially being an accomplice to his actions? Dominic already had an insane night before all that happened. He was in a different mindset and his rage was flaring. Apparently, I didn't make the situation any better. He would kill me if he knew I tried to snitch on him. You don't know what kind of man Dominic is," Drake proclaimed.

Jesse thanked his again for his time and the information before walking away. He left the apartment complex and headed back to the resistance hideout, arriving before the curfew began. On his long walk back, he had reached into his pocket several times and took out his cell phone. Jesse tried to resist calling his good friend to tell him about what he had just learned about his family's murderers. He finally took out his phone once more when down in the alley of the Resistance entrance and began dialing John's number once more. The phone rang a few times before John finally picked it up and greeted his friend, as he was deep within reading the bible he had been given by Jesse. It was becoming his happy place, where he was starting to find himself and come closer to God. There was a small pause on the phone as Jesse tried to gather his thoughts on what to say to John and how to phrase it all.

"I hope I am not disturbing you," he stated. When John noted that it wasn't a big deal and that he always had time to talk to him, Jesse had a sigh of relief. He then started off by telling John that he couldn't go into detail over the phone, but that they needed to meet in person. John could tell that there was something bothering Jesse and asked him what was wrong. "Nothing!" he answered in short to keep the conversation brief.

Jesse had to think fast. He knew that telling John face to face was the best thing to do. "It's just that we really need to meet. Can you get together tomorrow at the diner near my old house around three o'clock in the afternoon?" Jesse continued. There was crack in his voice while talking to John. He sounded scared and his close friend could tell there was something seriously wrong as he knew him best. John confirmed that he would be there. "Whatever you need buddy!" he affirmed. Jesse was relieved to hear how he responded to meeting on short notice. He knew that his tone had created a kind of urgency, but with a small pause after John's reply made it seem like he had other intentions. "It better not be related to joining the resistance!" continued John. Jesse chuckled at John's comment, though assured him that it had nothing to do with him trying to convince him on joining. He hung up the phone as he approached the Resistance's sewer cap entrance. As he came down the tunnel, he noticed Chance with a suitcase by her side as she was talking with several other Resistance members. He walks up to her to ask her what is going on. She tells him that some things came up with her immediate family that she just found out about and it was imperative that she go take care. Jesse was bewildered by what Chance was telling him, considering that it was the first time he had heard about Chance having any relatives. He offered for her to have her family come and stay with the resistance in hopes that that would salvage her issue there. Jesse reminded her of how intricate she was to the resistance. Chance told Jesse that she didn't think it was a good idea for her to bring her family around here. "You just don't understand!" she added. Chance assured him that she would return when things were completely handled, but that she had to go for now. Jesse could see that she didn't want to go into detail and that when she was ready to tell him more information that she would. She gave him a big hug and told him that she loved him and all of the Resistance members that have helped her along the way.

"Be safe!" Jesse remarked as he watched her head down the poorly lit tunnel with her luggage. Stacy came out of her subway cart and walked up to Jesse and asked him where he had been. Jesse explains that he went to follow up on a lead that had some information about the person responsible for killing John's family. Stacy's was shocked to hear what he said, but also felt like Jesse might be stirring the pot, considering how much hurt had been inflicted on John from the loss of his family. She told him that he should just leave it alone, though he insisted that it was the right thing to do. Jesse had always been someone that wanted to help other and he was also someone that had always been there for John. He felt like she just didn't understand their history or their friendship. Jesse told Stacy that everyone deserves the right to know about something like that, because it makes things just that much tougher not knowing. They argued about it back and forth, although Jesse didn't seem like he was going to budge on the matter. She knew it was his friend as well as his decision and if it makes things worse, then Jesse would learn from the mistake of telling John the kind of news.

The next day at the Dine-In diner, Jesse sat at a booth waiting for John to arrive. He looked around and noticed that Margaret wasn't at the diner and must have had the day off. Another server walked up and greeted him. She asked what she could get for him, though Jesse acknowledged that he was just meeting a friend and wasn't staying long. He told her that he would get two cold glasses of water filled with ice and if they decided to order that he would let her know. Just as the waitress walked away, John walked through the front entrance of the diner. Jesse signaled to him for him to come over. John passed by a few occupied tables and as soon as he reached Jesse's table, he greeted him with a friendly handshake. "This better be good!" John says as he sits down at the booth. When John had a seat, Jesse asks him not to get mad at what he did, because he only did it to help. John gave him a disgruntled look. He knew that whatever it was, it was important and was definitely going to be problematic either way.

"That is a terrible way to start off the conversation. What is this about?" John asked. "I got a lead on the guy responsible for murdering your family!" Jesse responded adamantly. John sighed as he demanded that Jesse let it go. He seemed angered and bothered that Jesse seemed to be consistently prying into things more than he had wanted him to. John had his own way of dealing with everything and to cope with the loss of his family and he was just starting to find peace after coming closer to God from reading the Bible. He stated that he didn't want to live in the past.

"Why do you go to the cemetery every day? You mourn and hurt from the loss of your family. That isn't the sign of a man that is not trying to live in the past. A broken past isn't the path to a happier future," Jesse raved. John was bothered by Jesse's statement. He knew that his friend was right about him still being broken by the loss of his family, but still didn't feel he needed help being healed. "Goddammit Jesse! Just for once stop trying to play savior. Stop trying to be the guy that helps everyone or helps me. Put less focus on others and focus on yourself. You care too much about everyone else! When will you take time to fix what is broken in your life?" John yelled back.

"I am just trying to help and I think you are going to want to hear what I have to say!" Jesse exclaims. The waitress came back and asks the two if they would like to order, but could tell she had come back at the wrong time placing herself in the center of a heated conversation. They both told her that they were fine for now with a bit of distaste towards her as a means to shoo her away. As she nods with a friendly smile and walks away, John turns back to Jesse. "Alright, go ahead and say what you want to say, because this is all about you. You want to help people. You want to be known as the guy who brought change to everyone. You forget that it isn't your place all the time to do so," John raved. Jesse looks at him in confusion as he asked what makes him thinks that. John continues on stating that he has gotten over what happened and that he only goes to the cemetery because it's the one place that he feels comfortable at. He could free his mind by talking to them and knowing that they were up above, looking down on him

"I just wanted you to know who is responsible, because you deserve that. The person that murdered your family isn't some random criminal. Well, maybe he was then, but he definitely isn't now," Jesse yelled before ramping himself up to spill the beans. "Okay, then what is his name? Who is the guy?" John retorted. Jesse turned his head looking over his shoulder and he leaned in towards John. "His name is Dominic Harvey. The President of the United States! He was a common criminal, breaking into houses a long time ago. I spoke with one of his former friends who admitted to being there the night that he saw your family murdered," Jesse confirmed.

John gave Jesse a look of disbelief. "So what do you want me to do? You want me to go after the President. I don't fight crime anymore. I found God and am saved. Look around you. This is not a world where criminals are brought to justice for the crimes they commit," John banters as a retaliation to the news. He stands up infuriated by what Jesse has told him about the person whom killed his family. "Bc there for me to help me get through the traumatic event. Don't go out and find ways to help me relive it," John screams out in rage. He turned around and stormed out of the diner bumping into a man standing at a nearby pay phone with a hoodie on and dark black sunglasses. Jesse tried to get him to come back and discuss the problem versus fighting over what he thought was great news. He threw down a tip and stormed out after John who got on his motorcycle and took off down the street. The man at the pay phone turned around looking out the window watching Jesse on the side of the street.

"I've been following Jesse, the leader of the Resistance. He is currently at some crappy diner on the western side of town near Nickels Street. I can follow him until you get close-by, Mr. President!" the man suggested to the person on the other line. As he hung up the phone, he walked out of the diner and began following Jesse down the street. He followed him for several blocks as Jesse got closer to the Resistance hideout. When Jesse got to the alley where the hideout's entrance is, the man watched Jesse enter around the corner of what was a dead end. He started to follow him as he took out a cell phone and made another phone call to the President. His voice calmly whispered to the person on the other line telling them that Jesse did in fact return to the Resistance's hideout and where its formally undisclosed location was.

Jesse came down the tunnel and saw Stacy talking with some children. He ran up to her in frustration and interrupted her as he began raving about what happened between John and him. She grabbed both of his shoulders and tried to calm him down recommending that they go somewhere else to talk. Stacy suggested that they go up to the alley and get some fresh air to help him breathe better. She ran to get a jacket and told Jesse that she would meet him back at his subway cart and they would head up above to chat. Stacy walked away as Jesse entered his subway cart. He walked over to a desk and turned on a small lamp. He sat down at the desk and noticed some photographs lying on top in the upper right corner of the wooden furniture. He began to look through them. They were photographs of him and John. It brought back many memories, causing Jesse to smile as he sadly reminisced. He pinned a few of the pictures onto the nearby pushpin board hanging on the wall. Jesse then opened a drawer from the desk and pulled out a book that had maps of Washington D.C. in it. He tore out a specific page and placed the book back inside the drawer. Jesse wrote a few words on it and circled something as he was interrupted by a knock on his subway cart. "I am ready Jesse. I thought we were going to chat. Are you ready?" Stacy voiced. Jesse dropped the marker and grabbed his coat after nodded his head. He turned off the lamp and exited the subway cart.

They both headed to the top alley to talk. When they got there, they stood near the dumpster by the sewer cap and Stacy asked Jesse to explain what happened. Jesse told her about how he met with John to inform him about what information he obtained about his family's murder. Stacy shook her head as she tried not to tell Jesse that she told him this would happen. She knew that John hadn't gotten over what happened even if it was twenty years ago. Stacy saw it as a woman's' intuition. Jesse continued with his story about how John got upset and stormed off enraged by the news. Stacy gave him a hug trying to console him as she explained to Jesse to give it some time and that John would get over it and they would come back to talking. Jesse nodded in agreement as he turned his head and noticed a figure walking down the alley. As the figure came into the light, Jesse realized that it was President Harvey accompanied by Jarvis, Sky and several military soldiers. Jarvis stood on the right side of Dominic as Sky was standing to the left. Both of them stood there boldly with a handgun drawn to their sides.

"Well, if it isn't the infamous Resistance leader Jesse Dean. I have heard a lot about you. You and your band of

Resistance members had created much hardship for me and are constantly in the news," Dominic snarled. Jesse placed his arm in front of Stacy as he safely pushed her behind him as he asked Dominic what he wanted. "You think standing against me with this resistance would accomplish something. It was only a matter of time before I found you and your fucking bandwagon of friends. You try to stand against me and all I see is you standing there alone," Dominic stated as Stacy walked forward to be beside the fearless Resistance leader.

"Fuck you Dominic!" Jesse retorted. Dominic took out a gun that he had holstered under his jacket and pistol-whipped Jesse, sending him crashing to the ground. He was bleeding from his mouth as he looked up to Dominic grinning above him. "You're a coward! You're a fucking coward! You have strived on trying to become powerful to hide from a world you were incapable of living in. And now you create this awful hell that you built to make others incapable of living in too," Jesse contested.

Dominic demanded that Jesse shut his mouth because he was tired of hearing what the relentless Resistance leader had to say as his response was given back spitefully. "I am a GODDAMN legend to this world! I have built a society where anyone can have whatever they want. I have created a tax that is affordable by all people and have given them a choice to pay it and live here with complete and utter freedom. No one has to worry about jail, or being homeless, or struggling. You run around the streets of what I created supposedly saving souls that need it and giving them a place to live. You think that you are creating your own utopia for them within my hell. You call yourself a leader to them and one that will lead them to salvation. There isn't enough room on this planet for two rulers. You are an insignificant piece of shit! You're an ant waiting to be squashed in my ant farm!" Dominic dominantly expressed to Jesse.

Jarvis and Sky looked at Jesse on the ground as he bled from his mouth and they nodded in agreement to Dominic in reference to his comment, whom gestured back the same response for them to soon take action. Jesse stood up and took a few steps forward into Dominic's personal space. The soldiers began to raise the assault rifles, though Dominic signaled them to stand down while standing there without any sign of fear on his own part. As Jesse deeply stared into Dominic eyes, he spit right into his face. It was an act of complete disrespect. Dominic pistol whipped Jesse again, sending him straight back down to his knees. "Don't worry Stacy, I will save you!" Jesse proclaimed. Dominic gave him an awkward look as he turned back to the soldiers and chuckled.

"Save her motherfucker! Save yourself!" Dominic raved as he shot Jesse in the chest in cold blood. The sound of the gunshot echoed throughout the alley. Stacy began to scream hysterically as she dropped to her knees and held Jesse in her arms. "Noooo! Why! Why did you do that, Dominic? Jesse, hold on! Stay with me! JESSE!" she cried out. Jesse looked up and smiled as he whispered something into her ear. "There's still hope!" he mentioned as they became his last words. Stacy's face was red and covered with endless tears as she held Jesse in her arms after he lost conscience and his eyes slowly closed. She could no longer feel his pulse. Stacy stood up and rushed towards Dominic as Jarvis stepped in and grabbed her by her throat and threw her up against the wall. Several military soldiers approached the sewer cap and climbed down the ladder.

Many gunshots and screaming were heard below as the soldiers eradicated most of the resistance members that occupied the hideout. Some soldiers came back to the surface with several resistance members as they placed them in handcuffs. Dominic walked over to Stacy and jammed his pistol into the right side of her neck as he stared into her eyes. "I'm not going to fucking kill you! I see you as a messenger. Now run back and tell that motherfucker, John, that I am looking for him next," Dominic deemed with his daunting message.

Stacy stared into the presidents' eyes in confusion and asked how he knew about John. Dominic remained brief in his explanation. He told her that he had someone follow John and Jesse and that that person had been gaining information about the two of them and the Resistance for quite some time now. He admitted that he does remember that family and how much that family meant to him as he glanced back to Sky and paused for a moment "One mans' trash was another man's treasure. I know what John treasured most," he suspiciously added with the pun cryptically intended.

A black limousine had then pulled up to the only outlet of the alley as Dominic continued talking with Stacy. "That person I had following them got me information and I gave him a place in my Presidential cabinet," Dominic stated. The limousine door opened and Carter, Stacy's husband, exited the vehicle. Her eyes lit up as she was shocked to see him side by side with the deranged President Harvey. Carter approached her as he noticed Jesse's lifeless body on the ground and several soldiers continuing to bring up resistance members from down below. Carter glared Stacy in her eyes with a demented stare as Jarvis kept her choked up against the wall and he began to speak. "I loved you, but I have been blessed with a new path in life. I don't expect you to understand that. I lost my family and now you all know what it is like to lose yours. I have a new home in Dominic's cabinet and look at you! You're clock is ticking. Every second belongs to me," he attested to his wife. Stacy began to cry even more as Jarvis released his grasp and she dropped to her knees. Dominic signaled to everyone to finish up what they were doing and headout.

Jarvis, Sky, Carter and Dominic all got into the limousine. The darkly tinted back passenger window rolled down, as Dominic peeked his head out and yelled back to Stacy reminding her of what message he demanded she pass along to her newly found friend, John. The limousine immediately bolted off down the street. Soldiers passed Stacy with the last few resistance members that they had room for in their armored trucks that were used for transporting large groups of passengers. Only a few resistance members were left behind and not taken as prisoners or executed.

Some children and some adults came up from the sewer cap and noticed Jesse's body on the ground surrounded in a puddle of his own blood. Justin parted his way through the crowd with Sarah as he quickly placed his hands over her eyes. Justin tried not to look over as well at Jesse's body, but couldn't help it. He noticed Jesse on the ground after being murdered, as tears began to trickle down his face. He wiped the tears away and looked over to Stacy and asked her what they were going to do now. "We have lost everything!" he continued. Stacy looked around to the remaining people of the resistance as she suggested that they find some wood and build a coffin to place Jesse's body in. She told them that she had to go deliver a message

and that they would have a small funeral for Jesse the following day before finding a safe place to bury him.

All of the resistance members quickly returned to the
subway station and gathered whatever they could find to
build a casket for Jesse. Stacy stood up, covered in Jesse's
blood, and looked down at him on the ground. She turned
away unable to continue looking at him as the sight of
his lifeless body made her cringe. The man responsible for
saving her life long ago in the alley and same man that
was helping the resistance to grow after Samuel's death
was now gone. Stacy exited the alley as she made headway
towards where John was staying. As she approached the
motel, she noticed the lights on through the transparent
curtains. She walked up and knocked, hearing a television
playing in the background on the other side of the door.
"One second!" John yelled out. He opened the door to Stacy crying and also covered in blood. He quickly asked her
what was wrong and why blood was splattered all over her.
As more tears began to fall down her face, she explained to
John that Dominic had just killed Jesse and many other
resistance members. John stared at Stacy in disbelief as
he asked her to repeat herself. He couldn't take in what he
was being told to him and needed to hear it again for confirmation that he wasn't dreaming.

"Dominic killed him. He's gone, I said! Dominic told me
that he wants you next and that you know where to find
him," Stacy stated as she wiped several more tears away.
She told him that he needed to do something and fight
back. There was a sense of agitation in her voice, but knew
that John was the last resort "This isn't a fight for God to
take part in. We need you! We need more than ever right
now. What are you going to do," she asked. John began to
stammer over his words in complete confusion from just

after hearing the news of Jesse being murdered. "I don't fight anymore. It's...I just don't fight anymore. I found God. I am saved and don't want to hurt anyone!" he exclaimed while holding his bible. Stacy became even more upset with John's statement considering her state of mind after Jesse had just been killed right in front of her. "Forget it! I guess I came all this way just to tell you that the funeral is tomorrow if you wanted to come pay your respects since that doesn't involve fighting!" she criticized sarcastically before snatching the bible from him and tossing it onto the ground.

"God isn't fighting this war. He let it happen. Consider it a testament to you that he wants his child to step up and fight for what is right. I don't need you to search for God as it's obvious you found him. We need you to search for vengeance," attested Stacy. John's eyes began to tear up as he genuinely asked what happened. His mind heard what she said but his heart couldn't fathom the loss of Jesse. "I hear ya, but how did he die? I want to know more about my friend," pleaded John for answers. It was hard for her to talk about, but she knew he deserved the truth. Stacy explained everything up to when she found out that her husband, Carter, was responsible for everything that had transpired, including how he had been following John and Jesse for a while. She then asked John to do something to make things right, though he kept to his promise not to fight anymore, even after her jarring comments.

"Being someone that doesn't fight hasn't helped stop the killings! You need to do something about this! We aren't asking for you to be a new leader of the resistance. We are asking only for your help. It's what Jesse would have wanted," Stacy replied as she reached into her pocket and took out a photograph and handed it to him before walking away. John glanced down at the photo and realized it was a picture of him with Jesse from a fishing trip they had gone on twenty years ago. The news of Jesse's death didn't fully process to John instantly. It was definitely going to be a process. He closed the door after Stacy left and sat down on the edge of the bed, contemplating the news quietly to himself. His body stood stiff and his hands began to tremble some.

The television was on and a breaking newscast was being delivered by Adriana Hart in the background. John wasn't paying any mind to the television, though he heard the young reporter's voice explaining how President Harvey had just killed the notorious resistance leader, Jesse Dean. The newscast continued to play as an endless stream of tears cascaded down John's face. He reached over to turn off the television, when all of a sudden a photograph of Jesse popped up on the screen as the newscast continued. John set down the remote and glanced at the picture as he reminisced about the good times he had with his friend. He was heart-broken that the last time they had spoken wasn't on the best of terms. His mind was filled with regret, as he wished he would have had said something more meaningful than the hurtful comments he last remembered saying to him. John looked on as the newscast as it steadily played in the background.

CHAPTER 20
EXTINGUISHED

"Infamous resistance leader, Jesse Dean, has been murdered in cold blood by President Dominic Harvey. Jesse has been known for deliberately disregarding all laws put into place by the President, creating a separate world to escape what many refer to as Dominic's madness. Many military officials had been in search of the now deceased resistance leader for his belligerent act of preaching a sense of revolution to people that there could be a world outside of the very one that Dominic has created and for their non-payment of the enforced crime tax to break any laws they may have broken.

Jesse Dean was known for wondering around after curfew hours helping individuals who were in need of help or shelter from the chaotic world. This was one of the specific laws that one could endure severe punishment for. Jesse was also caught giving shelter and aide to hundreds of people within an underground subway station. President Dominic Harvey is said to release a full statement within an address to the nation in the next few days about the incident at hand. This address to the nation is said to be a breaking point within creating a more free world to its inhabitants.

New laws may be put in place to ensure that no others create a resistance, considering that the President finds it to be a direct act of treason against him. He also commented on how a lot of active and inactive military bases were being robbed and it's steadily looking into the matter. He briefly spoke with me about the issue in an exclusive interview, stating that a shit ton of weapons, aircraft and highly sensitive materials had been fucking stolen. His words quoted exactly! He believes it could have been the resistance strategically planning such events to do so as an act of war. No weapons have been found or recovered from the raid that transpired at the underground resistance hideout, though officials are still investigating.

Dominic did acknowledge within the brief statement that anyone claiming to be a part of the resistance would be killed. Many walls around town have been tagged with phrases like 'Love Live the Resistance' and 'There's still hope!' The President intends to have all of the walls that were tagged with graffiti be painted over as he acknowledges that it isn't a form of the adulation that he feels that he deserves.

Is this NOT the world that you created I ask him to ask himself, and now there is conflict by the creator about living in it? It would be like the devil creating HELL and complaining that it is too HOT! This isn't freedom! It's servitude! This isn't a Utopia! It's a Dystopia! This is heaven! THIS IS HELL!"

CHAPTER 21

TAKING A GODDAMN STAND

The next day in the afternoon, John made his way into the Dine-In diner. He was dressed in a black suit, fitting for his friends' funeral set to take place within a few hours. He sat at a nearby table and waited for someone to come over to greet him. Margaret looked over and spotted John sitting down at a table in her section, she politely told the couple that she would be back in a moment and headed over to sit down at the table that John was at, placing her hands upon his. "I heard about Jesse on the news. I'm so sorry!" she politely stated as her eyes began to water just at the mention of his name. She, too, had a strong connection with Jesse, so the news about his death had been one hard for even her to handle. John thanked her for her sympathy and told her that the funeral was in an hour if she would like to go. Margaret apologized for not being able to attend on such short notice considering she was working a double.

"I don't think I can see him or the shell that once was him anyway, lying inside a box. I rather remember him how I remember his. Alive and full of life! He meant the world to me. You just don't know how much I have been through and how he had been there. I felt lost after hearing the news as if I was now alone, but now here you are sitting in the same section at the same table he would. That brings some joy to me," she dully noted. Margaret did acknowledge that if she could get someone to cover for her that she would try and make it out. John gave her the location where the funeral was going to be held at.

"Do you know where the resistance hideout was?" he asked. Margaret shook her head, chuckling before explaining to John about the many times that Jesse had come in and adamantly asked her to join. They laughed together as he agreed that Jesse would ask him several times as well. "I never joined, though I should have been there for him for that resistance," Margaret stated with a face full of tears and he facial expressions strangled with apparent sad emotions. "I was going through a rough time when he asked. He knows I wanted to be there for him, but fighting and running those dangerous streets wasn't the best option for me. Sometimes one has to think about more than just themselves. I have no regrets though. He was always in good hands and had good people around him. He talked about you all the time and how much you meant to him. I was hard on him at times about everything he was going through, but I soon came to realize that he found his peace and I found mine, Margaret continued. John placed his arm around her to console her before telling her that she should let it out. He knew how close both she and Jesse were. They spent every waking moment together after him and Marie split up, when he wasn't out handling resistance affairs. Margaret thanked him for his kind words as John spoke up with what was on his mind. It was almost as if he had been holding in his thoughts, but felt comfortable around the young waitress he had befriended.

"I have dealt with the loss of family to a point where I don't think Jesse's death has truly hit me as it should.

Death changes you. Hell, it can change anyone and everyone. That fact alone lets me know that from how strong of an affect that death has on us is why we don't truly appreciate the importance of life," John remarked. Margaret could look at his face and see that he was hurting from the loss of his beloved friend and had to be the voice he needed. She thought about what Jesse would say to him. "We may run from our past, but we never walk alone," Margaret stated to remind John that someone will always be there for him. She kindly told him that she had to go check on another table, but acknowledged she would return with a cup of coffee on the house. Margaret got up and walked off to greet a table that had just come in to sit down in her section. John looked out the window and noticed all the chaos unfolding on the other side of the glass. Everywhere he looked, people were committed crimes and no one stopped them. Nearby businesses chased criminal vigilantes down the street with bats and chains in their hands. In a world that is supposed to have complete freedom, more people seemed afraid for their life than to feel somewhat safe. Though it is the world that we have conformed to, something just didn't seem right about it all. People lost their lives by following the rules of this brutal society that had been molded by President Dominic Harvey. All they had to do was pay a simple crime tax and even after that it seemed like more lost their lives for not following that rule. It was a domino effect that was breaking down the foundation of our own humanity. Who knows what we stand for anymore? Who knows what purpose we have? We are robots, programmed to cause unthinkable and violent acts on either ourselves or others.

John could just look out the window, realizing that nothing had changed for the better, but yet to have only gotten worse. Margaret came back with a cup of coffee and set it on the table in front of him. John told her that he was only having one cup and he had to get going before the funeral was set to begin. Margaret nodded and smiled as she reminded him that the coffee was on the house, but to make sure he stopped in to talk to her sometime soon as a means to help fill that empty void that held a special place in her heart when Jesse would stop by to chat with her. "Don't look back on what you could have done in the past, but yet what you can do in the future. You are allowing your pain to take up a residency in your head and I can see it hurting you. You have to learn how to destroy what you allow to destroy you!" she stated as she leaned over and kissed John on the cheek. She told him to take care of himself and walked off to attend to her other tables as business was starting to pick up.

A group of kids came close to the window that John was at and began spray painting gang symbols on it. Margaret and another server ran out of the restaurant and told them to scram. They came back into the restaurant and continued working as if this was the normal day routine for them to chase off the everyday criminals and riff raff. John looked down at his watch and noticed what time it was. He took a few more sips of coffee and set the mug down as he rushed out of the restaurant, but not before leaving a significant tip for Margaret. John headed down the street, passing posted wanted signs all around on every light post with his face on them.

Apparently, Dominic had issued a bounty on John for a large reward, whether brought in dead or alive. John figured it would be smart to get off the street away from soldiers and other civilians that may initially recognize him. He crossed into a nearby alley and began taking back roads towards the resistance hideout to avoid detection.

He climbed down the ladder and walked down the tunnel into the main lobby of the station. He looked around and saw a group of people gathered around the wall that was spray painted with Samuel's name and other martyrs of the resistance on it. Many of them laid flowers and candles down as they were currently spray painting Jesse's name on it, in big letters, underneath Samuel's.

A large box sat at the front of the room where Jesse and Samuel would preach to everyone about how there would soon be a brighter day. The box was built as a coffin containing Jesse's body, and was sealed closed to avoid people smelling or seeing the gruesome and grotesque disfigurement from the process of his body decomposing . Other resistance members walked up to its side and laid flowers on top of it. Stacy walked to the podium that stood behind the casket as she announced that she was about to begin the ceremony and for everyone in attendance to gather around.

Everyone stopped what they were doing and began crowding in towards the front of the stage to hear Stacy speak. "I want to thank everyone for attending and showing their respects. Jesse wouldn't want any of us to hold our head down through a time like this. He would want us to celebrate. He used to tell us that the war is not over until the last one of us takes our last breath. To some, Jesse was like a father, a brother. To some he was a friend or a mentor, but to all of us he was a legend. He will always be remembered for whose hearts he touched and the lives he saved along the way. He will be truly missed. I will allow a few people to come up and say a few words," Stacy stated as she stepped down from the podium.

Justin then quickly decided to be the first to speak. He walked up onto the stage to state a few words that were on his mind. The young teenager approached the podium as he looked around the room to the hundreds on eyes that were glued to him as they clamored to themselves quietly. When he began to speak, the room suddenly broke to silence as they listened to what he had to say. "I was one of the first few in the resistance as they grew to the family that stands before me today. I have watched different kinds of leaders preach about a new day. One preached about a day where we would be free in a world where crime would almost become the best way of living. A way to be equal and free from consequence! Other leaders, like Samuel and Jesse, preached about a new day where we all come together to help one another. In a day like this we become equal and less fearful of consequence. No matter which day comes and goes, not everyone will see it to be the best way of living. Jesse preached to us about hope and faith and how important it was for us to have both in order to remain strong. Never forget what the wise man told us, but most importantly never forget about the wise man himself. He is just as important as his words spoken," Justin stated as the room arose with applause. Justin stepped down from the podium as Stacy came up and asked if anyone else wanted to come up and state a few words.

Several other resistance members approached the stage and lined up to share stories and memories about Jesse and the impact that he had on them and their lives. Many brought tears to everyone; while others left them all laughing hysterically from the fond memories Jesse had left behind. When the last person came up to speak, Stacy was about to end the ceremony. She asked if anyone else would like to come forth and say something considering how the service was coming to a close. The room was quiet for a moment seeing as most people had spoken already, giving their verbal bereavements. John yelled out from the back of the room that he had a few words on his mind that we wanted to voice. He passed through the crowd that was near the staged area. Stacy recognized him as he got closer to the podium. She grinned in happiness that John decided to come and pay his respects to his close friend.

John stepped up to the podium and looked around to many faces he didn't know and recognize. He then looked over to the wooden casket containing Jesse's body that was surrounded by several beautiful assortments of flowers. John quickly composed himself as he looked back out to the crowd to speak. "Jesse asked me to be by his side several times, but I found it very hard to stand by his side after losing my family twenty years ago. Though, here I stand after having lost another family member that was important to me. I can't say how things would be different if I would have actually sucked it up and joined, but I know that I would have spent more time with him while he was living and that would have been the plus side. I appreciate life more because tomorrow isn't promised to any one of us. You don't appreciate something till it is gone or taken from you. That is the only regret I have. I have thought about it many times and it hurts me because there is nothing I can do about it now, but a wise person once told me not to look back on what I could have done in the past, but what I can do in the future. A time for mourning may seem appropriate for today, but tomorrow is a day when the resistance will prove that Jesse was right about a new day to come. Tomorrow I will take a stand and fight for what we all want and believe in...A New Dawn!" John boldly stated as the audience began to cheer for him. Many didn't know who he was, but familiarized John to have the same desire to take a stand that Jesse had. Stacy came up and thanked everyone for coming after John had delivered his speech and ended the ceremony with her final remarks. She reminded everyone that it was important for them to pack up what they wanted for it would be their last night at the resistance hideout.

Since Dominic knew about this location, it was vital to protect the remaining resistance members that didn't want to live in the chaotic world above. Stacy and the other resistance members were intending on moving to an abandoned house that was several blocks away from the subway station. John went over to where Stacy was after her closing words and gave her a hug. He thanked her for being so tough on him, because it allowed him to open his eyes to stop living in the past. She couldn't be happier to see John as she thanked him for coming by and saying a few words.

"What caused you to change your mind?" she asked. John responded, "I wouldn't have missed it for the world." Stacy smiled and asked John what he meant by how he is going to take a stand and that tomorrow will be a new dawn.

Just as John was about to respond to Stacy's question, he sees a familiar woman in the distant crowd coming towards the casket. He leans to the left as he notices the woman's face as she turns around. "That's Marie! Jesse's wife," John affirmed. Stacy turned and glanced behind her as John pointed to the woman she thought he was referencing to. He mentioned that he hadn't seen her in almost twenty years and asked Stacy to come over to meet her. The two began walking towards Marie as she turned her head slightly and noticed them approaching her. She smiled and ran up to John to give him a hug.

"John, it's good to see you. It's been a long time," she affirmed. John agreed with Marie that much time had passed since they had last talked. "I don't want to be rude, but this is Stacy. She was a very close friend to Jesse. Stacy greeted her by cordially shaking her hand. "What are you doing here, Marie? How did you hear about Jesse's death?" John questioned with an inquisitive grin. "My daughter invited me to the funeral," she responded. John looked at her with sheer confusion. "You got remarried and had a kid?" John asked. Marie shook her head as she explained that the only man she had ever slept with was Jesse. Marie looked over John's shoulder and noticed a girl walking towards them. "Here comes my daughter now!" she stated. John and Stacy turned around and saw Chance making her way towards them. Even though the two were shocked to see her, many more questions had arisen in their minds.

"Chance is your daughter!" he expressed as she walked up to them to say hello. "Yes, Chance is mine and Jesse's daughter," Marie stated in response. John denied that that could be true because Marie hadn't talked to Jesse in almost twenty years and Chance was only seventeen. Chance quickly intervened to explain to John the truth behind the situation. She added that she had initially lied about her age because she felt Jesse might figure out that she was his daughter. "I didn't know how to tell him. I didn't even know that he was my father until about a week after Samuel had died. My mother had shown me pictures back when I was younger and I knew that I recognized him from somewhere. One day I had gone out to see my mom after being rescued and asked her what my father's name was. I was able to piece it all together when she told me him name. I was going to tell him but never got the opportunity to," Chance retorted. John looked to Marie and asked her why she didn't try to find Jesse to inform him that he had a daughter.

"I had found out the last time I had seen him. It was the night he came home drunk and discharged his gun into the ceiling. He could have killed me or both of us that day which is why I left him. He was becoming reckless. I had awoken one night a few weeks before that night and taken a random pregnancy test. It came up positive and I was going to tell him the news, but had prolonged telling him. It was a surprise to me as well and I was waiting for the right moment. I didn't feel safe with a child around him; just by the way he was acting and everything before that, so I had left him as that night was my drawing point. I came back to Washington D.C. when the world started to go mad, but the house was abandoned and he was no-where to be found," Marie vocalized. John told Marie that Jesse still deserved to know that he had a child even if she didn't feel that he was stable enough to be around her or the kid at that given time.

Stacy expressed to Chance how she, herself, should have at least told Jesse that she was his kid at the given moment that she found out. Bit was then when both Marie and Chance knew that they did not do the right thing and now it was too late. Marie looked to John for his advice or thoughts, though there was nothing he could possibly say. This was the moment that she knew that he was the right person for helping initiate change and continue the very legacy for this country and around the world that Jesse had in mind. She wanted him to see his worth and what he brought to the table, so she told him of a comment she remembered that a man once told her of how you can't look back to say what you should have done in the past, but what you can do in the future. John grinned as he proudly shook his head, knowing that that man was him that she was referring to.

"I get how I need to do my part and you need to do yours as well. So what do you intend to do to make things right, Marie? It's obvious you can't go back in time. So what now?" he asked. Marie explained to the best of her ability that she came there to help finish what he had started. "I don't have the right answer for you about what I can do as I am sure you don't have that answer for what you should do. All we have is what we think will be best," she retorted. Marie didn't want it feel like the script was being flipped by John, but saw his point that if she was asking him to take initiate and change and to help fix things, that she should do the same on her side of it all. She continued on talking about how things had been going rough in her life, which is why Chance had left to come home to help her. She felt that the best place to be though is around her father, Jesse, and the people that he cared the most about. "That is the best change and reason I told her we should come here together. Being around now is too late and there is no excuse. I get that! Not telling him abou this child is too last and that is no excuse as well. That doesn't mean I don't love him. I searched for him and found him. I am here and being here when it is deemed too late isn't the best response, as it is something I will live with for the rest of my life. Though when I think about it, I rather live with being too late than to have not been here at all. I am proud I came and was here for his send off. That is my change or at least where I can start for now!" Marie ended her verbal thoughts as a means to her own closure.

Chance saw that everyone in attendance was getting things off their mind and she wanted to do the same. She apologized to John and Stacy "You all have spoken your peace. I need to speak mine," Chance insisted. Marie had tried explained how they both were there to try and make good of the situation, but now Chance wanted closure as well as to speak up in her own defense and say how she really felt. "I value what my mom has said and I have no excuses. I understand that I should have spoken up and said something the second I knew that Jesse was my father. And like she said, there is no going back now. It's another scar placed upon our body by our own choices made that we will forever be reminded by when we look down and see that defining mark left. I want to not only do something about it, but continue the work he started. I can't ask for my father's forgiveness and for the advice of what to do from here on out, but I can ask both of you for your thoughts on what direction we must go together. What is next for us?" voiced Chance to her comrades.

Stacy knew that they were both sincere. She thought to herself for a moment on how to respond and gathered the appropriate wording, as she was the next resistance member with enough high ranking power after Jesse had passed away to assume leadership rank and role. She told them both that they could start by helping the other resistance members get their things together before they completely move out of the subway station. Marie and Chance were happy that John and Stacy were able to forgive them and began to quickly walk away to assist everyone with packing up their things. John grabbed Marie's arm as he forgot to tell her one more important thing. "I almost forgot. Jesse gave me something that he had bought for you and wanted to give to you himself on your anniversary. I hid it in a very safe place. Come with me, I want to show it to you," John stated with a smile. Marie agreed to go with him as she hugged and kissed her daughter before dismissing herself from the group. John told Stacy that he would be back before it got too late. "It will only take a minute," he added. John and Marie left the subway station as they traveled through back alleys so John could avoid any problems after being accused of treason and having a bounty placed on him. They walked several blocks until they came to the cemetery that John's family was buried at.

"What are we doing here, John?" Marie calmly asked. "I told you that I hid Jesse's gift for you somewhere safe," he responded. They walked through the graveyard until they made it to the head stones of Julie, Jennifer and Sky. Marie noticed the names of John's family members above their respectful graves as she asked him why he brought her here once more in pure dubiety. John took out a hunting knife that was concealed and strapped around him under his suit jacket. He used it to dig up the grass and dirt that was in front of his wife's headstone. "I brought the very important thing that Jesse gave to me here because I figured that no one would ever look here, but me!" John stated as he continued to dig up the soil.

A military truck sat near the fence of the cemetery a several feet away. The window of their vehicle rolled down and Stacy's husband, Carter, peeked his head out and spotted John in the cemetery beside Marie from a distance. He told the soldiers traveling with him that the guy in the cemetery was the one that Dominic had placed the bounty on. The soldiers then grabbed assault rifles and exited the vehicle as they began to walk over to where John and Marie were located.

John continued to dig further down into the ground, unbeknownst to the soldiers approaching, until he hit a hard platform. He scraped away the dirt and pulled out a very small metal box, almost similar to a small safe. John opened it up and inside was an even smaller jewelry box.

He handed Marie the box as he stood up and dusted the dirt off of his suit. "This was for you from Jesse for your anniversary," he stated. Marie opened the jewelry box and pulled out the small silver bracelet. She read the inscription on it. "Once a guiding light!" she read out loud as she snickers and cried simultaneously. Marie told John that she used to always tell Jesse that he was like her guiding light when things were tough as he did the same to her. Another few tears ran down her face as she admired the bracelet before placing it onto her wrist. Two soldiers abruptly approached John and Marie and asked them for identification. As John turned towards the two soldiers, one of them noticed the hunting knife in John's hands. The solder quickly pointed his assault rifle towards John and demanded that he drop his weapon. John complied, dropping the knife on the ground and placing his hands up into the air.

"I know who you are," one of the soldiers stated while smiling. He divulged to them both that he was going to turn John into Dominic to collect to reward placed on his head. The soldier began to reach into his back pocket to grab a pair of handcuffs as he moved slowly towards John. Marie stepped in front of John and that the soldiers leave him alone, playing the role as the spokesperson meant to ease the tension amongst everyone. "Leave him alone! We have done nothing wrong, leave us be!" she begged. The other soldier grabbed Marie as she began to tussle with him crying out for them both to be freed. "It is way before curfew time, and we have fucking done nothing wrong here!" she protested. The soldier swung Marie aside as she fell to the ground onto her back, twisted her ankle. She slowly got up and hastily hobbled towards one soldier to push him down as she screamed out for John to run. John stood there with his hands steadily raised in the air as he told Marie to relax. He knew that resisting would only create more problems. Marie could look into his eyes and didn't see the change he had proposed to make. She saw that he still thought of himself to be a God faring individual with no fight visible inside of him.

One of the soldiers that remained infuriated by Marie's belligerence stood back up after trying to regain balance and pushed her to the ground again. He pointed his assault rifle at her and shot her multiple times in the chest. One bullet after the other plowed thrown her body and into the gravel. John stood there stunned by the happenings, responding instinctually. He moved in closer to the soldier and grabbed the front of the rifle lifting it towards the sky as he swept the legs of the soldier beneath him. The butt of the gun hit the ground with the barrel still pointing towards the sky. As the soldier fell forward, his throat landed on the tip of the barrel, piercing through his throat as a bullet prematurely fired off through his neck into the air.

The other soldier began turning towards John as he shoved him to the ground beside the now lifeless body of Marie and dived directly for his hunting knife. As he spun over onto his back and sat up, he threw the knife at the soldier. The knife spun through the air and into the soldier's chest, piercing through his rib cage into his beating heart. John rushed over to Marie to try and help her even though she had already died from the several bullet wounds inflicted. He placed both of his hands on her chest to try and stop the bleeding and even tried CPR though it was too late. Her body laid there cold and lifeless on the ground in front of Julie's headstone. "Why?" John screamed out as tears poured down from both eye ducts. He unlatched the bracelet from Marie's wrist and placed in in his pocket and immediately left the cemetery in case more soldiers passed by after hearing the gunfire. Carter was leering out from his vehicle seemingly unnoticed as John scurried away leaving out of the cemetery. He knew that John had to be stopped and wanted to be responsible to for collecting the bounty. He promptly got on his cell phone to call Dominic to inform him what had just transpired.

John ran to the motel that he was staying at, that was close-by, around the corner. He swiftly opened the door to the room and ran over and opened the air conditioning vent. As he reached towards the back of it, he pulled out two silver nine millimeter handguns. He stuffed them into the back of his pants and ran out of the room down the street to a nearby church. John walked in the house of God and made his way down the aisle to the second pew from the front. He took out both of his pistols and kneeled over the first pew to pray silently to himself.

A priest walked in, taking notice to John at the front of the church with two handguns in his possession. He yelled to John, confessing that he didn't have anything of value worth taking and should just leave. John turned towards the priest, yelling out back to him, "I just need a place to stay that is all. I mean no harm!" The priest recognized John's face after the short interaction, from seeing him on the news, as well as the postings around town about the bounty and reward money. He told John to how he realized the severity of such proposed punishment he could sustain for letting him stay there and wanted no part in what he was bringing to his house of peace and worship. It was obvious that there was a soft spot in the priests' heart for John just by the tone he used. It wasn't one used to scare off John or even one that would pose him as being a threat. He knew what the news had reported about him and of his rebellious ways towards the President and his regime. The priest introduced himself before making an offer to John that he could stay the night. The risks were high and consequences immeasurable.

"My name is Father Kirkland by the way. However, I know that I could be killed on the spot for letting you stay here or even associating with you. I may not have a family that would miss me if I was gone; however I am NOT yet ready to leave this earth. There is much work left to be done and people I must spread the good word to. I will allow it for the night, but you must leave tomorrow in the morning," the priest continually insisted. He explained that he would set up an extra cot and give him a warm meal to eat. The priest headed into the kitchen returned several minutes later to inform John that food would be ready soon. He saw John still hunched over and praying to the large cross at the front of the church with the bible he was given by Jesse sitting on the pew beside him. The priest walked over and sat down next to John and asked him what he did that had caused so much trouble between him and the President. "I can see that you are a man of God, but you come into his house with weapons and I only assume that you will depart with bad intentions in mind.

John briefly explained the whole story to the priest from the beginning about the involvement with Dominic and the murder of his family, all the way up to him coming to seek sanctuary in the church. The priest wasn't shocked to hear the news about the President considering how he had always assumed that something just wasn't right with him, but prayed he would find himself and be given forgiveness for his sins. He tried to console John by telling him that everything was going to be alright and that he would pray for him as well and all the ones whom had lost their lives fighting for a better tomorrow.

"Never give up! It will show your enemies that you stopped trying. Never stop fighting! It will show your enemies that you are weak. Never lose hope! It will prove that you lost faith!" the priest stated sincerely. John looked up to the priest as if he had just been struck with an epiphany. He asked the father if he had a computer and copy machine somewhere inside are the church. "Yes, in my office. It's just around the corner," he noted. The priest then took John to the back and down a hallway as he approached a large wooden door that was bolted shut. He unlocked the master lock on it and opened the door as the two walked in. John looked around the room and saw all of the antique furniture inside all covered in plastic. The place appeared as if it hadn't been used in years. The priest pointed out the copy machine and computer and asked if he needed any help using it. John shook his head as he walked over to the computer and blew off much of the dust. He booted up the computer and began drawing up a bulletin similar to the one around town of him.

After a few hours, he completed the flyer and printed up a copy of it. He took it over to the copy machine and had hundreds of copies printed up. The night grew on and the next day was soon to arrive. John had fallen asleep and was awoken by the sunlight gleaming through the stain-glass windows as he heard a knock at the door. When he answered, he was greeted by the holy messenger of God, Father Kirkland, which stood before him holding a bulletproof vest. "Get dressed and meet me in the nave of the church!" Father Kirkland requested. John threw on his button up shirt and jacket and headed out of his sleeping quarters.

When he came face to face with the priest at the designated meeting area, he asked what he was called there for and the purpose of the bulletproof vest. Father Kirkland placed the vest atop a table next to a small can of red paint. He took the brush that was set beside it and dipped it into the paint before drawing a large red circle on the vest.

"I thought about what you said and I want to make sure you are good to go on your mission. I know that you have been away from the Bureau for a while. Your shot must be horrible and after being saved, I know that you have been away from violence as well," noted the priest before dipping the brush into the paint and drawing another circle inside his first circle. John took what Father Kirkland was saying as knowledge in preparing for his encounter with President Dominic Harvey. He wanted the father to know that he was ready for whatever comes his way, within this soon to be hard fought battle. "I have been thinking too Father, and I know that I must do something. I would hate to call it revenge more so than doing what is right. This is a manno one can reason with. So option two becomes both mine and his final option," stated John.

Father Kirkland took the brush and dipped it in one last time and drew a bold bullseye dot in the center of both circles he had previously drawn. John peered over in confusion, while still holding the casual conversation. "I ask again Father for the purpose of that bulletproof vest with the target you have drawn on it," he inquired once more. Father Kirkland approached John and asked him to hand over one of his pistols. John grabbed one out from his left holster and handed it to the priest who proceeded to take out the clip and check his ammunition before placing the clip back into the weapon. He then cocked the gun a few times and handed it back to John, who was impressed by the knowledge that the priest had within handling the firearm. "How do you know so much about guns Father?" John asked to where he only gained a smile as a response.

The non-fearing priest headed back to the table to obtain the bulletproof vest. He put it on and re-approached John. "You need practice firing that weapon, so I am here to be your target," offered Father Kirkland. John stood there appalled by the suggestion for him to sacrifice his body by becoming target practice. He hoped there would be another way. "I am NOT going to shoot at you. That is insane! Let's just set up a couple glass bottles that I can shoot at like normal people to ensure no one gets hurt. Plus you are considered the Lord's messenger. What happened to you saying that there is still work left for you to do?" asked John.

Father Kirkland tightened up the strap on his bulletproof jacket. "There is work left for me to do and I am doing just that. I can't say that I condone you going out to murder the President, but I also know that I can't stop you from doing so, so the least I can do is make sure you're prepared for this fight. Setting up bottles won't prepare you. You need a moving target. You need a person that is equivalent to the height and weight of the man you are going after. You need the mentality necessary to reach down and focus that hatred when going up against such a powerful man that is backed by a military of soldiers willing to do his bidding," voiced the priest while turning around to walk away and a lot a significant distance between the two of them. With his back turned, he continued to address John in hopes to convince him to a point where he would be comfortable using the priest for target practice.

"God saved your soul and here you are before me with the devil's intentions. All I can do is pray for you. Stop seeing me as a priest and see me as the enemy you desire. Harness that and focus so that your aim is precise. Imagine that I am President Dominic Harvey and I just...," added Father Kirkland while turning around to face John. At the mention of Dominic's name and the eye contact made between the two, John didn't hesitate after firing two bullets off that struck the center bullseye of the bulletproof jack sending the Father flying backwards onto the ground. John walked up to the priest whom was caught off guard by the attack. He had patted himself down to ensure he was not hit anywhere else and bleeding. John, now standing above the priest, shot three more bullets at Father Kirkland hitting him directly in the same bold bullseye. He screamed out for John to stop before realizing that the mention of the President's name had become the trigger word to his rage. Deep down the priest knew that John was ready and prepared for the fight of his life.

John holstered his weapon and extended his arm to help the priest up off the ground. Father Kirkland looked down seeing that all five bullets had hit the bullseye. "Next time, we should maybe count to three first so we know that we are both on the same page. I can definitely look into your eyes and see a different person. You have changed. You are willing to kill another man and I understand that you think this is what will salvage the problems of today. Are you still a man of God?" inquired Father Kirkland.

The tension grew strong as John slowly made his way closer to the priest. "Am I still a man of God? Dominic Harvey killed an innocent pizza delivery boy. He killed my daughter, my son and my wife. He went on to kill my best friend and last known leader to the Resistance. My pain only exists because of him! You ask me if I am still a man of God. Oh....NOT TODAY FATHER! NOT TODAY!" he expressed in response. John thanked him for allowing him to stay the night before grabbing his stack on flyers he had constructed and printed up. The priest stopped him just as he was exiting. "One more thing I want to tell you before you go," he stated as he grabbed John by the arm before he walked out the door.

Through this short time span, a relationship as well as trust had been established between the two and Father Kirkland felt comfortable talking more with John after learning so much about him. To him, this may be the last time they would speak or cross paths, so he wanted to share something that grew steadily on his mind. He wanted to send him on his way with a message that would give him strength. "Let me tell you a story. A story that changed my life and I hope changes yours. This story is about the impact we make by the choices we make. This world needed Jesse and now it needs you. Once upon a time, there was a completely blind girl who hated the fact that she was blind. It bothered her every day of her life. At one point, she met a man that she fell in love with and he became the only individual she absolutely adored and was enamored with. He desperately wanted to spend the rest of his life with her and asked her to marry him. She said that she would do so if by some miracle that she was able to no longer be blind and gains the ability to see. Weeks passed and it appeared as if her call had been answered. Someone came through and donated their eyes to her, giving her the ability to have the sight she had always dreamed of. Her boyfriend was ecstatic about it as he approached her and asked if she would now marry him, considering that she was no longer blind. He was shocked by her response when she turned him down. She had say 'NO' to him after realizing that he was blind and she just couldn't bring herself to it. She couldn't marry someone that had the same disability she had. If only she had known he was also blind, she thought to herself. He boyfriend was let down by her response, but respected it. He walked away from the one person he loved and a few days later wrote a letter to her that only had one sentence written on it. It read 'Just take care of my eyes, dear!' The message is about what we do and sacrifice as people to help others in need. I may not believe in murder, but I think about the lives that will be saved by the death of this one man, being President Harvey," the priest continued.

John took on a full understanding by the message trying to be relayed to him. He thanked the humble father for his kindness and knowledge as he left the church with one thing on the mind and that was to take down the man that destroyed every inch of happiness he had stripped away from him. While parading down the street during the midday hours, he came across a large telephone pole which had a poster with John's face on it, requesting a reward for him if captured. John ripped the poster down, crumbled it up and tossed it aside into the streets. He reached down and took a bulletin out of the cardboard box and pinned it onto the pole as a replacement.

The bulletin read: Bounty for Dominic Harvey Dead or Alive. Cash reward will be issued. John walked around town tearing down all of the bulletins with his name on it, replacing each of them with his copy of a new posting that had placed a bounty on the President's head. The word got around and eventually, it became the talk of the town on every radio and news station. Dominic ordered all soldiers to take down any bulletins claiming a reward for him captured dead or alive. He looked out the window of his office building that was located on the fifth floor of an abandoned building within the inner city. It began to rain vigorously outside as one hour passed by another. Dominic was in a huge panic of concern when his assistant rushed in and apologized for rudely intruding.

"Soldiers have spotted a man a few miles away headed in this direction. They say it's John Lewis and that he is responsible for placing up the bulletins that had the bounty on you! I know that you don't want to be bothered with this matter, as you have other affairs to tend to overseas," he said nervously. Dominic demanded that the assistant tell the soldiers to stand down and allow John to make it to the building. The assistant then rushed out of the office to pass the message along to particular high ranking military officials as Jarvis and Sky entered through the door, passing him by.

"What is going on?" Sky asked immediately. Dominic briefly explained to Sky that there was a man seeking revenge and how he was currently headed towards the building at that very moment. Jarvis looked over to Dominic, aware of the identity to the man he was describing, and was positive that it was Sky's biological father in which he was referring to. President Harvey told Sky that they had to go and leave the premises just before he had directed his right hand man, Jarvis, to head out of the office towards a secure portion of the building until he could gather some sort of transport to a safe house. Dominic walked over and turned on the television as it ran a news report about John's actions by heroically standing up to the President and even initiating a hit out on his life. He walked over to his desk and pulled out a coveted berretta of his as the newscast continued to play in the background.

CHAPTER 22
BREAKING THE RULES

"Rumors are spreading around that a local member of the resistance named, John Lewis, has placed a bounty on the President's head. John Lewis was spotted walking the streets whiles making headway towards the President's downtown office to collect on the bounty himself.

The bulletin states that anyone can be rewarded by fulfilling the bounty's requirements before John, if they reached him first and were to bring the President before him, dead or alive. Though many people are scared to even go up against such a powerful individual, it is the biggest news in the history of the last twenty years since Dominic took office and put the nation in the state it is in.

I, myself, would definitely collect on the bounty if I had a stronger stomach for blood and gore like many of the other rapscallions. The question becomes what will be the nation's condition under the possibility of the President's demise. Since President Harvey has no Vice-President, no one could immediately take his place within the dictator's office in the event of his death. The former speaker of the house, Phil Plezna, is one of the few governmental officials alive under Dominic's reign of power that could take control of things until a new President is selected if Dominic is murdered. We spoke with the speaker of the house earlier whom said, and I quote, "Fuck Dominic! His time is up!"

Another person of the few that could play a role within taking over is known as former Senator, Walt Michaels. He was named a high ranking official that had cared for several matters of particular countries overseas for the last seven years. We hear little in the media about Walt, as he is more of a messenger with some form of power that had been rectified by Dominic, himself. Senator Walt Michaels had been in South Africa and unavailable to comment until most recently, after returning today. It is questionable how things will play out, but it appears to just be John with the guts to take on the powerful world leader.

In the event that John doesn't succeed in his mission, then things will just go back to how they used to be until someone else gets the testicles to stand up against this chaotic President. Hopefully if this becomes the case, the message will go out to the people of this nation and nations around the world that we need to take a stand against the corrupt system and those of power that run it as so, like John did!"

CHAPTER 23

A NEW DAWN

John was focused on the task at hand. He trotted through the streets, while the rain continued to rapidly fall from above. The raindrops hit John and slowly rolled down his face onto his finely threaded suit. He saw many soldiers begin to take notice to him approaching, while they anxiously sat in their vehicles on their walkie-talkie's awaiting confirmation of an order to take action upon him. John got closer and closer to the office building Dominic resided in. No order had been given yet. Dominic ran over to the balcony window, looking down to the street only to spot John in the near distance coming his way, dressed in an seemingly expensive black suit. When John got close enough to where he was now standing just a few feet from the entrance of the building, several guards stood at the front door of the building blocking the entryway. A voice is heard over the radio wave, commanding the soldiers to step aside from the entrance to allow John to pass through. Dominic walked over to his desk with the radio in his hand to spout off more orders. He told several of the awaiting soldiers in the lobby of the building to kill John when he enters and is fully surrounded. John saw the men separate to allow him passage as he had a gut feeling that Dominic was setting him up to fall into a trap that was all too obvious.

The rain continued to fall harder on him, while he had to make up his mind on if he was willing to fall for the trap or not. When he approached the front entrance to get out of the rain and fully enter the building, one of the soldiers gave John a disgruntled look as he passed by. John caught notice to all of the soldiers standing at the front entrance, being armed with various shotguns or assault rifles and he had only shown up with two hand guns, a few extra clips and a hunting knife. The odds were stacked against him. The soldier that gave John the disgruntled look had walked over to open a secondary door to allow him to enter. As John began to walk past the soldier, he aggressively grabbed the shotgun from the grasps of his hands and unloaded several shots at the armed soldiers before they were able to return fire or react. John looked down at the soldiers' bodies, before dropping the shotgun onto one of them. He walked into the main lobby as several more soldiers ran out and jumped into positions behind cover.

Tables and large pieces of statues were scattered around the lobby floor. Debris floated through the air as the soldiers drew their weapons towards him perilously. John quickly dashed behind the front lobby security booth as they opened fire at him. He kept his head low to avoid being hit, while reaching for the hunting knife that was tucked away underneath his left pant leg. John poked the knife out around the corner of the security booth, as several bullets whisked above his head. He glanced into the reflection to see where each soldier was posted up as most of them tried to move in closer.

While the soldiers continued to open fire, John reached into his inner coat pocket and pulled out a laser as he attached it to one of his Berettas. He inched his hunting knife back out around the corner of the security desk at the same time as pointing his handgun over the top of the desk. John moved the gun around until the laser was centered in the middle of one of the soldier's chest. The soldier looked down at his chest and spotted the red laser dot slowly moving upwards towards his chin. Before the soldier had time to react, John fired the Beretta as the bullet erupted from the weapon and pierced through the soldier's neck. Blood began to squirt out and he quickly tried to place pressure on the wound, though before he knew it, he had taken his last breath just moments after falling over onto the ground.

A few of the nearby soldiers had directed their attention towards John after seeing their fellow soldier shot to death. They immediately radioed for some back up assistance. John used the laser and reflection in his hunting knife to take out several more soldiers. One by one, John picked off each military official with his creative tactical advancement. One soldier remained within the lobby, close by the elevators, to prevent or slow down his plan of attack to reaching President Harvey. John came out of cover and walked towards that soldier, whom squeamishly tried to reload a clip in his assault rifle.

As John raced towards the armed soldier with his weapons aimed towards him, he yelled out demanding that the soldier not make any sudden movements. The soldier continued to struggle trying to change the clip, ignoring the directive. John fired a warning shot by the soldier's head as he dropped the gun and clip, before placing his hands up. He asked the petrified soldier what floor he would find the illustrious President Harvey. He nervously responded, "Fifth floor!" John thanked him for the information before he pulled the trigger and executed the man right where he stood. He entered the elevator and pressed the button to go up on to the fifth floor. John took pride after looking around at the carnage, while the doors of the elevator began to close. He knew that now was the perfect time to change the clips to his guns and prepare for the second wave of possible soldiers he predicted to be waiting for him on the other end upon arrival. The doors closed behind him and he proceeded up.

Soon after riding the elevator up, the light inside had lit up red indicating that he would be making a stop at the second level along the way. Someone obviously had disrupted him from reaching his destination, when he was forced to make this unsuspecting stop. What he would encounter could possibly be a slew of more soldiers or even the President himself, he thought to himself with much concern. The doors opened slowly as a surprised Jarvis was met with an awkward stare to the aggravated John Lewis. Jarvis begin to reach for his handgun, as John quickly raised his hand holding his weapon up to fire a bullet into Jarvis' skull, sending him falling backwards into the hallway. John stepped out to where he was standing over Jarvis' dead body and fired off several more shots into his corpse. No man was meant to be left alive on this heroic suicide mission of his.

John backed up into the elevator after peeking around the corner to see if there were any other enemies in sight. Jarvis apparently was by himself. No one else was seen with him. John could see the saved man he once was becoming a deteriorating shell that was cracking and breaking apart piece by piece. He wasn't even the man he once was before then as a federal agent that would save people. To him, he was starting to see himself as a vengeful murderer. Was he becoming the same monster he was chasing down? John had to remain focused and couldn't lose sight of his mission. He waited patiently as the elevator rose up a few more stories towards the private Presidential floor. Thoughts ran ramped though his head not only about Dominic and how much hurt he had caused John by killing his family, but the things he intended to do or say once confronted by his family's murderer. He also thought about the memory he had from when he came home to his house in a blaze of flames and of the more recent memory when he found out his best friend had been murdered. All of these things became the center point and fuel to his rage.

The elevator door opened once again after reaching the fifth floor and John stepped off and moved further into the hallway. He began checking several nearby rooms on the floor for any hostiles. John opened each door, one by one, screaming out Dominic's name. "Dominic, I know you're here! Come out you fucking coward! YOU FUCK-ING PUSSY" he yelled. John strolled down each hall on a rampage until he came across a room located on the other side of the building that was locked. John stepped a few feet back for a running start and charged towards the door ramming against it with his shoulder.

The doors flung open as a terrified young teenager turned around and saw John standing there at the door with a handgun. It was Sky sitting in this room by himself behind the locked door. To John, he recognized the young teenager, but not as his own son that was his flesh and blood. He recognized this boy from television as he was always seen beside Dominic. To John, this made him a target and imminent threat to be associated with his nemesis. John quickly drew his weapon towards Sky assuming that he was a hostile, no different than any other soldier he had previously come across. When he realized that the boy wasn't armed, he quickly lowered his weapon. In a bold voice, John told the teenager to leave the building and never return, allowing him to be the only person thus far that he had come across in that facility that left on their own will to live and see another day.

Sky had little hesitation with his response to John's order as he quickly exited the room and ran down the hallway. As he approached the elevator, he ran into a portrait hanging on the wall. Some of the wooden and metal parts were protruding out and had ripped the necklace off him. The frame cut the side of Sky neck leaving a small gash that immediately started to bleed. The necklace fell to the ground next to the elevator that John had rode up. It was the same necklace that he had bought for Sky over twenty years ago that had his name inscribed on it. Without recognizing that the frame had snagged his necklace, Sky immediately got onto the elevator and took it down to the bottom floor and quickly exited the building as directed.

John came towards a double door that had a gold plated sign on the right door that read, 'Presidential Suite.' John kicked in the double doors as they both flung wide open slamming against the inside walls of the room, almost ripping themselves off the hinges. John entered into the room and recognized the man standing behind the desk. The man knew he who was and had been waiting for his arrival. There was an intense feeling between the two that was so strong that it could drive a nail into a metal plank with ease. John had been waiting for this very moment, thinking about what he would say, more so than what he would do.

"If it isn't the infamous, President Dominic Harvey, finally standing right before me! It's weird meeting you face to face, as I have always only seen you on television, but this is more up close and personal. You look different though. There is something about you that doesn't strike me as the same asshole I have seen on television, but I figure you will be less recognizable once I am done with you motha fucka," John boldly stated.

Their guns were steadily pointed at each other as John walked further into the room while waiting for a response. "Well, if it isn't John Lewis. How are the wife and kids?" he replied, sarcastically asking with a sadistic chuckle. John discharged his weapon, firing a bullet that missed his target as both men fell back to cover. He reached behind his back and pulled out his other Beretta, while dodging behind a nearby couch. The two opened fire at one another, as John dodged behind a nearby couch for better cover. Several more shots were made at each other until both of their guns were empty. Both men began to reload their weapons diligently hoping to the other person and gain the upper hand.

"Don't be a fucking coward, Dominic!" John yelled out while he reloaded his weapon. "Take a look around you, John. You don't live in the same world from twenty years ago. That specific world where there were rules dictating where you are able to smoke a cigarette, who you were able to marry or even what drugs you were allowed to put in your own body. It was one where you were forced to pay thousands of dollars in order to continue to be alive if you suffer from a terminal illness or disease and if you didn't have the money then it was as if your life wasn't as priceless as someone with a larger and more stable bank account. The same world that put people behind bars for life or gave them the death sentence based on evidence obtained and not the evident truth. A world where obtaining a job was harder than maintaining one! And you called that type of world a free one! You referred to it, like so many other fools, to be better than the vision I had for us all. The people that looked down on the common folk, like myself, and had passed judgment are initially the ones whom need to be judged. I don't plan to be a messenger or messiah, yet I would like to be a withstanding vision that a stronger nation is one that isn't ruled by a judgmental government that claims to know what is best for all people while making huge decisions that only affect some people. That's the world we all deserve, John! That's the world that seems truly free!" he stated while pouring out his thoughts to John.

The words held so much meaning, but it was apparent that John hadn't come there to negotiate or hear his political standpoint. A war was meant to be fought and revenge was meant to be had. He switched his clip while talking to John further and fired off a blind shot into the air, as they two exchanged a few more shots between each other. John responded in a bold voice to the comments made. "What we had almost twenty years ago was less fear. No government is perfect, just like no person is perfect! Though we did have order within our nation. The same fear that you have put forth within not paying a crime tax is the same fear one has about speeding, or robbing a liquor store. I can't say that either world is better or worse. It is just a world, nonetheless, that we have conformed to. The rules and laws are different, but it seems like the action to give consequence based on one's decision hasn't changed, but the consequence itself has. In retrospective, you have done nothing to give back a sense of freedom or to even call yourself a legendary figure in my opinion," John clamored.

A bullet whisked by John's head as he returned the fire. Smoke and bullets flew through the air as the two continued to shout at one another in rage. "What do you think about that Dominic? You sound different too! Scared! But different! Is it the truth that I speak that bothers you, Dominic? I can hear it in your voice. You don't even sound the same when I hear you speak!" asked John to his evil foe that shouted back, demanding that he stop talking as if he knew what he was talking about. His response had to be impactful, though it was clear that John just wouldn't understand the message, so he tried to help clarify "I am a legend! This world was in shambles before I took it and nurtured it with freedom and power like a newborn baby. The people that were in power back when you were a family man tore this nation apart. Instead of becoming a stronger nation, we fell to our knees and were bewildered as to how to recover from disaster and turmoil. Those people played God, as to what they thought would fix things, when it only brought us further down. People act like they are GOD, but we as people, are only as knowledgeable as the guy living before us. Don't preach to me motha fucka like you are some idealistic prophet! You're nothing to me! You're a nickel trying to be a fucking dollar," he belted back in retaliation.

John retorted with anger as he screamed out, referencing to him as being a coward. "That's all that you are! You're a caitiff playing dress up in a presidential suit!" he continued. They both eventually stood up from behind cover with their guns still drawn sternly at each other. John came from behind the couch first, followed by his villainous antagonist. "You took from me something that can't be replaced. You took lives of people I will never see again. You took everything away from me! And now I am here to take from you!" John stated as he pulled the trigger and it clicked, but no bullet burst from the barrel. John had realized in that moment that he was out of bullets and was ridiculed for his poor observation as a former law enforcer. "Out of bullets, I see! It's a shame!" John's foe noted, as he pulled his trigger and it clicked as well representing that he too was out of ammunition. They stood before one another at a stalemate.

They were close in proximity and this proposed a dangerous environment. John was close to a tattered grand piano that was residing in the room as he passed it by rolling the barrel against some of the keys along the way. "Your move!" John said malignantly. "My move? It's far from my move. In this world I am considered the fucking king. And to me, you're just my fucking pawn!" he responded with poise. John looked on with a slight grin. "Well, in thatcase... CHECK MATE!" John responded as he pressed the button on the side of his Beretta releasing the clip from his weapon. The gun fell towards the ground as he reached into the back of his pants pocket and pulled out an extra clip he had for emergency purposes. He secured the new one into his Beretta and fired off a few consecutive shots. The bullets passed through the air from John's gun, as it pierced through his archenemies right shoulder. Following the violent theatrics of the attack, another bullet had pierced its way through his skull and chest sending his falling backwards through a window to where he would plummet to the ground.

John had stormed towards the window, while continuing to pull the trigger, emptying most of his clip into his assailant's chest as he had fell out from the fifth story of the building towards the first. John grabbed a hold of a pipe next to the window to catch himself from falling with his deranged foe, as he leaned out and he fired off the remaining bullets into the body of his enemy. He then leaned back into the room just shortly after the body collided with the cement, dropping the Beretta on the floor. A sign of relief passed through him. He felt as if a huge weight had been lifted from his shoulders and much of the pain off his conscience. In his mind, he had exacted the justified revenge on the man responsible for killing his family. John took a deep sigh of relief and smiled to himself before he somberly exited the room. While he was walking down the hallway, he stopped to take notice to the necklace he saw on the ground near the elevator. It was familiar to him. He recognized it, as he read his son's name on it. He bent down and picked it up glancing at the necklace as it sent him into immediate shock. The jewelry didn't appear brand new, considering the condition it was in, though it remained assuredly recognizable. He was confused as to how the necklace had found its way back into his life, especially after all of these years. He assumed that Dominic kept it as a keepsake from twenty years ago as he didn't think anything past that. He placed it into his pocket and stepped onto the elevator to take it down to the ground floor.

As John walked out into the lobby, several soldiers were seen carrying the bodies of their fallen comrades out of the building to a coroner's truck. When they saw John exit the building behind them, they quickly raised their weapons towards the door at him. "There he is!" said one of the soldiers. "Lower your weapons. It's just John Lewis!" another replied. They all followed the command of the higher rank officer and lowered their weapons to let him pass. It was a strange interaction, but it seemed as if the soldiers came to the understanding if they weren't already aware that their President was no longer alive. John exited the building and was greeted by several resistance members and many locals that stood in front of the building as they watched a different group of soldiers quickly carry away their beloved presidents' body.

Justin gingerly ran up to John and gave him a hug, thanking him for allowing people to obtain a new start in life by assassinating the President. John told Justin not to thank him, because the real work of creating a new dawn should be given to Jesse as well as Samuel and all that they did. He asked Justin where Stacy was and why she didn't come by, to which he quickly responded. "She knows what happened. It's all over the news, but she isn't that far away as she had to help a lot of the resistance members get settled in their new home," he replied. Justin went on to recommend that John go over to visit, as he gave him a piece of paper with the address written on it to where she was located. John placed it in his pocket and thanked Justin. He turned around and walked away, passing through the crowds of people still celebrating and joyfully thanking him. John Pushed his way by person after person shaking hands and receiving hugs until he had finally reached the exit to the mass crowd. Upon reaching that point, he bumped into a young man, brushing his shoulder up against his.

"Excuse me! My Apologies!" John stated without even looking back at who he had ran into. For if he had, he would have realized that the young man he had just crossed paths with again could potentially be his son, Sky, unbeknownst to him after piecing together the clue from finding his necklace. Sky turned around and gave a discourteous stare to John, whom hadn't even turned the other cheek, while continuing down the street on his way to meet up with Stacy. When he arrived at the house several blocks away, he saw her and several other members of the resistance bunched around the television as they celebrated the President's death. Stacy turned around and spotted John standing in the near distance. She immediately called out to him and told him to come over to join them. John began making his wayover, greeting some familiar faces along the way that he had been introduced to before. She met him half-way through the crowd with a hug and kiss on the cheek, yet closer to his lips this time. "Jesse would be proud," she stated with a glamorous smile.

John was still a little caught off guard by her intimate gesture by kissing him. He began to blush, turning bright red, before responding. "Jesse believed in a new dawn. A day that was to come and prove that people didn't have to live in fear or commit crimes to be considered free! I wish he was here to relish in such a glorious day," John responded back. A resistance member entered and announced to everyone of how people were heading down to the City Hall to discuss who would run for office now that Dominic was dead and could become the new World Leader. Stacy asked John to come join her down to the City Hall and be in attendance. "This is meant to be a monumental day. Picking someone new that is more suitable for the office is a day I don't want to forget. We will have no more days of hatred and lost lives. I wonder who will be running for office," she voiced.

One resistance member intervened to make a valid point arguing a proposal to Stacy that she should consider putting her foot in the race to power. "We could make a great case as to how you would make for a great representative running for President. You are considered the next leader in line after Jesse to speak from the resistances' political point of view of how things should be. You are that reasonable side that creates a more liberal point of view. There is already someone representing the Republican Party and Green Party, though there is no one representing the Democratic Party," the resistance member raved. The idea was pondered for a moment as it was all so much to take in. "I'm not sure. I am okay stepping up as the person leading this resistance, but I don't know about world leadership," Stacy added with a sense of confirmed content.

John felt as if she was being modest. He knew that she was ideal for the role, especially considering that no one has presented a voice for the Democratic Party, so he quickly spoke up. "We shouldn't waste any more time. Let's go!" exclaimed John as if the decision had been made for her. Several resistance members grabbed their belongings and began heading over to the local City Hall as John and Stacy followed out behind them. When they walked to the building that the meeting was being held, there was a massive number of people waiting in attendance. Way more than what Stacy had anticipated, which inevitably made her more nervous and unwilling to stand up in front of a large crowd like that to announce that she was running, even though she hadn't really decided that she was. It was more decided for her by her peers. Adriana scurried in with her cameraman to gain the scoop, as she quickly set up her equipment to begin a live newscast before any other reporters were to arrive at this tentative town hall meeting. Her hair was yet again still in disarray and her clothes mangled as usual, as she dusted herself off and cued her cameraman to begin rolling. A channel 6 promo played prior to going on the air as a man walked out to the front podium to calm down the audience and speak to those listening.

"I am a spokesperson and representative to the Speaker of the House. I am here today to speak on his behalf. Today, we lost our leader!" he stated as the enamored crowd cheered. Many had shown up as unfaithful followers to Dominic's regime. They were ecstatic when discovering that he had been killed and were only in attendance to find out what was to come next as far as the world-wide leadership. The man continued with his speech, "...but we have to move forward looking for someone to lead us in the right direction. We have lived in a Utopia to some and a Dystopia to many others. We don't know which world is best for us, but neither world that we have been accustomed to have initially led us to the world peace we desire. We ask that representatives, either selected unanimously amongst your decisive party or those as volunteers, step forward that feel that they will be eligible and best fitting to fulfill such a prestigious leadership role. We would like someone whose views are comparable to the two separate worlds' that most of us have been exposed to within the last several decades. We will vote on the likely candidate, if there happens to be several people running that would spark debates, then we will have a national vote within narrowing down our selection for our new President."

A man came forward after he had raised his hand, approaching the podium, shouting that he was the best suitable candidate for the Green Party. He stepped onto the stage and approached the microphone. "My name is Walt Michaels and I used to work closely with Dominic as I was a former Senator. I feel that the world he has created has a good direction, but definitely has kinks in its system that could be worked out. I know what most of you disliked about what Dominic Harvey had done to this world and its inhabitants. Though you have to open your eyes and realize that there is so much more to the plan he envisioned for us. With Dominic's former path, I can lead this nation to its most promising destination," Walt vocalized as many of the audience members began to cheer for him.

Another lady raised her hand as she approached the podium, passing by Walt Michaels and giving him a look of disgust. The woman walked onto the stage and took another microphone from the stand beside the podium and began to speak to everyone. "My name is Lenore Graves and I am one of the former Washington senators representing the Republican Party. I have watched the nation develop cancer. I have seen that said cancer spread from country to country and person to person like the infectious and deadly disease it is, although I have come forth today to be that miracle cure. I want to be that cure that will bring this world back to a healthy state. I am against the idea of taking away our right as Americans to bear arms and only having that right given to military. I love our military and consider myself highly patriotic, but I also love my guns too and protecting my family. I am against the idea of paying taxes that support crime so others can blindly have what I have without working hard for it like I did. Stop letting people come in and tear down the strong foundation we have built up. I can't even see this as the United States of America anymore. I am straight forward and won't bullshit you on what I think and hope this great nation can one day return to. I see a world of dictatorship we are leaving behind and hope to get to a more conservative world we used to live in with laws and rules, and most importantly a constitution. No more crime! No more suffering!" she stated before recognizing Stacy was standing in the audience.

Lenore called out to the humble newly elected resistance leader and asked her to come up to the stage. "Is that Stacy? Stacy Parks? I thought I recognized you. Ladies and gentleman, I would like to introduce you to Stacy Parks, the current leader of the resistance that fought hard against Dominic. I would have to say that that is a tough job to hold as the leader of that group, seeing as how not many that have held that specific position live longer than a few months or so," she sarcastically continued with a cruel undertone of her ending snide remark.

Stacy snatched the microphone from Lenore's hands, giving her a cold-hearted stare that could pierce through her soul. "Shut the FUCK up Lenore! Just because I used to work for you doesn't mean I have to sit up here and listen to you spew out feces from your filthy whore-like mouth. I figured I would come down here and take a gander at the other arrogant individuals, like you, that try to live in Dominic Harvey's shadow claiming to be a leader!" Stacy retorted candidly. Lenore turned her nose up at Stacy's blatant comment and asked if she felt she could do a better job.

"Of course I do! I know that we all miss the capitalistic world we once lived in. I know that if I was to run and be elected that I would do much more good than damage," Stacy continued. It was clear that Lenore was trying to coax Stacy into running for office, not knowing that that was her intent anyway by approaching and speaking out on behalf of her people that didn't have a powerful voice similar to hers that had been given to her by being granted the title of Resistance leader.

Lenore looked out to the audience, "There you have it! The current resistance leader is deciding to run for Presidential office within the Democratic Party. That's all we need is to take two steps forward and five liberal steps backwards," Very few people raved at the possibility of her running for office and winning as they screamed out all kinds of things. Stacy looked around the room and saw the same kinds of faces she saw in the resistance and others that would normally be on the streets committing crimes. She knew deep down that the people wanted to live without fear for their lives. They wanted to believe that things could get better. Stacy took back the microphone and announced that she would run for President and give back a sense of hope and faith to the people of this nation and around the world.

"This world deserves better; however, let me drop some knowledge on you. Lenore and those here and around the world need to listen up. I want everyone to pay close attention to what I am about to say because it will be the hurtful truth that is unbearable to all people belonging to any political party. Stop handing out a liberal or conservative label. It isn't helping anyone by doing so. It is only creating two sides. What good does it do for you to stay strongly opinionated with your side and me with mine till the day we die? We pass these points of views onto our kids, which means that nothing will change. Those kids grow up arguing, debating and hating those that have opposing views. You may see that it is good to have your opinion and argue that. You may see it as good to stay true to your beliefs and NEVER stray from them, but let me build you this logic. Think of it in terms of construction workers deciding on building either a house, a shed or a trailer. Should they build it out of brick, straw or wood? If all the construction workers continue to argue and never come to a cohesive decision, then that house will never be built. If we argue who is a manager, a regular employee and who has been there the longest, even though the same end result is to build a home, then more conflict will happen and surely slow down the process of building the home. When your opinion never changes mine and mine never changes yours, then time is frozen. Until we look for new ways and compromise, then we will never in turn move forward. This is my message. I may represent the Democratic Party for the purpose of running in this election, but I don't see myself to represent any party. If I represent the political ideas that support a particular party, how can I ever become a leader that represents ALL people?" she rhetorically asked. Her speech was one that held much weight and opened many people's eyes. It became logic that couldn't be argued with and an idea that had to be sat on bye every person that walked the earth. Stacy stepped down from the stage and headed back to be by John's side as the audience continued to give mixed reactions to her speech.

John was impressed, himself, by what she had said. He saw so much wisdom and those leadership qualities that one would need to inspire and lead. John was even starting to have feelings for Stacy. He saw her heart and how kind she was. These were qualities he was attracted to. He gave her a hug and acknowledged that he felt she would make a wonderful President. "I just have a good feeling that we won't find anyone better for the position. Wait a second, it just hit me. Where is Chance? John inquired. He realized that he hadn't seen her since the funeral. Stacy could only remember the last time she saw her and stated that to John to help ease his worry and concern for her. "Chance said she wanted to be alone after everything. She saw a newscast about her mother being murdered when you decided to head out to kill Dominic. It is difficult to lose both parents like she did, so I get it!" Stacy uttered. John told her that he thinks he knows where Chance is and concluded that he was going to go out looking for her.

Stacy was well aware of how important Jesse's daughter was to him. In such a short amount of time, they both had acquired a genuine love between the both of them as if Chance was his own flesh and blood. He had taken her even more under his wing and became protective of her after Jesse died, being a sole promise and vow to himself. Stacy made it clear that she was going to remain at the City Hall a little while longer. The two parted ways, as John exited the building and began walking away. Stacy then stayed at City Hall, when the announcer came back to the stage and asked if anyone else wanted to come up and speak. At that moment, a gentleman's' voice was heard in the crowd proclaiming that they had something to say as he pushed their way through the audience. When approached the stage, he aggressively took the microphone from the announcer to speak about what was weighing in on his conscience. "My name is Sky Harvey and I am another former Senator appointed by my father, Dominic Harvey. I am here to state that I intend to continue his legacy. He taught me that a legacy is a legend's story. I realize what his legacy is and whereas many people may not like or understand his vision, know that you must get wet to cross a river with no bridge," Sky boldly stated as many in the audience that supported Dominic's viewpoints and politics had cheered and applauded his speech.

The ceremony continued and John missed another interaction with his biological son. The thought of hearing that speech and the name Sky could have possibly resonated with him that his son was still alive, although John was on a different mission. He had set out in search of Chance, to make sure that she was safe, especially after all she had been through and the loss she endured. When John approached the alley where the former resistance hideout was, he climbed the ladder and walked down the tunnel. He immediately heard audio from a television coming from one of the subway carts. John walked into the suspected nearby cart as Chance turned around and greeted him. "I see there is no hiding from you John. Come! Take a look for yourself at this!" she responded as she turned up the newscast about her mother being killed as well as John going out after Dominic to kill him. He watched the newscast that was re-covering the events that transpired today, as they brought back many mixed emotions.

Chance turned back to John in replied in a soft voice, "I lost my family! I lost everything! It's like my body is covered with millions of scars. And even though my scars don't bleed, they also never fade! I am stuck with them as reminders. They can heal, but these scars always hurt!" Tears ran down her face, as John walked closer and kneeled down beside her. He placed his arm around her and pulled her close to him as his way to console the young grieving teen.

"Jesse and Marie both loved you! Jesse considered you his daughter without even knowing that you actually were. Jesse gave me something to give to your mother to show how much he loved her. I have faith that he would have wanted you to have it though," John stated as he reached into his pocket and pulled out a silver bracelet. He handed it to Chance as she read the inscription on it. John informed her that it was an anniversary present for Marie from, her father, Jesse. He also explained to her what he felt the inscription meant.

"Jesse wanted Marie to know, just like he would want you to know, that no matter what; if a day came where he was gone too soon that he hopes he left behind enough knowledge to lead you into a new dawn. A new dawn that would be far brighter and more hopeful than what he could imagine!" John stated with a solemn smile. A few more

282

tears cascaded down Chance's face as the newscast continued in the background. Adriana Hart wrapped up her news report with a few closing words. She stated in a calm voice, "This day is not like any day. It is historical one. It is one that we will remember by the masses. I hope, through these newscasts, that this legendary story was told and the message easily conveyed. We need to stop battling one another about politics and come together as people to battle the problem. Don't be someone so wrapped up in taking from others that you forget to give! Not one party can get what they want, but we can compromise and make some sacrifice and grow to become better people, individually and as a whole. We lost many people along this journey. There were people that risked their lives for ours to continue. People like Samuel Freeman and Jesse Dean! But don't be discouraged. There is still hope..."

CHAPTER 24

A CLOSED CHAPTER

"And even though a flame dies, remember that it was once a guiding light!"

This book is in memoriam of Jonathon Lewis White.

Made in the USA
Monee, IL
26 February 2022

91887107R00173